WHISPERS AFTER DEATH

REILY GARRETT

Acknowledgments

To Siobhan Caughey, for reading through my rough drafts. Your perceptions are spot on and always appreciated in delving into a character's mind. First drafts are always the roughest, but is also where changes in a character's direction take root.

To Rosie Amber for an in-depth assessment of character and plot, thank you for all your help. You can find her blog and services at rosieamber.wordpress.com/beta-reading-service.

To my readers, each one of you who selects and reads one of my books, thank you for the opportunity to share my work. If you've enjoyed it, please consider leaving a review. They are the best way to help your author share her work.

This book is a work of fiction. Names, characters, places, and incidents either are products of the author's imagination or used fictitiously. Any resemblance to actual persons living or dead, business establishments, events, or locales is entirely coincidental.

Chapter One

"Kendra Lea Bower, 'bout time you got your scrawny ass down here. You been helping Father McKinley at St. Marks again?" Daeron's rhythmic foot tapping signaled his pre-performance adrenaline rush, complete with the all-too-familiar hand gesture asserting, *"Today would be nice."*

"Yeah. He's still ragging on me to stay there." Kendra darted up two steps at a time, her beloved and battered acoustic guitar thumping against her back and snagging her hair.

The source of trepidation, a wary foreboding sandwiched between hope and confidence, dampened her mood.

"Maybe you should pray for patience, Daeron."

Their band manager, Wes, had indicated this might be a good break for them but remained stingy with details except the caveat of entailing a short night, more like an audition.

Money equals food in our stomachs.

Jutting up from the serene landscape, immense castle-type walls portrayed a primeval struggle between the virtuous and immoral, the results determined by each individual passing through the arched gate to hell.

Deep-set windows on either side of the wood-plank doors beckoned the intrepid to press a curious nose against the smoked glass and bear witness to the activities occurring within the darkened interior. Wes had also warned them this club was like none other, his ironfisted grasp of details something no one could dislodge.

"If I prayed, it'd be for the strength to toss your sorry ass in the sea." Slightly crooked front teeth gleamed white against Daeron's sun-coppered skin to give him a certain backwoods charm. Aside from the worn threads, no one would suspect him to number among the teaming homeless.

Impatience stiffened his solid frame as he stood by the massive door. He was always game to try new things, willing to tempt fates who tossed them enough curves to enforce a demeanor exceeding his twenty-two years. A soft wash of silvery moonlight filtered through the adjacent oak leaves to add a layer of mystery which lacked definition.

"Wouldn't hurt you to stay there, you know." A lopsided smile softened his admonishment.

"Hey, you won't, so don't hassle me. What is this place anyway, a special retreat for the knights of old? How'd Wes get our first gig in a medieval joint like this? It's making my skin crawl." Kendra hesitated at the top step, doubt and curiosity warring for dominance.

"Wouldn't say. But, it's five hundred bucks. A hundred for each of us tonight, then less thereafter, but its steady work, which means a steady supply of food if you don't keep giving half of it away." Daeron yanked on the iron door handle to reveal a wide antechamber lined with assorted jewel-toned tapestries, each draped over tightly mortared blocks behind gleaming silver suits of armor.

Lifelike silver-plated figures dared the stouthearted to enter, lest some dark prophecy from within awaken to enslave their will.

"If you want to sleep in a real bed and not a condemned building tonight, you tickle the ivories."

Inside the door, a bull-necked man in black jeans and t-shirt nodded a greeting as they passed.

Focusing on music lent clarity of purpose despite her world having plunged into hell in the aftermath of tragedy three years prior.

The band members touting her a strong-minded street rat belied the contradictory evidence, her heartbeat resembling castanets flavoring Spanish music. Stoicism was a trait not yet perfected and, like any art, needed practice.

"Yeah, yeah. Just so they're not sacrificing virgins..."

Three men in dress slacks and pressed shirts stood near the end of the vestibule, each turning to give her a brief head-to-toe perusal which morphed into blatant interest. Of the three, the closest broadcast a curiosity understood all too well, a shark sensing prey in murky chum waters.

"Not likely, asshats." Words mumbled under her breath didn't catch the predator's attention.

"Ha! I knew it. That's why none of the guys have put any moves on you." Daeron's innocent comment drew intense looks, inquisitive, like heat-seeking missiles locking onto target. Her incrementally swelling anger.

In silent disgust, she named the first prick Saltie, reminiscent of salt water crocodiles, the largest of the reptile species.

"As if I'd fall for one of my own rat pack." Her playful bicep punch drew a round of silent chuckles from the sudden admirers. "I prefer a man, thank you very much."

"That's our girl. Just chafe in that chastity belt 'til you find the one." Daeron exchanged greetings, scowling in the face of the men's appreciative grins.

Inhaling a slow, deep breath, she let her gaze warp around the room, taking in the walls of impressionist art, couches lining the perimeter, and tables in the center bearing candles.

"Fuck me sideways. What is this place?" She didn't belong in the building, much less on its stage. "What the hell is Wes playing at?"

Understanding came too late that she'd walked into a trap with no clear escape. Daeron's second rule came to mind. *Never enter without first scouting the exit.*

"Hey, no cause for alarm, cutie. We're all here to relax and have a good time." Saltie held out a hand in greeting. "Hi, I'm—"

"Not interested, troglodyte. Have a good evening." Kendra wondered if the semi-advanced Neanderthal got the message. A glance at his expression dictated she'd started something, offending a guest within two minutes of arrival.

His scowl deepened. A touch of crimson infused his cheeks.

As if sensing her next move, Daeron reached back and stopped her arm reaching for the guitar. "We need to work to eat, Kendra, unless you want to sell this, which I know you don't."

Daeron was right. The guitar entailed the only tangible piece of her brother's soul in her possession. It meant everything, her lifeline to another time, another world where she and Billy sang wacky, nonsensical melodies until the entire family cried with laughter.

Family and laughter, two things her existence lacked, unless she included the chittering, hissing rats in the abandoned buildings where she slept.

"I don't need this shit." Empty pockets and a bottomless pit of determination kept her rooted in place. She might end up cold and hungry tonight, but her integrity and self-respect would remain intact. No one would ever break her again.

7

"Kendra, no. We need this gig. Broke, remember?" Daeron's frustration radiated out concentrically as a pebble hitting water, each ripple adding a thicker layer of indecision to the air. "Where are you gonna sleep tonight?"

On a deep sigh, she dropped chin to chest, shaking with frustration. Like a tree that couldn't bend without breaking, she couldn't weather the storm. How would she survive?

"Stop." The disembodied mandate issued from her left prevented further consequences of her faux pas. "What's going on?" Deceptively calm, the interrogator's rough tone left no room for argument.

It never had.

Of the two men approaching, the tallest one commanded her attention the same as when she'd been a teenager caught sneaking out of the house. Regardless of time's passage, she remembered them as family during a different err. Her brother's best friends, Conner and Marc, had accepted her into their pack.

In the back of her mind she remembered Conner's voice, so much like her brother's, from a period of fanciful dreams and great aspirations, pigtails and ribbons which gave way to eye shadow and lipstick, exciting adventures, and warm smiles.

Billy followed Conner into the military, consigning her world to a hell from which she'd never recovered. It'd taken years to overcome expectations of a surreal past life.

Instead, she'd learned to navigate the hazards and pitfalls of open-air living, the real world. Resentment swelled and intertwined with the yearnings of yesteryear to leave her thoughts as gnarled as her gut.

The weight of Conner's stare, heavy as a prisoner's chains, locked her gaze to the floor.

What the hell is he doing in a fancy place like this?

The thought of her brother's death destroying other lives was one she hadn't conceived. Conner stepped forward, crowding her. His unspoken, unfulfilled demand to meet his gaze preceded a deep rumble from his chest and a small smile to her face.

She'd always loved defying him to the limits of his strength and sufferance.

"It's been a long time, Mongrel. Welcome to Ambrosia. Good to see you."

Kendra's gaze swung like a pendulum between Conner, and others now gathered awaiting the outcome.

The previous version of Conner wouldn't have raised his voice to her, but the new and devolved adaptation remained a question mark.

Score one for the deviant. A deep breath, intended to clear her mind, succeeded in aiding his scent to enhance the band squeezing her lungs.

Among the bystanders, a top-heavy refugee from a misbegotten makeup counter sneered in regal smugness, sure of her station by Conner's side. Her verbal footnote of "dregs of the gutter" earned Conner's sharp visual reprimand.

"Go." Conner's monotone could slice through steel.

The bottled blonde scurried away amid mumblings of vagrants, beggars, and hobos. If that was his preferred type of woman now, he'd fallen further than anyone could've imagined. Another one of Billy's casualties?

Wait!

"You? You own this animated freak show? Conner, what happened to you?" A decade ago, he and Billy had filled her head with fantasies only an innocent could dream, back when sex in a t-shirt carried the easy grace of a natural predator and filled her head with delusions of eternal love.

"You always talked about owning a sporting goods shop. What happened?"

Time lent fuel to her imagination. Like a boiler that continued to build up too much pressure, her thoughts skated along the razor's edge of a volcano. The age-old longing persisted despite current reality's intervention and the memory of how he had led Billy into the military, to his death.

"Times change," murmured with a shrug. "It really is good to see you again. I look forward to hearing you play." That sweltry intonation could curl an iron bar, yet there dwelt a deep sadness, as if memories pulled him down a road too often traveled.

An audible gulp. Her mouth opened and closed several times with no sound issued.

She couldn't look at him, not when her face flamed with the memories of first infatuation. The disappointment invading her mind now stung the back of her eyelids.

"Why would you buy a place like this?" It was too much to bear. She needed the quiet and peaceful white noise of the street; wind chimes on someone's front porch, a car backfiring, a breeze sifting through the trees and blowing the road's detritus in small dust devils.

"Seemed like the thing to do at the time."

"Nice place you have here, Mr. Crofton." Daeron, ever the peacemaker, stepped forward with outstretched hand.

"Yeah, all it needs is some spider architecture, pointed hats, and a pentacle drawn on the floor. Oh, and I think you're missing a vat of boiling oil." Mumbled words lost the bite of her intent.

"Can't say spiders do much for me, but I could come up with scented massage oil. I hear women think of it as magic." Conner's husky laugh scorched the knot in her throat like melted sand, changing its consistency until acid threatened to spew forth.

"Looks like a damn interesting club you have here, very niche." Daeron's comment would earn him an all-out brawl later.

Freaking traitor. Men always stuck together.

After a moment, Conner's words sank in.

No.

It seemed bystanders thought her a comedian or imbecile, their laughter creating more blazing heat to encompass her face.

Marc, brother of her current tormentor, took pity as he stepped forward. "Hi, Kendra. It's been a long time."

Sympathy radiated from him in waves to envelop her in a maelstrom of cloying, sickly sweet flashbacks she couldn't handle. Of the four brothers, he'd been the nice one.

"Hi, Marc. Let me guess, you're also part of this zoo?" Regardless of their intended sincerity, she couldn't rest her gaze on either man.

"You got it, hon. Ready to work? I've missed hearing soft jazz." Marc stepped forward to offer a hug yet stopped short of contact.

No. She couldn't abide the company of men whose lives had been twisted by pain and despair, the last men to see her brother alive.

Conner's presence ushered Billy's last words to fill her mind before ditching her for another military stint, his final tour. *"You're being selfish, Mongrel. I need to do this, protect my brothers. You'll be safe here, but they won't be unless I go back. When I return, we'll start a new chapter in life, together."*

She got a new version of life, all right. Just not the one they'd planned.

The physical ache in her heart wasn't relieved with the pressure of fist against chest. She turned and ran, as she'd always done when the agony of memories washed over her. She would never again allow anyone to witness her suffering.

Chapter Two

"Kendra, stop!" Conner's voice had commanded Special-Ops forces during dozens of top-secret missions. Assignments her brother had followed to his last breath.

But not her, not anymore. An arid mouth prevented her from licking her lips or offering a retort. The words swirled in her mind like particles of sand in a dust storm. She no longer accessed common ground from which to communicate.

Several gasps from onlookers drifted to her ears as she bolted back through the hallway and snatched the heavy, oak portal open. The door attendant greeted an incoming guest who stood frozen with mouth agape, not unaccustomed to women fleeing the perverts within.

Cold wind blasted her face yet failed to clear her mind. True escape would never come while she drew breath. No one could outrun their inner demons.

Down the steps and over the dewy lawn she flew, skidding before botching a leap over low shrubbery bordering the parking lot. Landing on hands and knees cost precious seconds, time she couldn't afford. Instinct told her he'd chase.

He'd always been fast.

Her feet scrambled for purchase before traction yielded distance. With the woods twenty yards away, she heard his booted steps over the blood roaring through her veins right before he tackled her to the ground.

Panic seized her with the force of her landing. The abrupt jarring depleted her lungs of air. Desperation curved her hands into claws to gain traction in the slick grass despite the fire shooting through her right wrist. The heavy weight of a large male body on her thighs thwarted her attempt to stand.

Even before he spoke, she knew it was Conner. It was always Conner. Though she wouldn't hurt him with it, if she hadn't lost her precious knife months ago, she'd give him second thoughts.

"Damn it, Kendra. You *will* listen to me."

"No, I won't."

His tone settled the matter in one of their minds.

Fighting someone with a hundred-and fifty-pound advantage didn't shake her perseverance for freedom until his weight once again bore her flat despite her attempts to twist free and landing an elbow jab to his midsection.

Jerking her head back to connect with his nose equaled her next miscalculation. He'd moved.

She froze when his teeth clamped down on her neck. He'd always been one step ahead, just like now, anticipating her moves and countering them with little effort.

"Settle down, Mongrel!"

His muttered admonition breathed new strength in her scuffle for independence.

A simple task in using his weight to stifle her movements, it likened to a hefty chunk of steel squashing a fly.

With a disgusted groan, she relented and played possum to create a false sense of submission. He had a lot to learn about the new and improved mongrel.

Once his weight lifted, he still bested her struggle to shake him off. He'd thrown one heavy leg over both of hers, which equated to lying under a tree trunk. The best she could manage was a string of foul curses.

Fresh mown lawn, onions, and musty earth—calming aromas which normally induced an aura of peace—didn't compare to the warm scent of Conner surrounding and filling her mind with memories she couldn't handle. A time of innocence and unspoken promises that would shred her insides like glass if she allowed those long-ago images to surface.

Harsh breath in her ear preceded rough hands on her arms, holding them behind her back in one meaty paw. One hand banded her wrists before he hauled her upright with her back against his solid chest. Her fingers, bound behind her, skimmed soft denim over steely thighs.

It felt like security despite the restraint.

Genetics gave her the right height.

Rage gave her the requisite attitude.

Fate threw her the specific scenario.

She leaned back into his frame and issued the small noise of a wounded animal. His grip loosened as breath from his shushing murmur brushed her ear.

"You're gonna be all right, sweetheart." More soothing words.

Right moment.

Years of guitar practice added strength to her endeavor. Seizing as much semi-soft groin tissue as she could grasp, she squeezed with all her might.

His choice of expletives rivaled anything her mind could ever hope to conjure. En route to doubling over, he shoved her forward, which gave her a few yards head start.

Like a released rabbit, she took off.

Still, he was faster.

She didn't get far before he hauled her back against his hard frame, careful this time to maintain a little distance between her hands and his prized bits.

"Do that again and you won't sit comfortably for a week, sweetheart." The endearment was a curse, halting words forced through clenched teeth.

She struggled against his hold until he gripped her shoulders and shook her like a rag doll. The next minute, he'd turned her to face him, pressing her head against his chest, and brushing his lips across her hair.

"I'm not a criminal. You're not a cop. Let me go."

"Not until you hear me out. We *are* going to my office, and you *will* listen. I have things to tell you. What the hell have you been doing on the streets all this time?"

"Anything I damn well please." His heart thumped hard under her cheek while heaving breaths warmed her forehead and cocooning heat stretched her nerves. She wouldn't cry, not in front of Conner.

His flipping the switch to gentleness forced like in kind in her. Daeron had taught her there was always more than one way to fight a battle. There was no contest with strength.

To gaze at him now would destroy her. She shifted to absorb a little more of his warmth, the slight arching of her back forcing her breasts against his granite-like chest.

Strung-out caffeine junkies moved slower than Conner when he recoiled and eyed her like an infected leper. As if taking the offensive to hide his reaction, he added, "Do you know how long it's taken me to find you?"

"Street rats become invisible." Her mutinous glare had no apparent effect.

"Huh."

His nudge in the club's direction signaled her temporary defeat, but she'd grown hard, no longer the sweet kid he'd labeled her long ago. Like the cichlid fish lurking in muddy lake water, she'd roll over and play dead, biding her time and planning.

He wouldn't be so easy to fool in round two.

"Especially when you have such loyal friends." His voice was rich and deep, blending admiration with affection, beguiling and all-consuming. His mood flashed from pariah to friend with a swing of the pendulum, a sharp blade that eviscerated with one stroke.

"Yeah, you'd know all about that, wouldn't you? Your friends followed you right into hell." Her intended barb hit its mark.

He flinched. If she hadn't known him so well, she'd have missed the tightening of his torso and narrowing of his gaze.

"You okay?" As if needing physical confirmation, he ran his hands up and down her arms.

"You hurt me, you big oaf." She didn't need his tenderness or close proximity. Even in the wide-open space, he seemed to suck up the very air she needed. Surely her heart raced from exertion and her scrambled brain couldn't easily sort his words because his presence blindsided her. "My right hand."

"Come on, we'll take a look at it inside where I can see better." Dirty, leaf-filtered light dissected the shadows to reveal a sadness she'd never witnessed. The years may have been kind to his body, but his spirit failed to conceal a poignant heartache universal to human suffering.

That, more than anything, brought the full weight of their shared past down around her shoulders. "Let me go, Conn. There's nothing you can say that I'd want to hear."

Surprised he'd let her jerk away from his touch, she shivered from the cool air washing across her long-sleeved t-shirt, damp from her tumble on the dew-covered lawn. Quivers rattled her teeth in the all-consuming presence of Conner and the aftermath of their encounter.

"It's about your brother. And you will listen regardless of what it takes." A shrug and twist slid his jacket down his arms before he placed the supple leather around her shoulders.

Heat from his fingers lingered at her neck as Conner's scent filled her mind. A tremor ran from shoulder to shoulder.

He smiled.

At least his coat covered her damp shirt. Tears pooled in her eyes as she mounted the steps again. When the door swung open this time, she knew what waited on the other side. One man remained in the vestibule, nodding at Conner as they passed.

Just as they entered the great hall, the top-heavy blonde who'd voiced her contempt now radiated a thinly veiled hatred, as if every evil ever perpetrated on the planet originated from Kendra. The promiscuous shrew tallied one more thing on the long list of things to avoid.

"*Hmm*, I see you didn't go far and collected a little trash while gone."

Whether the bitch referred to her as trash or the dirt that smeared her face, didn't matter.

Regardless of the circumstances, Kendra's dignity remained intact. "I'll be with you in a minute, cur." Leaves clinging in her hair, dirt and grass staining her shirt, she portrayed the criminal, back-alley urchin condemned by the bitch's arrogant gaze. It didn't subordinate the rock-hard defiance filling her soul.

"Her name is Cindy, and she normally knows how to comport herself. Tonight is an absolute exception."

Conner's husky voice in her ear prompted fantasies from long ago she could no longer contemplate. Given no choice as to direction, her stiffened frame shuffled into a smaller hallway where several closed doors likely gave way to large offices. The closest one on the left opened when he leaned around her to nudge it wide.

Chapter Three

The massive executive desk fit Conner's lifestyle, but not the deep leather sofa and side table bearing an intricate medieval lamp. Bookcases filled with leather-bound volumes lined the adjacent wall. What took center stage—a large expanse of pictures taken long ago.

Emotional waterworks threatened again as she jerked away to pad closer to the largest photo, one where her brother and his unit all wore camouflage and sported wide grins. Mixed in among the shots were pictures of the Crofton brothers, Billy, and herself standing in front of a Ferris wheel at an amusement park. It'd been one of the best days of her life.

Billy's eyes condemned her for withholding the secret she couldn't reveal. His last letter, posted from overseas, contained a time bomb that, if acted upon, would threaten her very sanity.

"That was taken just before he left." Her stomach contracted violently in its attempt to refute the serenity radiating from those paper smiles.

Years of anger had denied her tears release, but seeing Billy beside Conner and his team sporting that trademark grin, induced the urge to cry until her soul lay desiccated.

"Yeah, I'll never forget that day."

Venting in front of Conner wasn't an option. She fought the pressure behind her eyes, since the restrained torrent could fill a moat around his castle.

Conner turned her, pulling her against his chest as his hands smoothed down her arms, removing the jacket and tugging her close. "You've never cried for him, have you, sweetheart?"

"N-no. He left me. He left me to go back to hell, and you." Throwing a solid strike at his stomach felt good—until her injured wrist struck a solid wall of muscle. "Ow, damn it."

He didn't flinch, a sigh the only indication of her outburst.

"You have to grieve in order to come out whole on the other side. Otherwise, the darkness will fester like an infected wound, growing and spreading until it consumes you then turns you into someone you're not meant to be."

A pointed look around reinforced her recognition of his insight. "So, I see. Always setting the perfect example." Had Billy's death consigned Conner's soul to the same sludge-filled nightmare that comprised her existence?

Only a slight frown declared she'd nailed him. He was intuitive and would now understand she blamed him for her brother's death.

"He did what he needed to do, Kendra. We all did. Here, sit with me on the sofa." More of a command than a request, he gripped her waist as if she'd fly off at the first chance, and then sat, pulling her down beside him.

Shock and wrist pain prevented a physical reprimand.

Taking her right hand, he examined it as the doctor once had after her attempt to climb a tree. "Just like the time you fell out of the old oak, remember?"

Delving through her memories, he extracted a past trauma and how he'd soothed a frightened girl. The gentle touch used to examine her wrist so contrasted his earlier tackle that she questioned her judgment until the images of him carrying a gun into battle resurfaced. The man he'd grown into was nothing like the one she remembered.

"Seems all right." He flexed it back and forth before continuing, "If it's still bothering you tomorrow, we'll have it X-rayed."

"Dude, its fine. I've had worse falling off my skateboard. 'Sides, I can always punch you with the other fist."

The deep baritone chuckle softened her heart as much as the calloused fingers sifting through her short choppy hair. Each molten graze tightened muscles on her traitorous body which had never responded in such a way.

"The hair cut suits you."

"Best I could do with my knife." Life on the streets changed her ways she'd never imagined. Cutting her hair had taken part of her soul but made it easier to manage. The waist-length ponytail equaled one of the first casualties of street life.

If unable to hold onto her anger, she'd end up panting after him like the bottled blonde. Inside, the quivering snarl of a long-standing grudge twined with desire and fogged her brain to leave her confused.

"It appears we've gotten off on the wrong foot."

"We've never gotten off at all, but if your piece on the side doesn't mind..." she said, pointing her chin toward the door and the bitch who'd be listening at its seam.

"Enough. Don't assume anything." Thick brows slammed down over his gaze, warning her as he never had, not in the old days. He switched gears faster than anyone she'd met.

"How'd you find me, and why bother?" The pleasant scent of leather, books, and Conner beckoned her to relax, but she couldn't, not with this new and aberrant version of her previous infatuation sending her emotions skittering hot and cold, reversing on a dime.

"With the skill set learned in the military, it seemed a natural progression to private investigator after discharge. The club is something my brothers and I started as a... stress reliever. Even so, you've been difficult to track."

"Huh. Once a dick, always a dick." The hurt deep inside claimed him a traitor to an unspoken promise and compelled her to wound him at any cost.

"I prefer the term private investigator. Your mouth has gotten dirty over the years." His grin spoke of infinite evil as the swirling motions of his fingers down her arm induced a shudder. "From sass to foul mouth. Seems to me I described how I'd cure that, something involving my hand on your ass."

"Still a pervert, just all grown up. Of course, if you wanna give it a go, we could—" She smirked when he covered her mouth with his hand, then jerked it away before her teeth could clamp down.

All the threats he'd delivered to her younger self and how Billy had always intervened, claiming it was the nature of a young girl coming into her own and testing limits. The image of Billy standing between them brought a wad of bitter acid to her throat.

A sob escaped. Then another, until a flood of unspent tears overwhelmed her mind and threatened to spill into the real world. Conner's world. He tightened his arms around her, pulling her to his chest, whispering encouraging words and stroking her back in light circles.

She wouldn't cry despite him wrenching her into his universe. This was temporary. Emotions bottled so tight they filled her chest to bursting forced a growl hissed through gritted teeth. Anger at her brother for leaving and at Conner for not protecting him scorched a painful swath through her soul.

Conner soothed her as she struggled to gain control.

From beyond the door, sounds of music and Palmer's voice signaled the beginning of her band's performance. She shifted her weight to stand, but Conner held her back.

"No, hon, they'll take care of things tonight."

"But I need this gig to eat." In her pocket, a bit of loose change and two one-dollar bills entailed all her worldly possessions, except for her guitar.

"Don't worry. I've got you covered."

Of all the ways she'd earned her keep, she'd remained on her feet, refusing to sell her soul or any part of her spirit, much less her body. Images of dark corners and his secluded instigated a wide assortment of scenarios.

"I don't do charity. I work, Conn. Honest work."

"It's not charity. I've hired your band for three months. We'll consider this a little break. You and I need this time together." His calloused fingers brushed hair from her eyes, then stroked along her cheek in a warm and casual benediction.

"C'mon, Mongrel. This isn't a handout, just a hand up. We all start life with nothing. I'm offering a chance with no strings attached. What you do with it is up to you."

"God, I can't. I just can't. I'm like ground hamburger inside." Her confession cut deep, a razor-edged knife slicing pain through her heart and leaving furrows for the acid of his betrayal to burn ever deeper. For, in her mind, Conner had drawn Billy away and to his death.

Why did life have to turn upside down?

Despite her mind's objection, she rubbed her cheek in circular motions against his chest and inhaled deep. If she could pull some of his strength into her lungs, maybe she could see past the pain. Maybe she could survive.

Again, his low, whispered words comforted even as she absorbed the heat of his large frame.

"Billy extracted a promise from me before... not that he needed to. I'd intended to look after you as soon as I got back. I thought you'd moved away with your parents. I hadn't spoken with them since the funeral—not until a month ago." His words caught, hitched with the pain they both endured.

"You spoke with them?" Years had passed since she'd seen her parents. At the time, she thought they'd loved her, but they turned on her. They'd turned on each other, until her mom spoke the unthinkable.

A sliver of hope tinged her senses in thinking perhaps, one day, she could return. Like they'd approve of the gutter rat she'd become.

"Briefly, yeah. I've lacked the courage to follow up. I was supposed to protect him, bring him back to you. I failed." Such gruffness had never entered his well-modulated tone, at least not in her presence.

"How'd you find out I wasn't with them?" The pain of accepting his comfort almost outweighed the burden of loss squeezing her heart. Bittersweet memories persisted in flooding her mind. How many times had she wished she'd been the one to die, if for no other reason than to escape the endless bite of loneliness?

"We all made out wills before we left, a standard. However, Billy posted a package from overseas to his attorney and deliverable to me on your twenty-first birthday. I didn't know about it until receiving the special delivery. It's been in my safe, waiting for you." Conner tucked a lock of straight hair behind her ear before continuing. "On your birthday, I tracked down your parents. They said you'd run away."

His gentle caress stroked her pain as his words gave life to the images of how Billy had died. Control of her body came in slow degrees of halting breaths.

"When they realized you weren't coming back, they moved, said their house held too many memories. They couldn't bear living in a home minus their children. Your mom said she's never regretted anything more than the things said to you."

"Took you long enough to find me. Some dick you are."

She smiled at his groan.

"Careful, little one." His very presence dominated the space with such a casual air he wouldn't realize it. "I would've searched right away had I known you'd taken off. Why, Kendra? You know they love you."

"Before Billy left for his first tour, he said he'd move to an apartment when he returned and I could live with him." Several minutes passed before she gained enough control to continue.

"Then, when he came home, he said he had to go back with his unit, they needed him more than I did. I waited, and just before his tour was over..."

Spicy aftershave and minty aroma permeating her senses wasn't like the false comfort she derived in her dreams. This instigated a poignant ache sending her mind back to older and simpler times. An era when she hadn't worried about strange men attacking her while asleep or where to find her next meal.

"Jesus, Kendra. Why didn't you contact me? You know I would've helped. I'll always help you. Instead, I ended up chasing you from one bolt-hole to the next." The deep rumbling in his chest filled the room.

"You remind me too much of him." His smoothing circular caresses on her temple then down the bridge of her nose and cheek quieted the worst of her turbulent thoughts.

"So, you've been on your own all this time? Dear God. You've hidden right under my nose." As if trying to negate his own culpability and pain, Conner pressed her cheek against his chest while kissing her forehead. "I'm eternally thankful you've done whatever necessary to survive, but you're safe now. It's time to let go of all that and start over."

"I don't need you. I do fine on my own." The lie tasted acidic in her mind and on her tongue. The last thing she wanted was to leave, but if she stayed any longer, her heart would detonate, so conflicted, so wrapped up in this man who'd changed in ways she couldn't define.

"We'll discuss that later. Right now, we need to get you settled."

"I'm okay, for Chrissakes. What was in the envelope Billy sent? And why wait to open it?" Curiosity drove her thoughts forward while pulling up memories of how Billy had always protected and supervised, guiding her actions and nodding approval of her choices.

"Don't know what's inside. It's still sealed. When it arrived, that's when I found out you were in the wind." Self-recriminations and a certain emptiness seemed to writhe within his tone as his caresses momentarily stilled.

"So, let's see it." She understood Conner's perception on an elemental level since the same agonizing torment lay within her heart, as if seeing Billy's legacy would reanimate pain and restore her anguish to its former heartrending capacity.

"Since it's waited this long, a little longer won't hurt. I have a proposition for you."

Her body tensed. This new and twisted Conner held more than a shadow of something ominous beneath the surface, something dangerous which led far from her desired path. Just because she accepted a few crumbs of comfort didn't mean she'd trust him.

"Jeez, haven't heard that one before. No, thank you. I was just kidding earlier." She curled forward and away from his body.

A small shake accompanied his admonishment before he pulled her back tight to his chest. "Knock it off." Immediately, his touch softened.

"I'm twenty-one. I've grown while you've been away. Do these look like puberty-induced pimples to you?"

Either self-preservation or cowardice prevented her from lifting her shirt but placing her hands beneath each breast and pushing up proved her point. Although she'd matured into a woman's body, her small breasts didn't compare to his blonde, capable of breastfeeding a small village.

"Yeah, like I said. You're young." Seizing her chin between his thumb and forefinger, he turned her face to meet his gaze.

Regardless of the decades spent, she would never fathom what depraved schemes warped through his mind. He hadn't been like this when she was younger, when Billy was alive.

"You're going to spend the next three months working for me. I have need of an assistant in my PI firm." Determination in his gaze matched the force of his grip.

This version of Conner she feared, the one who lurked behind the fierce scowl and foreboding aura.

"A dick's assistant? Wonder what that job entails. Sorry, I don't look good in knee pads."

As the oldest of four brothers, he'd looked after them even before his father murdered their mother and left them alone in the world. He'd become protector, advisor, and parent to three younger siblings. It became his way of life.

Determination and something unfathomable vacillated in waves to insulate them from the world while at the same time spreading uncertainty and a tinge of fear. "It's the only way you'll get the envelope."

This time, her entire body threatened withdrawal. Gray edged the periphery of her vision, fighting to take control. Could she run and leave a part of Billy behind? The last part he'd intended to share? If not for street seasoning, she might've caved—until another thought occurred.

A standoff ensued as neither could proceed nor retreat without exposure to a crushing defeat. For him, the danger was failure to coerce her as he'd always done.

The menace to her was much greater and entailed a broken spirit. The resultant tension knotted her stomach just as his jaw tic radiated conviction.

There's more than one way to skin a cat. "No. Now, let go of me." Shocked when he relented, she scrambled to her feet while examining his expression, dissecting it. She didn't like what she saw.

Cunning. Determination. Victory. Then the damned smile, the one she could never resist that declared him master.

Why?

The ensuing silence unified years of grief, fear of the future, and dread over what final method her dead brother had devised to tweak her mind. It resulted in a point of no return and no moving forward.

The present was too painful to live in. Delving into the past would kill her spirit in an instant.

Flinging the door open, she rushed out to the vast hall until her forward momentum was halted by the scene on stage. Palmer was wicked on the drums as Cliff, their bass player, sang a slow ballad. They sounded good, real good.

Daeron's gaze found her, friend to friend, visually inspecting as if seeking assurance of her safety. She nodded then gestured toward the front door, knowing he'd discern her need to go.

Like Conner, he understood her. Unlike Conner, Daeron never inspired fanciful dreams of white picket fences and long, hot nights filled with melting kisses and bodies joined in ecstasy.

In less than an hour, the night brought death to her dreams of a new beginning while throwing her into a living nightmare fashioned from her own horrific past.

The blonde bitch who'd visually dissected her earlier stepped into her path, the evil gleam in her eye spelling a type of trouble no one needed.

"Where're you going, sweetie? Obviously, Conner wants you to stay. I'm Cindy, by the way, his girlfriend."

"Listen, slut. You can have him. All of him. I don't want him, don't need him, and wouldn't have him, especially *that* part. All yours. Have fun boning the dick." She couldn't force any more vehemence in her rejection.

"Oh, hon, green just isn't your shade. He's already mine. Always has been and always will be. He just needs a little push now and then as a reminder, like tonight. 'Sides, there's not enough of your skinny little ass to keep a man like him satisfied. Tell me, why didn't you stuff socks in your bra for tonight's performance? Must be awful to be mistaken for a guy..."

The room held no comfort and no future. Pivoting, Kendra ran through the entrance hallway in need of the cool, fresh air to snap her reality back into place. At least Conner didn't follow.

He thought to manipulate her? Ha, he was in for a big surprise.

Though almost dry, her thin shirt afforded no protection against plummeting temperatures and accumulating dew. The jacket she'd tossed aside in her bolt-hole would've felt good about now, but the distance to travel and retrieve it would ruin the evening's plans.

If only she could see the look on the smug bastard's face once he discovered she'd outmaneuvered him. Wes should have been inside by now, which meant his vehicle was on the lot. She hadn't seen him yet and wouldn't search for his truck. The risk of being seen as a delinquent lurking about was too great.

Still, she had a plan.

Chapter Four

The parking lot held more shadows than comfort as row after row of vehicles fostered the look of soldiers at attention, lined up and oblivious to the castle's barbarians seeking untold perversions.

How could Conner submerse himself in a glorified bar? Had war twisted him into some distorted and demented creature so foreign to his previous character? During her younger years, he'd existed as a beacon of light.

Understandable the younger Croftons would follow his lead. Some things never changed. Marc had seemed perfectly comfortable in the dark surroundings. Even Daeron, whom Kendra had called friend for three years, cast an appreciative glance around the interior. How could Conner lead them all astray? What happened to his sense of direction?

The way he'd jumped away from her after their bodies collided relegated her to the status of filthy animal. That realization imparted freedom to view the world in a different light and from a different perspective, one she'd never considered. Perhaps she *had* sunk to the level Cindy's gaze condemned.

Smooth hardtop met damp grass beyond the last row of cars, a perfect place to sit and ease the roiling emotions driving her heart rate skyward from conflicting thoughts. Something about the surrounding woods made her avoid their silent offer of anonymity and shelter from the wind. The night's temperature was dropping, yet the emotions boiling inside her would provide warmth until the band finished.

Lower temps forced her to look around for Wes' car, finding it locked and near the middle of the lot. Strange that she hadn't seen him inside. Where was he, and why hadn't he helped them set up? Wasn't that what managers did?

A black SUV in the lot's corner offered a much-needed windbreak from the slicing breeze along with back support as she sat and rested against the wheel while praying for sanity's return along with a plan. Tilting her head back, she closed her eyes and took a deep, cleansing breath.

Thank God.

Minutes passed as the cold breeze seeped through her pores to encase her new reality in virtual ice.

"Hello, sweets. Need a little warming?" Underneath the thin veneer of civility, menace and syphilitic intentions lurked in the disembodied voice.

Her gaze snapped open.

Two encroaching shadows moved with stealth born of dark intentions. Blood roared in her ears to override the breeze's sibilant sloughing through budding oak trees. In her life, threats often approached from a twisted angle seldom seen without good peripheral vision.

She'd known better than to have her head up her ass and ignore her surroundings. A rapid vault to her feet landed her in a fighting stance with knees bent and fists ready. She may not have attained Billy's level of black-belt expertise, but she'd spent years on the street, and had Daeron's training to hone her skills.

As panic settled its talons deep in her chest, the danger creeping forward took human form. Black-clad, masked face, gloved hands, the thugs stalked from the woods to extend the fingered, inky darkness in venomous degrees of menace. Despite the cloudy veil, she detected slim, wiry builds as faster, stronger than her adrenaline-flooded frame.

Viewed minutes ago as a threat, the castle stood too far away to furnish safe haven since a flood of adrenaline compromised her mind's order to run. She couldn't override the increasing tremble in her legs until she got control of her breathing and heart rate. Daeron's words echoed in her mind: *"Assess your situation, control your response."*

A deep breath. A mental shake. Her head cleared—somewhat. Her first opponent's rigid stance prepped her mind and body for the brawl ahead. Six feet away and out of reach, he still towered over her.

I will survive this.

Her personal boogeyman motioned to an extended threat.

A shorter man stepped up beside him.

Jesus. Two-to-one odds.

This isn't good.

Shorter, stockier, and dressed like his companion with the addition of a black trench coat, the newest peril kept his communication nonverbal, albeit more threatening. Ambient moonlight reflected his knife's glimmer weaving a figure-eight pattern in the quiet night.

Oh, shit.

Her glance flicked to the castle.

"Yeah, you could try, but you'd never make it. I'll bring you down like a small deer and maybe snap your neck." The leader snorted as he stepped closer, further assessment underway indicated by the way he cocked his head side to side. Four feet separated them, not close enough for a strike. His height gave him a longer reach, another disadvantage.

"What do you want, asshole? The rest of the perverts are inside. Why don't you join them?"

Calm likely inherent to his degenerate personality, he gave her chills, something not many could do.

"Just what your brother stole, the envelope. We've watched you, waiting for you to exploit the contents, then realized you didn't even have it. Probably never did. Your bastard brother must've mailed it to one of his team. We've never been sure."

"You've waited years and still want to collect it? Must be important. Let me guess, pictures of your boss screwing his secretary? Probably worth millions in alimony payments."

"No dawdling, sweets. I'll have what's mine." Three feet and almost within reach.

How about a kick in the teeth instead?

Kendra took a soft step left, but both men mimicked her move. "I don't have your envelope."

"Maybe not, but you can get it from one of the Crofton brothers. Otherwise, they'll be having accidents and end up like your big brother." The verbal blackmail held no hesitation, only the desire to fulfill a promise, an unspoken need for violence.

"If it's in a safe deposit box, I can't get to it. Looks like we're in the same boat." Street smarts only carried one so far. She didn't want to bet a Crofton life on being able to crack it.

"The way I hear it, no lock can stand in your path. However, if you prefer the easy way, use your charms, but be careful. The oldest brother has a terrible temper and has killed many times." A glint of light off a false gold tooth provided the only distinguishing feature through the mask's openings. "My boss wants this done now and without a mess."

"I've never been one to screw around, asshole."

"Well, then, looks like you need a tutor. I don't mind helping a girl in need." Glancing over his shoulder at his partner, he added, "Brac, keep a look out while I take this little morsel in the woods and guide her in the art of sucking dick and spreading her legs."

She couldn't place the foreign accent, some form of Asian dialect.

Affirmation wrapped in the same foreign intonation defied definition but not clarity as his partner rubbed the front of his jeans. "Save me some."

The woods lay twenty yards behind the second man. If she ran, regardless of the direction, they'd catch her. If she screamed, someone might come out and receive a crimson necktie during an attempt to intervene.

When the first dirtball stepped close, she dropped her shoulders and relaxed her hands in a show of defeat.

His gloved fingers flexed into fists.

Another step forward.

Fear clouded her mind, disconnecting thoughts firing at random while the rapid beat of her heart shook her body. The sound of it echoed in the roar of blood through her ears. She remembered how terror smelled after one time in its grasp. The memory now left a nonhomogeneous sour reminder in her throat.

She was experienced. She was strong. She could survive.

A stiff blast of chilled air dried the moisture beading her brow before his foul breath boiled down her face and shrouded her mind with its filth.

A dark chuckle accompanied rough hands pulling her forward and rubbing his hips back and forth against her.

A quick step back prepared her for action. A deep breath to clear her mind. She'd use the SUV for leverage.

Introducing her knee to the pervert's nards lent its own satisfaction.

"Looks like this chilly weather has had its own effect. Sorry, I don't carry tweezers."

The hard ridge of his manhood received a wakeup call, street style.

Her attacker doubled over as she shoved him to the right and off balance. Her step to the left gave her a clear line of sight to thug number two.

A low snort accompanied the second man's immediate countermove. He'd anticipated and again mimicked her step.

She stood no chance against a knife.

Hoarse words followed a groan from the first asswipe. "Shit. You're gonna pay for that, whore." Harsh breaths punched thin trails of vapor in the moonlight.

Delight sprinkled his partner's tone in chiding. "Christ, man, you can't handle a half-pint like this? What good are you?"

The taunter's sudden grunt took her by surprise when unseen hands jerked him backward, the knife flying from his hands to clatter on the stones at her feet.

A third unknown had joined the party from hell, one she hadn't sensed. Damn. Again, with a mask, this one wore a trench coat and made no sound in his ghostly movements.

The split-second reprieve offered no clarity of the situation. Who the hell was helping her? And why?

Regardless of the temporary remission from purgatory's northern theatre, she was now hunted. Not by a random sexual deviant, no, she had to go for the deluxe stalker, one with a complicated agenda.

Figures.

The first assailant caught the blade's glimmer before she could recover it. He struggled to grasp it even as he groaned. Due to her first knee-jerk reaction enforcing his bent posture, he was closer and scooped up the blade.

Shit.

His fumbling the knife in raising his arm allowed her to reach under and around to grab the outer part of his hand. Using her other hand to grab the inside of his palm, she rotated them to apply a joint lock.

Had pain not incapacitated her opponent, even her adrenaline-flooded system wouldn't have been able to enforce the restraint. There was no space to afford a step back, so she planted her foot against the SUV's fender as leverage and shoved forward with all her strength.

The resultant gurgling and warm spray across her face and chest betrayed the dark, slick evidence of her success. Copper scent induced a dry heave as her heart hammered and an icy chill penetrated her mind. In all her independent street time, she'd never faced a knife, yet minutes after rejoining polite society and letting her guard down evolved into murder.

A widened gaze further exposed his sclera and betrayed the victim's shock as he scrambled to stem the flow of blood from his neck. A strangled bubbling sound confirmed his compromised airway. He jerked in random spasms even as his body thudded to the ground.

The new view unveiled the second thug's struggle against her unknown rescuer. The crack of fist connecting jaw preceded a heavy grunt, but she couldn't discern aggressor from defender. Undeterred by darkness shrouding finer points of the struggle, they appeared evenly matched in weight and skill when neither wielded a weapon.

Insufficient light and knit hoods foiled her attempt at identifying either. When she stepped forward to help, her rescuer—identifiable only by his whisper—warned her off in a harsh, low voice, "No, Kendra, back off. Go to Conner."

In his moment of distraction, her dark knight took a solid thrust to his midsection. Air wheezed out in an explosive heave as he stepped back and shook his head.

With prick number one bleeding out, two-to-one odds didn't suit the second asshole, who turned tail and raced back to the woods, followed by her rescuer after his re-issuance of the command. "Go back to Conner, Kendra. Go now. I'll handle this."

Shit, shit, shit.

Post-fight adrenaline rush overwhelmed her mind and body. Shaking hands reached for the SUV as her stomach acids scorched her throat in their successful bid for freedom. The sour taste reminded her she'd survived.

With the end of retching came ice seeping through her marrow to provoke convulsive shudders. Her thoughts congealed into a fuzzy backwash of panic. Blood spatter painted her face, hair, and clothes. Who knew dying could be such a messy business?

A small swath of moon glow glinted off staring, glassy eyes and burnished the pooled under his head. Looking at the now lifeless cadaver, she couldn't force her feet closer.

Identification didn't matter. She didn't know any Asian types. Unable to turn her back for fear of some new unnamed horror taking shape, she backed toward the presumed safety of the building.

Less than five minutes changed her world, yet the surrounding area remained quiet except for the raw breeze sweeping her stiffening hair across her face. Who'd helped her? Should she follow into the woods to see if her guardian angel needed assistance?

Hell, one masked man fighting another? She wouldn't know whom to aid since both appeared equal in build and attire.

As the sky gathered more clouds to foil the meager light, she used shadows to creep toward the club. Existing shrubbery surrounding the structure would offer concealment until the building emptied. Her original plan remained in play despite the ghastly twist in her life. Now, more than ever, she needed that damn envelope.

Whatever Conner held in his safe made him a target. He'd declared ignorance of its specific nature with untainted honesty. Despite the way he'd handled her earlier, she owed him for protecting her in the past and the misguided attempt to do so now.

Tonight's close call involved Billy's legacy, dragging her into a seedy underworld where she held no knowledge. At least street life was honest.

One seldom recognized the why of evil's approach but could react accordingly. She wouldn't allow Conner to take responsibility this time. Throughout her self-imposed exile, she'd remained the same person with the same moral code, ethics, and honest heart. The only difference now—stone encased all three, permitting no one to alter the foundation.

Deep in the crevices of her darkened spirit, she'd always known the day would come when she'd have to face Conner, praying a childhood crush hadn't morphed into hatred for breaking a sacred promise.

Whether fortunate or disastrous that her feelings remained intact despite his failure didn't matter. She'd see the new threat ended then find another city to haunt.

Whatever Conner had become, the concern knotting his expression earlier was sincere. He still considered her a responsibility.

Chances were good that with enough time, she could break into a pure combination safe but wouldn't be sure until she tried.

For now, she'd wait, hidden by the night and scantily clad shrubbery while trying to figure out how her life had gone to hell without the slightest nudge.

Using the bottom of her long-sleeved t-shirt to wipe her faced smeared more than cleaned. Prickly yew bushes bit into her shivering flesh while her teeth chattered until she clamped her jaws shut. Behind her, witch hazel would've made for a better-smelling camouflage but lacked enough lower foliage to accomplish the job.

Each minute felt like hours as she reviewed the confrontation with Conner in her mind, anything to prevent the image of blood spray covering her face.

Conner admitted her brother had posted something, which meant it originated from overseas. What had the team done to warrant foreign assassins? Searching her mind, she replayed her attacker's accented dialogue, trying to determine national origin.

Nothing.

Harsh whispers had disguised much of the cadence and timbre.

None the less, she was a murderer. Heedless of the predator's intentions, she hadn't wanted to kill.

Chapter Five

Kendra shivered with the gusty breeze piercing her damp tee.

In counterpoint to the assailant's words, Billy had never been a thief. Even more mysterious was the man who'd saved her life. The fatal encounter had taken place out of the security lights' range, leaving no illumination to aid in identification.

Too short to be a Crofton.

What purpose did hiding his identity serve?

Staying huddled at the base of the bristly yew bush offered little protection other than the fallen leaves under which she'd burrowed. The jacket stashed in the abandoned building now kept the dust bunnies warm. *Damn.*

Blood stiffened her shirt, with harsher wind adding to the cold filling her joints. The bottom line, she lacked adequate preparation for street life.

Sporadic opening of the heavy doors discharged guests at the height of fashion, clothes she'd dreamed of wearing once upon a time. Short glimpses revealed silky dresses and satins with hair in fancy styles.

Departures by twos and threes trickled down to singles as the parking lot slowly emptied. She caught a glimpse of the SUV where the body had fallen, out of sight.

Where in the hell was the band? Tonight's performance was supposed to be short. Perhaps the group stayed to make up for her cutting out or even decided to join in a late-night drink.

* * * *

"How hard can it be to terrorize a little girl? I have a dead body and no merchandise." Cheol's anger seethed over the mic.

Brac thanked providence he relayed his failure through radio waves and not in person. He'd live longer. Cheol's fist slamming against something solid transferred the dull thud's sound through his transmitter with a surety words could never convey.

"In my country, such incompetence ends with death," the leader continued his rant, unaware his puppet considered losing himself among the masses of a distant city.

Coming to this land of vast opportunity grated Brac's nerves with the leash that remained so very short. Everything felt—wrong. Slipping his mask off, he took a deep breath of crisp air. "But the message was delivered despite not getting the intervening bastard's identity." In reporting failure, he expected repercussions regardless of their form or timing.

"I lost him in the woods, but he was well-trained." Eying the clock in his van, he wanted nothing more than to curl up in the back and sleep. First, he'd have to rectify his mistake.

Pale shafts of moonlight sifted through low clouds to reveal the dirt road's exit ahead. The stillness, but a moment in time, stretched out before him while he contemplated his boss' foul mood.

"*Did our boy in the band interfere?*" Cheol's threatening growl did nothing to set his minion at ease.

"No, this prick was built thicker. Our intermediary is skinny. Shall I bring him in for questioning anyway? Perhaps he has some new information." Having an office a short commute from Ambrosia meant his boss kept a close eye on every detail.

Brac preferred a hundred-mile commute.

"*No. I have a better approach. The girl knows what we want, and just as we've figured all along, she doesn't have it.*" Notorious for his patience and intricate strategies, Cheol laid out a plan using his prey's own friends against him. "*Tell our male crooner I want one of Conner's weaknesses, one of the feminine persuasion, under my control. I have difficulty believing he's held our merchandise for so long and not indulged, but then again, I've found many men here to be high on their moral horses.*"

"Okay. What should I do with the body?" Brac hadn't liked his partner and had returned to hide it in the woods. The idea of chopping him to bits and tossing the chum to sharks held little appeal considering the time and mess involved.

"*Burn him along with another. Leave a trail to Conner.*"

"Why not just burn the informer since he's been of little use?"

"*No, not yet. This will be his warning. We still need him for now. I've instigated a plan to instill terror in our little gutter princess while warning Conner at the same time.*"

As his boss outlined the basics of his strategy, Brac prayed he remained in Cheol's semi-good graces, the antithesis being unthinkable and deadly. He didn't take a deep breath until hearing the line disconnect.

At least rain wasn't pouring down. A short text to their mole set the next phase in motion. Relief washed over him as he snapped his cell shut and exited into the cool night air. The same deer trail through the woods leading to Ambrosia's parking lot once again bore the weight of his passage. This time, with a distasteful task ahead instead of sampling a tasty piece of tail.

Time spent waiting further soured his mood. He'd much rather be inside enjoying the delights offered. He'd been inside before. When he finished the job and collected the substantial pay, perhaps he'd find a club to join.

"Where the hell you been? I've been waiting." Brac's skin crawled with the current company. So willing to betray the little bitch in hopes of getting his hands on her, he might just decide her not worth the risk. The nest he called home featured the extent of his obsession, the sick bastard. Pictures of Kendra sleeping, helping at the church, playing her guitar when she thought no one watched, all stashed in a secret hideaway.

"Hey, I had to wait until we finished. It was supposed to be a short night. I'm here now. What do you want?"

"Do not outgrow your usefulness as a spy. Just because we're sure Kendra doesn't have what we want doesn't mean she can't find it. We've searched that damn club along with the Crofton homes, but my boss is now convinced one of them has it."

"What exactly are you looking for?"

"A flash drive."

"Then why not just take one of the men and *question* them. Should be easy enough to do."

"Because if we're wrong and they don't have it, we've tipped our hand at a most inopportune time."

"Must be important. What's on it?"

"Data and details. That's all you need know.

"So what do you want now?"

"Information and help moving a body I've lugged to the wood's edge. Hurry, we'll work and talk at the same time." As much as Brac wanted to shoot the mole, struggling to carry a corpse by himself wasn't his idea of a good evening. They had much to accomplish.

"What've you done?"

"Been entertaining. Now, shut up and get moving." Brac's mood didn't extend to pacifying the closet degenerate.

They made good time despite briars and thorns snatching at their burden not yet stiff from rigor mortis. Along the way, Brac outlined his strategy and made his demands, promising more money and exclusive use of Kendra in return. The money hadn't been necessary as nothing outweighed the use of the little whore's body.

Chapter Six

Grumbles snatched by the breeze with the band's descent from the castle warmed her heart. No one wanted to leave without knowing her whereabouts. Each blamed Conner.

Daeron's voice emerged as the group's common sense, assuming his lead role. "Come on, guys. You know she'll head to one of the abandoned warehouses she occupies when avoiding us. Let's go find her. I'll see if I can finally convince her to stay with Wes."

"Speaking of our fearless leader, where is he? Hell, he dropped us off will little more than an adios," Palmer complained.

She hadn't seen Wes arrive earlier. Then again, she hadn't seen much of the inside, not past the cozy lights, large dance floor, and candlelit tables.

Lack of equipment being lugged down the steps meant they'd accepted the three months' work. Her first gig with a chance to make money, and she'd blown it good and proper. How could she face Conner again?

Fuck a duck.

She had the talent to start a new band in a new city. Decent backup and sound equipment would take time to acquire. She'd have her instrument back in a few minutes.

The guitar was Billy's last birthday gift to her and traveled everywhere. She'd entertained Daeron for three years, her blues music a medley of solemn hope and sad memories.

The parking lot cleared, but she waited, listening to her teeth chatter. She didn't recall Conner's deep voice among the deviants leaving, but figured he'd caught a ride with one of his brothers parked in back.

He'd always been a cunning bugger. Time in the military would've sharpened his talents while adding a few more to his repertoire, increasing her risk if tonight's intended maneuver went south.

If she told him what happened on the lot, he'd go commando and someone else would die. At the very least, he'd draw his brothers into the sordid mess. There'd been enough death. If she could steal the envelope and return it to the foreign pricks, maybe fate would see them all safe.

Life as a street rat held advantages in honing skills of technique and covert activities despite risks involved. She'd gotten better at picking locks and reading people, but like Daeron, refused to steal.

Well-oiled hinges denied evidence of her intrusion while no blaring security system announced her presence. It felt good to leave the wind's bite behind, but maybe too easy.

Inside, a deep blackness obscured visibility and held the building in thrall as she crept along the block wall.

Her whole body shook, whether from fear after the savage skirmish or anticipation of someone catching her didn't register. She needed to get her shit together.

Wet, worn-out tennis shoes pealed slight telltale squeaks from the hardwood as she padded along the perimeter. The two-tone *gurgle-eek* discord lamenting drier climes and times echoed in the massive space.

"Oof." Her face made hard contact with the edge of something solid, the cabinet containing a fire extinguisher.

In gradual degrees, her eyes adjusted to the varying shades of black within the tomb-like structure. The lighter cast of shadows created by high windows admitting ambient light perpetuated the ominous feel of her break-in and offered no real guidance.

What would Conner do if he caught her? He'd already proved faster. The wad of nerves inhabiting her throat refused to lend an easy breath with the thought of tripping some type of silent alarm in his office.

Tactile examination advanced until falling through the invisible plane of a hallway leading to the offices. Earlier, Conner had led her to the first door on the left.

She moved forward, each quiet draw of breath reverberating in the stillness.

When the faintest of breezes brushed her searching fingers, she realized the recessed seam of a door lay underneath. Probing the dark, she found the door handle and twisted.

Locked, of course.

Pulling her pick set out again breathed new life into her ultimate goal of protecting the Croftons. Billy had coached her to do this in the dark. Feeling her way now provided no physical barriers, just the twinge of uncertainty over invading Conner's private domain.

As pick lifted pin, pushing the driver into the upper chamber of the cylinder, the knob turned easily under her gentle touch. The door's hinge joints rotated without sound on their pins to refute the idea of neglected maintenance. Warmer air, now associated with Conner's scent, drifted to her, a soothing calm for the next phase of her plan.

Letting her fingers inch forward along the wall, she searched for a switch. Common sense dictated its placement near the door. Conner was nothing if not practical.

From earlier, she remembered this office had no windows, so no one would know of her legal infraction, as if she hadn't already killed a man. Bile roared up her throat once more with the image of glassy eyes staring into the night sky.

A little fumbling and she found the switch. A deep breath fortified her nerves.

"Hello, Kendra. You must know there's a price for burglary." Conner's sotto voice coincided with the click of his desk lamp. He'd made no sound, no heavy breath to give away his presence.

Aw, fuck.

She should've expected it.

* * * *

Conner's mental tally of the little hellion's nonverbal cues earlier dictated she'd return for the envelope, the only remaining link to her brother. Defiance and anger had shadowed a soft underbelly of vulnerability, traits he'd exploit and manipulate to see her safe. She'd played right into his expectations.

He'd also helped teach her to pick locks years ago.

The fact she froze with the light, her mind searching for a plausible explanation, priceless. From the back, her short hair held an array of torn leaves. Not expected.

"Turn around, Mongrel."

To see her shocked expression when she pivoted was a gift he'd treasure, until his mind registered the dried blood smearing her face, neck, and shirt.

"Jesus, Kendra. What the fuck?" Lunging from his chair, he bolted around the desk to grab her arms, taking note of her shaking body. "You're in shock. Where's the injury?" Without visible confirmation of active bleeding, he searched her head and neck then let his tactile exploration spread to her shoulders and arms.

"Hey, hey! What the hell? Hands. Hands. Hands." Her voice shook as much as her body.

She tried to back away, but his grip held her firm.

"I'm not in shock, I'm cold. I didn't bring my jacket since I thought I'd be entertaining guests inside with the keyboard, not the dirtballs outside with my sass. 'Sides, Wes said he'd give us a ride home."

Ineffectual shoving ceased with his pinning both her hands behind her back, putting them chest to chest. Distant alarm bells sounded in his mind, but he paid no attention in his panic to assess her wounds.

"Hold still, Mongrel. I'm trying to see where you're injured. Nothing more." Unable to see any holes in her shirt for the grime covering her, or gain any degree of cooperation, he released her, letting her take a deep breath before proceeding. There was more than one path to his goal.

"I'm not a mongrel, you big oaf."

With a two-handed grip on her shirt collar, he ripped it from top to bottom, exposing some type of cloth binding across her chest.

"A pressure bandage? Really? Fuck me." Blood caked to the cloth and down the center of her chest sent his thoughts in a tailspin.

"Shit. How could this happen?" He'd promised to look after her. Instead, stiff, dried blood smeared her shaking body while her teeth chattered. "Damn it."

Chest wounds seldom ended well. No wonder she mumbled in shock. Sputtering and choking accompanied her obvious panic. Several of her blows hitting his shoulder distantly registered as insignificant.

41

He'd failed her brother but wouldn't abandon her, regardless of her foul mouth and hedonistic ways. Despite her attempts at twisting away and pounding his head and shoulders, he unknotted the cloth binding her breasts and yanked it away. Underneath, her skin remained unbroken to his probing fingers.

He saw no gashes, no broken skin, and no more blood. Somewhere in the back of his mind, alarms blasted furiously, but his thoughts focused on smeared crimson across her chest.

"Where is it, Kendra?" His searching fingers found no jagged cuts nor elicited sudden screeches. It wasn't until she huffed a deep breath and settled her hands on hips he realized what he'd done. Holy hell, it wasn't good.

As if burned, he snatched his hands back then crossed his arms over his chest, taking the offensive in nonverbal form.

"You own a night club, standing in front of a half-naked woman, and you still can't find them? Jesus, man. You really are hopeless. They're called boobs, Conner. No wonder you're with a top-heavy bimbo and not someone with midget earmuffs."

"What? Earmuffs? What're you talking about? Where. Are. You hurt?"

"I'm not. This isn't my blood."

It wasn't until the last word shuddered out that it sank in, his list of errors. Still, his brain filter continued to misfire. "When in the hell did you grow them?"

Despite her shaking, despite the tears pooling in her eyes, she looked at him with the most poignant sadness he'd ever witnessed.

"I've had them for a while now. Glad you're able to figure out what they are." Desperate words whispered to fill the room.

Her legs buckled under the onslaught of shaking limbs, but she didn't make it to the floor.

Instinct and something deeper and more intimate saw him not only sweeping her to his chest but also holding her tight as he sat on the leather sofa. He snagged a blanket from the back and tucked it around her. "Kendra. I'm so sorry. Jesus, sweetheart. Tell me what happened. From the start."

Like a bludgeon to the head, he realized with a few careless words and thoughtless actions, he'd just beaten her raw, not with a baseball bat or two-by-four, but with the lash of his tongue and instinctual maneuvers. He'd done more damage tonight than any knife could ever accomplish.

"I went outside and sat at the edge of the parking lot to wait until you left." A broken sob disrupted her account of the horrific event. "Two guys came at me. One had a knife. They wanted my brother's package. Said if I didn't get it for them, you'd die, just like Billy." Dry heaves necessitated her sitting up.

Brushing the ragged locks from her face, he held her close until the spasms passed. Only then did he notice the amount of leaf litter and dirt clinging to her hair. Her earnest and innocent intent to keep him safe had forced her to burrow in the dirt, confirming her strength of character.

She'd hand over the envelope in hopes of protecting those for whom she cared, regardless of how deep she buried her feelings.

"They said you've killed many times and were mean as a snake. Told me to use my charms. Looks like they weren't good enough."

"Shit. Goddamn it. I'm so sorry, hon." She had no idea about the effectiveness of her charms.

"I told 'em I wasn't a whore. They said they'd coach me. The one called Brace, or no... Brac, said he'd show me the ropes. He was gonna take me into the woods and rape me. No, wait, Brac was the second one." She took her first unbroken breath while rubbing her eyes, as if she could wipe away the memory along with the crimson smears. "When the first shithead stepped forward, I kneed him in the crotch."

"Jesus." It was all he could do not to smother her, locking her to his side for the foreseeable future. Here was the girl he'd sworn to protect, now terrified, abused, and starving, considering her frame's bony protrusions.

"I've learned a good bit about street fighting in the last three years."

"Thank God for that. Then what happened?"

"Brac dropped his knife when someone, also wearing a mask, came to my rescue. The first asshole picked up the knife and jabbed at me. I

43

grabbed his wrist, twisted, and pushed off the SUV into him. The knife cut his neck."

More dry heaves.

"Blood sprayed everywhere. I couldn't scream. The other two guys, I was going to help whoever intervened, but... I couldn't tell one from the other. It was too dark. Clouds had rolled in heavy."

"It's all right now, Kendra. You're safe. You didn't recognize either voice?"

"No. The second dipshit ran into the woods. The guy who helped me chased him. I couldn't place the foreign accents of the scumbags who attacked me."

"Then?" Conner ran his fingers over her scalp, face, and down her arms, needing the assurance she remained physically unharmed. She still shook from the post-adrenaline rush of her ordeal and his manhandling, but her clattering teeth had settled. This would give her nightmares for months, maybe years to come. "Jeez, I kept three younger brothers in line for years."

Now, I can't handle one small waif.

It'd been his promise to a dying friend.

Snatching a candy bar from the end table, Conner ripped the foil and placed the chocolate to her mouth, ordering, "Eat," while wondering, *When's the last time you had a decent meal?*

Her hands fluttered toward the chocolate, then dropped to her lap as she accepted a bite of the offered bar. "I ran and hid, trying to figure out what to do. I waited, thinking I'd get the envelope and see what was worth rape and murder."

"Then, run?"

She'd been on the streets too long. Unless he was way off base, she could navigate the entire metropolis like her own personal rabbit warren, slipping seamlessly between shadows without disturbing a stone or alerting the smallest furry creature.

Her gaze slinked away while fatigue and fear etched lines in her face.

"Kendra? Not gonna happen." Thought gave way to fear, fear for the young lady she'd been and the woman she could become.

Her wince alerted him to his tightening grip. He tried to take a calming breath as excessive hormones pummeled his composure.

"I killed a man, Conner." Exhaustion laced her voice and glazed her eyes. She was nearing the end of her reserves.

"In self-defense. If you hadn't, I would've, regardless of the circumstances." He would kill anything and anyone who threatened her. "Where's the knife?"

An account of the evening from her point of view flashed through his thoughts, one trauma after another, insult on top of injury. He'd botched this mission from the start.

Hell, he should've known years ago she'd run, instead of thinking her better off without his presence as a reminder of her brother's death.

He'd waited until she turned twenty-one to check on her. Even so, it had taken time to find her and set up the elaborate band charade, knowing her time alone would've toughened her inner tomboy with an iron will.

Flashes of memory after exposing her body proved she held nothing in common with a male. That sight now lay burned in his mind forever and stirred his demons to needle him with the memory of silken skin and perfect breasts.

"I-I couldn't bring myself to—take it from his clutched hand."

"Neither are there now. Anyone finding a dead man near their vehicle would've reported it, and we'd know about it."

Finally, her muscles gave up their tension to his continuous petting as she took another nibble of the chocolate that would counteract her dropping blood sugar. Considering her anorexic frame, if she'd grabbed the candy like a starved vagabond, he'd have lost the fight to contain the moisture brimming his eyes.

"All right. I'll sort this out. You sit tight and rest now."

With the nightmare she'd survived, it came as no surprise when her breathing slowed to an even rhythm, the adrenaline washout leaving her unconscious.

Quietly, he unclipped his cell to enlist his brothers' help. Before he got the police involved, he needed more information. Nobody attacked his... exactly what was she to him?

Julien answered on the second ring, concern pitching his tone to one expecting trouble.

After recounting the evening's unholy mess minus holding a half-naked young woman in his arms, Conner asked his younger brother to bring Nika, his tracking dog, in hopes of ending the surreal nightmare fate had created.

It wasn't fair and galled the hell out of him to wake her, but his light touch on her shoulder snapped her eyes open.

"Sweetheart, we need to get you dressed before Julien arrives. Unless I'm wrong, he'll call Marc or Nate regardless of my order." He prayed Julien would keep things quiet, for once.

To see her in one of his chamois shirts would more than satisfy the primal instinct in him. It was selfish, but she needed something warm and dry.

Never the type to explain himself to anyone, he closed his eyes at the memory of his brothers shaking their heads in confusion over his hiring a jazz band until Kendra's less-than-spectacular entrance. It'd stopped the moment they recognized her.

None of them approved of her being in the club. Granted, this wasn't the type of place she should spend her evenings, but if he didn't keep her under his thumb, he couldn't ensure her safety. He'd planned on the band playing for a night or two, then reuniting her with her parents… where she belonged.

Even after the last strain of music had died and after they'd closed up for the night, he'd known she would return. Nothing could keep her away from the mystery of her brother's legacy.

Something akin to wonder had settled in his chest while she slept on the couch. No stranger to a woman's body, he valued them all, but Kendra had shocked him, transporting his mind and spirit to a calmer place once he'd discovered her in one piece and safe.

He hadn't wanted to notice her firm breasts flattened by that offensive strip of cloth. Again, primal instincts took over. He'd noticed.

Over and over in his mind, images of what homeless teens endured in hopes of survival ground his shame like shards of glass in his gut. All this lay on his conscience. If he'd checked on her after her brother's funeral, he would've known she'd taken off and could have avoided all the needless suffering. He had a lot for which to atone, regardless of the time and effort it took.

Chapter Seven

Marc strode through the door first with Darius, his shepherd, by his side. "How is she?"

Figured Julien would call him, probably before getting out of bed. "Where's Dani?"

"She's fine. The team's with her. Matter of fact, we all convened at Julien's house. The girls found out about Kendra's arrival tonight and decided to *help*."

"Oh, hell. I don't want them involved in this."

"Too late. Dani knows about Billy's death. Then his sister shows up looking like a street urchin?" Marc snorted. "Word spreads between the women faster than lightning. Hence, we all gather. That's how it works. Remember?"

Like each of his other brothers, Marc could go wheels up in ten. His pointed look at the ragamuffin dwarfed by an oversized chamois shirt morphed into sympathy after Conner's nod to the bloody clothing in the corner.

"She's pretty shaken up." Conner lowered his voice when Kendra stirred in her sleep. He wouldn't let her run again. "Easy, Mongrel. You know Marc." Like a kid wanting to avoid admonishment, she snuggled deeper under the blanket.

Billy used to brag about her brilliant mind and how she'd one day become a renowned surgeon or scientist when all she'd wanted at the time was to play her piano. Now, she was homeless, hiding her fear, and probably hungry as hell.

Damn her pride, anyway.

"Any further info?" Marc's hand signal released Darius, who whined before padding over to Kendra.

When she held out her hand, the shepherd rained pup kisses up her arm before stepping up, nuzzling, and sniffing her face.

"Aw, what a good baby."

"Damn, what is it about Crofton women and dogs?" Marc's uncensored comment snapped Kendra's gaze up, a priceless mixture of hope, shock, and something defying definition.

Conner cleared his throat. "Marc, how about you—"

"Um, no, man. Not this time. This is all you." Marc chuckled before continuing, "I'll work with Darius while you keep her safe." Devilment danced in his gaze with the last comment drifting softly into the still night. "Finally, big brother falls. We've waited a lifetime for this."

Constant ribbing from his siblings about not having a long-term relationship had grown old. He'd never been the type to settle down or be with one woman. For Kendra to hear the reference was unfortunate.

The situation's trajectory already deviated from his plan to see her settled and safe with her folks. It appeared the envelope's contents *were* worth dying for, or maybe tonight entailed collateral damage.

Either way, the unforeseen escalation necessitated drastic steps, ones she wouldn't like. Better that than leading this trouble to her parents' door.

"You're all right, Mongrel. We'll wait here until Darius is finished before heading out."

Julien appeared minutes later, his dog's heavy breathing betraying excitement and anticipation of work. Nika whined until allowed to greet Kendra. "I see Marc beat me here."

Should've expected a full response."

After subdued greetings and brief interactions, Julien left.

With silence gracing his domain once more, Conner inhaled deep, witch hazel, decaying leaves, and offensive copper odor filled his mind with death. She'd always smelled of vanilla and cinnamon shampoo, along with a uniquely scented body lotion.

Now, the faint whiff of stringent soap came to mind. He grimaced with the faraway memories of her preferences.

"I'm not going home, Conner. Not now, not ever." Her body tensed, but she didn't push to stand.

"My home. You're coming home with me."

A rabid raccoon would've been easier to manage. A solid kick landed on his flank before he maneuvered out of her range. Kendra snarled warnings he'd never expected to hear.

"Settle down, damn it! Nothing's going to happen. I'm going to see you safe until we sort out this mess. Someone's after you. For God's sake. You know I would never hurt you!"

Energy reserves diminished quickly after so much stress, which didn't stop the bite of her tongue. "Says the man who owns a night club. Though, I guess I should take comfort in the fact you can't recognize a boob smaller than a soccer ball."

He could ignore her barbed tongue as long as she calmed physically, knowing her mind would soon follow.

"When's the last time you ate?" The image of her malnourished skeleton doused him with another round of remorse. He'd seen starving children in the Middle East with more meat on their bones.

"Um, I'm okay. I just ate a candy bar."

Which would constitute a meal, or three, in her book.

The thinness of her voice sliced his gut like a razor's edge of shame. "Jesus. That's not food. That's just a bit of sugar to keep you from bottoming out."

"Sorry. It's just that you've changed a lot since you returned, and I don't know what to expect. I guess war had changed Billy, too."

He'd address the food issue at home. "Yeah, I guess it did. We don't realize it until something from the past forces us to face former realities. I'm not the only one who has changed, little one."

"How did it happen?" Whispered words, so innocent, pleaded from a heart in desperate need of healing.

There was no need to ask for clarification. "I don't know who shot him. We'd finished our exercise and were taking a break in Europe before coming home." He hated glossing over details, a necessary evil.

"You'd just completed a mission." Determination marred her brow and firmed her tone.

She deserved the truth.

"Yes. That morning, Billy said he needed to run an errand. Once finished, he'd drop a post in the mail and return. Didn't give any details, just that he'd be back by nightfall. We figured he'd gone to do a little shopping for you.

"Nobody heard the shot, so he must've hoofed it a good distance. He collapsed after stumbling through the doorway, died in my arms shortly thereafter. We searched and tried to backtrack his movements but failed. Our commander didn't shed any light on the situation, just ordered us home."

The biggest tragedy of his life had encompassed watching his best friend die while begging Conner to protect his sister.

"That's when I decided I'd become a private investigator. Your brother was a good man, an honorable man. Don't ever forget that, Kendra. He loved you very much."

The panic in Billy's eyes and the plea in his rasping voice inundated Conner's nightmares on a regular basis to leave him shaking and drenched with sweat.

"Promise you'll take care of her."

"He didn't love me enough to stay home."

With no physical way to refute her claim, he relived some of the antics they'd pulled as kids when she was a doe-eyed teenager enduring her first crush. He'd thought her a cute kid.

Some of her own stories from bygone years surfaced in a trembling voice. He wondered if she'd grieved before growing her virtual shield of armor. It'd take time and effort, but he'd pierce her shell and cocoon her in safety. He could at least do that much in the name of penance.

"His last words were about you, Kendra. He made me promise to take care of you." His eyes misted with the thoughts of her three years on the street, a sin for which he could never atone.

An uncomfortable truce ensued, the silence filling the room with expectations and possibilities, but most of all, regret. Still, her presence settled the demons inside him, allowing a deep breath as after swimming the length of a pool underwater, his soul grasping for equanimity instead of his mortal body gulping air.

Excited chuffing announced the return of his brothers with their dogs, each entering in a wash of cooler air. Julien leaned against his desk while Marc sat in the leather chair. Each dog pushed at the other to gain

Kendra's attention, a constant swirl of fur, noses, and kisses. Conner moved aside so she could pet, nuzzle, and coo over each one.

"Jeez, it's just like with Callie and Dani. Damn dogs have a sixth sense." Marc's perception of the dogs' reactions stemmed from years of Schutzhund training and understanding the shepherds' motivations and emotions. "They just know, don't they?"

Julien chuckled.

"So?" Conner wasn't in the mood for sibling shenanigans.

"No body. We see where he went down, but he's gone. Which means either he wasn't injured as bad as we thought, or someone provided a cleaning service." Marc frowned at Kendra as if debating whether to probe further into the night's tragedy.

"He was dead. I know it. You can see all the blood on me and my clothes. It sprayed everywhere when the knife sliced an artery in his neck." Her whispered confession silenced the room while pleading her case. Marc's dog jumped up, placing his front paws on her lap to rub his neck against her face.

"Kendra, we understand, and we believe you. We're just trying to figure this out." Julien's sympathy came as no surprise. They'd always seemed to understand each other growing up.

"What about the guy who intervened? Think he came back and moved the body? Seems someone is protecting her." Conner's ability to puzzle out complicated affairs usually served him well, but they lacked sufficient pieces to see how the current oddities fit.

"I don't know. I just don't know." Renewal of Kendra's shudders suppressed further questioning.

"Let's get you home, Mongrel. You need food and a hot shower." Conner held his hand out to help. Instead of fear, defiance, or anger, her expression registered acceptance and defeat. He'd never intended to crush her spirit.

"I don't want to go to jail."

"Whoa, Kendra. No. That's—" Marc's denial came fast, but Conner cut him off.

"Kendra. You will not go to jail. Eventually, we'll have to report this attack." He motioned to Julien to bring her clothes. "However, without a body, we don't have much to go on yet. Either way, it was self-defense and you're staying with me. Got it?" No one argued as he strode out beside his conflicted ward.

Chapter Eight

Light mist accumulated on the windshield to create a thin veil much like the frosted blocks Kendra erected to encase her heart.

Through those translucent bricks, Conner caught glimpses of her inner turmoil yet couldn't define the elusive fragments without further details. Unfortunately, shattering the glass barricade would leave her defenseless and force her to run.

Ensuring she stayed with him topped his to-do list with no ready solution.

"There's a storm brewing. You can smell it in the air." Her pensive gaze drifted to the passenger window, ambient light illuminating her frown's reflection. Nature's answer came in the form of a low, far off rumbling.

Tension coiled in her frame like a thousand-quilled porcupine waiting for a bobcat to flip it supine and rip into its vulnerable belly. Contrary to her behavior in the parking lot and his office, she now resembled a frightened animal, rattling her hollow quills in warning, her tongue a shield behind which she could hide.

If his memory served correct, storms generated a fear in her unparalleled by anything else.

"Yeah, unusual for this early in the season, but we're supposed to have a pretty good thunder bumper tonight." Did storms still terrify her? If so, had Daeron offered protection? He wouldn't contemplate why that thought disturbed him on a visceral level.

"No matter. What's one more?" Her muttered reply sounded disproportionately vague to the worry in her eyes when her gaze swung in his direction.

"You're gonna be all right."

Billy used to wake up during a storm to find her huddled under the covers on the edge of his bed. He wasn't prepared for that occurrence.

"Yeah, I know."

He wanted nothing more than to reclaim the long-forgotten, easy comradery once shared, not turn her into a physical plaything.

"Tell me, when was the last time you played a piano?" The thirty-minute drive home allotted time to formulate a plan, without which Kendra would vanish before morning. Back in Ambrosia, he'd read it in her eyes, as expressive as always.

"I play an electrical keyboard now." A tone filled with belligerence stymied further questions along that vein.

At present, she should be attending the private conservatory and sharing her prodigious talent among those who could appreciate perfection. Instead, blood smeared her face and neck, strain tightened her eyes and mouth, and a shadow stalker hovered in her future.

Death should never have touched her world at this age. The seamier side of life should never have corrupted her light.

"I've got some beef stew we can heat up at home. You need to eat something solid." He had little else to offer but vowed to send one of his brothers shopping tomorrow.

"From a can?" Humor nudged a little color in her cheeks.

He'd take it. "Um, yeah. I still can't cook."

"Lucky for you, I can." Again, she turned her face to the window. "But even I can't do much with cardboard containers and tin cans. Wanna stop at a convenience store for a few staples?"

Was she remembering the time years ago when she, Billy, and his brothers created an unholy mess in the kitchen? Even as a young girl, she'd cooked better than her teenage brother and his friends. "Nah, we can get groceries in the morning."

Heaven's tears washed the darkened streets, pattered the windows, and announced the coming storm when silvered by a barrage of jagged lightning. The road's convex slope facilitated runoff accumulating in the drainage ditches, gravity pulling it downhill.

Several years ago, he'd helped a friend suffering from PTSD out of such a ditch on a night like this, trembling and confused, frightened of phantom threats and imagined terrors. Prior attempts to help had met with firm denials until rock bottom lent no other direction to go. Would Kendra be the same? His heart ached for the young lady he'd known.

Turning into his driveway, he waited for her reaction. Years of harping on her older brother for a house by the sea where she could play music and commune with dogs had led to the boys' jokes about owning a seaside cottage. They'd all loved to snorkel and surf. Like his brothers, he'd done better than earlier expectations.

A quick, quiet inhale was her only indication of surprise.

"It's just a house, with windows, doors, siding, and floors." He knew she'd like it at first, not so much the house but what waited inside. The discovery might keep her from bolting tonight, which based on her tight posture, lack of eye contact, and closed-off expression, existed as more than a possibility.

"And a beach view. You've done well for yourself." Not an accusation, just a statement.

"I think you'll like it here. You'll certainly be safe." After he settled her down and saw to her comfort, he'd coerce the deal to protect and secure her future. It was the least he could do.

Her non-committal grunt boded ill.

"Come on inside. Let's get some food in your belly."

With the push of a button over his visor, a faint metal groan preceded the garage door yawning open to welcome in weary stragglers, bright light repelling the shadows seeking entrance.

Pulling inside and cutting the engine lent a finality to his course as the diminishing aperture folded them in their own world. Overhead lights illuminated his well-kept garage, organized tools, and projects in various stages of progress occupying the third bay. Despite several attempts by determined women, there'd never been a vehicle in the second space. He'd never found anyone who fit.

Her fingers trembled as she opened the car door. "I'm exhausted."

He couldn't wait to get her inside and cleaned up. The smeared reminder of her horrific night, visible in the open V of his shirt, chafed his thoughts.

Memory of how she'd turned her back to put it on, as if embarrassed, doubled his shame. She should never have ended up in such a situation.

Excited barking inside gave away his surprise as he stepped up to the back door and pressed his thumb against the security pad.

"Oh, you have a dog, too?" Finally, a bit of excitement in her voice, the included smile created little crinkles at the corners of her eyes. "What's his name?"

"Yep. Marc does the initial training, but we all work with them. This is Krystal." Seeing hope and passion lighten her voice gave him another idea. One he'd have to implement right away to keep his plan moving forward.

Before light spilled from the interior, Krystal's snuffling around the door's seam brought a round of chuckles.

Nature and nurture. The interactions between species hid as many mysteries as they revealed. In each instance of his brothers finding their better halves, it seemed their dogs instinctively knew, taking to the women as if by fated intervention.

They. Just. Knew.

Now, seeing Krystal swarm to Kendra in the same manner mocked his entire existence. This wasn't the woman for him. She deserved someone with fewer harsh edges, more patience, and a softer touch.

After two steps inside, she dropped to one knee to accept her due of pup nuzzling and quiet communing.

"Why don't you get a shower while I heat up some food?" Leading her to the spare bathroom, he stopped at the hall closet for a spare towel and washcloth.

"I'll leave a pair of sweats and another shirt folded by the door." Gesturing her ahead, he added, "Take your time."

Though he hadn't planned it this way, their situation could've been worse. Instead of the quiet conversation he'd intended, it could've ended with him at the hospital consoling a victimized Kendra or at the morgue identifying her body.

Cool air from the refrigerator cleared his thoughts as he removed a plastic container of stew and dumped it in a small pan. Canned stew should not constitute a meal.

He didn't expect her out in less than fifteen minutes. Then again, life on the streets altered a lot of one's normal activities.

"What's your end goal, Conner? What do you want from me?" Kendra, always to the point, cut through any subterfuge or misdirection, though now with a new edge depicting a wariness previously unknown. She kept her gaze on him as she took a seat at the table.

To see her take an aggressively defensive position so soon slaughtered his hope of resurrecting and strengthening the bond they'd once enjoyed.

"To keep you safe. I gave Billy my word, and you know I always try to keep a promise." Clinking dishes brought Krystal's attention to his filling two bowls with hot stew.

Her wary expression, reminiscent of a horse sensing a snake nearby and expecting it to strike, warned him to curb the hedonistic tendencies displayed earlier.

"Always nice and vague when it suits you. Where's the envelope?"

"In a safe place." A fact he intended to verify as soon as she fell asleep. Thick chair legs scraped the tile as he took a seat.

Doubt and wariness overtook her expression as if fighting an internal battle and the decision of whether to accept some small crumb of charity decided her ultimate fate. In a way, it did. Each step he planned would build on its predecessor, one block at a time. They had a long way to go.

"You planned on hiring the band before you ever heard us play. We're new and haven't performed anywhere other than Wes's garage. Ambrosia doesn't seem the type of place to normally have live music, much less jazz."

An accusation wrapped in practiced nonchalance betrayed her lack of trust while foraging for answers. "How'd you find me?"

He had a lot of work to do. Calling her a mongrel, one of the pet names bestowed in a different lifetime, hadn't helped. The fact she'd shared that name with Daeron held an intolerable significance.

"Come on. Let's eat while it's hot." Snagging the loaf of bread off the counter, he untwisted the wire tie and offered a slice before settling in across from her, stalling while deciding on the best approach to answer her question.

"Look. I located you but couldn't figure out your connection to Wes, your manager. Then I found out you were on your own. You've been hard to track. I just want to see you safe, nothing more. You know me,

Kendra. I've never lied to you." He met her gaze head on, determined to show he hid nothing, at least nothing that would bring her harm.

Again, she squirmed.

As if just noticing her surroundings, she whistled low, her appreciative gaze dissecting each appliance and smooth stone surface in his pristine kitchen. "Do you even know how to use these things?" Restless fingers drummed the table in contemplation.

In the next instant, she padded to the ovens and skimmed her fingertips along the stainless steel double ovens, as if the cabinet might sprout wings and take flight.

She'd earned the right to dole out trust in frugal scraps, one day at a time. Like a canine in a new home, she visually explored the open floor plan, agitation her companion for the near future.

"Well, I plan on learning at some point. Maybe you could teach me a few things. Otherwise, it'll be takeout or burned, crusty goodness." It surprised him to feel a smile creep into his voice.

She bit her lips, the corners tilting up, perhaps over a fond memory?

He let the quiet stretch out while she contemplated her situation. When she slid the bowl closer, something settled in her expression, a sadness he knew she wouldn't express. In words.

She's gonna run.

"I can't stay here." Regret shadowed her gaze as she scooped one spoonful of stew after another, tendrils of steam mimicking and blending with her skin's pallor.

And there it was. His fingers clenched on the spoon as he ate another mouthful.

"Yes, you can, and you will." He let just enough authoritative command enter his tone, testing her.

She sat taller in her seat. Defiance.

He'd begun the foundation of their new relationship yet needed to convince her of a better path. "Leaving is not an option. Not while someone is hunting you, and not while there's an unclaimed dead body out there." His reminder of her danger in the vagueness of a hand gesture was intentional and manipulative. A distant cannonade of thunder punctuated his statement.

She startled at the low rumbles, her entire frame condensing with a small convulsive shudder. "You're looking for a slave."

"I'm looking to keep my friend out of a rapist's clutches," he countered.

"So, give me the envelope. Let's see what's inside."

"Not for three months." Regardless of what favors he'd have to call in, he'd see the danger resolved before she got further involved.

"One." Resiliency had always existed as one of her character strengths. Tonight proved no exception.

"No, three. And this isn't a negotiation."

Silent fuming ended the conversation but didn't stop her from finishing every speck of food in short order.

"I'll get you some more." Adding fifteen or twenty pounds to her thin frame might alleviate some of the weight on his shoulders. Krystal watched his quiet and efficient movements before padding to her side and rubbing against her leg.

Again, Kendra applied an enthusiastic response to the food set before her. Silence thereafter represented a deadlock of sorts, an uncomfortable truce while she studied him, her frown declaring him some type of mystery or monster. He wasn't sure which. Each time their gazes locked, she looked away first.

In his career, he'd learned to wait.

When she pushed back from the table and stood, she added the zinger he'd been expecting. "I'm not sleeping with you. Not that you've figured out I'm of the female persuasion yet. But just in case you ever do..." The furious blush overtaking her face attested to the weight of her anger and hurt.

"Jesus, Kendra. You don't know me, not anymore. 'Sides, you're a young lady. Come on. I'll show you to the spare bedroom."

"I'm a street rat." Defiance straightened her spine. "A killer, just like you."

"No, babe. No. You're nothing like me." Three strides closed the distance between them. Unable to bear the weight riding his shoulders, he clutched her arms and urged her forward, his hands shaking with shame as he brushed his lips across the crown of her head.

"Kendra, you are nothing like me. I may not know what you've endured the past three years, but I do know this. You're still the bright light in my life, just as you've always been."

A whispered confession, a light kiss on her hair, his gentling caress down her back, she still remained stiff in his arms for long minutes as if afraid to accept the slightest comfort.

Maybe exhaustion wore her down, or maybe past memories invaded her mind. Either way, she softened in his embrace, accepting him and wrapping her arms around his waist before holding tight.

Uncounted minutes passed, a heaven he didn't deserve but would treasure for eternity. He didn't move an inch until she pulled away.

Never in his wildest imagination had he foreseen Kendra sleeping in his spare bedroom. Unlike his brothers, who'd learned to dodge their drunken, abusive father, she hadn't needed that type of protection, but he'd overseen her life as he'd done with his siblings. Yes, his conscience could accept their current situation in that mindset.

A thin bar of light spilled across her bed from the hallway with the silent door opening. Settled after a hot shower and full stomach, she looked adorable in his oversized t-shirt.

She eyed him with suspicion, pulling the covers to her chin in a gesture of self-protection.

Steam from the attached bath carried a faint scent of the hyacinth shampoo and body wash, unused toiletries he'd kept on hand. They weren't her current style, but better than the copper scent that had tenaciously clung to her skin. Damp tresses haloed a heart-shaped face not meant to withstand the horrors she'd known.

Curled up and snuggled against her shoulder, Krystal rested her dark head on the spare pillow as if they'd always slept that way.

He simply smiled.

She eyed him as an aquatic snake with tentacles that tricked its prey by rippling its flexible body and forcing the unwary into its jaws.

His heart ached for the easy friendship they'd once shared.

"Just wanted to make sure you didn't need anything. I'm an early riser, but I'll wait till you're up to fix breakfast. It's the one meal I can cook." He hesitated before adding, "You've had a hell of a night. Want me to sit with you for a while?"

"No, thanks." The cloud of black hair fanning out on the crisp blue sheets appeared as soft as her voice. "Maybe you should let me do the cooking. I can't afford a trip to the ER with food poisoning."

"G'night, scrub jay." Another nickname she'd adopted long ago brought back memories of her early teenage years when she'd balked at the name, Mongrel. Still a tomboy, she'd questioned her identity.

A shock of blue dye running through her black silk curls had reminded him of a western scrub jay. The mischievous streak, either endearing or annihilating his patience, never failed to bring out the gleam in her eyes.

No doubt, just like the winged corvids, she maintained scattered caches of basic necessities throughout her realm, pilfering when necessary and always vigilant. The moniker still suited her.

A mule's tenacity, hoarding stuffed animals, always dogs, and standing in front of anything which threatened someone she cared about had grown more pronounced considering her current behavior. Fierce and loyal, she'd personified the word friend in his mind, both then and now.

"My hair isn't long or streaked anymore." Defiance radiated from those azure blues in spades.

The streak of hair color had long since dissolved, but her underlying character had remolded, solidifying her stubborn nature until she could no longer bend without breaking.

"No, no it isn't. Sleep well." He'd almost called her mongrel. Something no young lady would want to hear, regardless of the affection lacing his tone.

Flipping off the light switch, he felt the darkness spread a melancholy to fill his soul with all the missed parties, close friends, school antics, and other things every teenager should experience. Instead, he tucked her into a hellish nightmare and wondered what Billy would think if viewing them from some ghostly plane, writhing in a purgatory of frustration.

Chapter Nine

She was preparing to run. He'd seen it in her eyes and felt it in his bones.

"Time for plan A." Sitting on his sofa, he'd waited an hour to give her time to sleep if in fact it visited her at all that night.

On his lap lay the reason someone killed Billy and now hunted Kendra. In order to solve a problem, one first had to define it. How could anything of great value fit into such an innocent-looking, battered manila envelope?

Unlike the thirteen-second fuse delay of particular Russian hand grenades, the *ssslp* of the seal reverberated in his mind like a bullet's short-lived flight.

A peek inside.

Aw, shit. He sent this to me, knowing I'd safeguard it and figure out what went wrong.

Rage shook his fingers and animated the darkness festering inside to dovetail long-standing confusion with logic in forming a coherent explanation for Billy's death, if not the specific details.

He expected some expensive trinket an older brother might send to his sister as a peace offering. This was far from it.

These items sanctioned Billy's death while threatening any lives connected, directly or not. In thinking back to the time after discharge, Conner flashed to the scene of coming home one night and realizing someone had broken into his home. The same thing had happened to each of his brothers.

Damn Colonel Kenson. His ex-commander had always played his cards close to the vest, but Conner had believed his superior's denials of sending Billy on a solo mission. The three gems and small flash drive were probably worth millions in the wrong hands.

Honor had bound him to delay opening the gift from hell, per Billy's last request. Why had Billy wanted his younger sister to be twenty-one before receiving it? It made no sense.

Innocent as a bomb without a fuse, it had occupied his safe at Ambrosia then at home, oblivious to time. Now it threatened a life for which he cared, another person he'd sworn to protect. Sweat moistened his brow as a virtual meat grinder churned his stomach.

The FUBAR scenario held so many possibilities for disaster. He wasn't sure which way to turn. Fucked up didn't come close to describing it. Trusting the colonel with Kendra's safety wasn't an option. Hence, the contents' existence would remain private, between brothers.

Late-night phone calls between the brothers received immediate attention. Tonight proved no exception after he hit the speed dial on his cell.

Fate would not kick Kendra in the teeth again. Damn if she wasn't due for a little good fortune. "Hey, Marc. Sorry to bother you so late. Need a big favor and real quick."

"No problem, I've been awake, thinking about her situation. We all care, though you were the one who semi-adopted her." His audible smirk now absent, Marc's tone had changed with Kendra's dire circumstances.

"Listen, she's got bolt written in her eyes. Anything new and promising on the market? This is a pivotal point, and I only know of one thing that might change her mind."

"Yep, I remember her biggest weakness, besides you. A silver sable I've been eyeing is ready to go. It'll cost me a favor, but that's not an issue. I can be there tomorrow morning a little after ten with the special delivery."

"Good. Thanks. I think that'll tip the scales in our favor. Now, for the nuts and bolts that started this goat-fuck."

"Fill me in on the background." Though the tone declared him wholeheartedly on board, it also bore the distracted traces of a puzzle solver.

"Well, it's a bit complicated. Before he died, Billy sent me an envelope for safekeeping. I hadn't broken the seal because, well, it was for Kendra, and I thought it was personal, his way to compensate for his re-upping."

"'Kay. And? What's in it?" Marc's virtual wheels would be spinning now, putting together the location, assignment, and timing of Billy's last mission.

"You're not gonna like this…" Conner rubbed a hand over his jaw bristle. What a clusterfuck. Describing the contents of the pouch culminated in his younger brother's expletives.

"Why in hell did Billy involve his sister?" Between quiet statements, the sleep-laced murmur of Marc's girlfriend posed her own suggestions.

"I have no idea. Maybe he thought he'd got away clean and wanted to make sure she came to me… He extracted a promise before he died, that I'd protect her." Further conversation failed to illuminate any reasonable explanation for Billy placing his younger sister in danger. Ending the call allowed Conner's brain to heap more grief on a conscience threatening to bury him.

The only time he'd ever seen his friend's eyes tear was after returning for his second tour. Kendra's harsh last words to him, said in anger, haunted them all. The entire team shared responsibility. But he and Kendra had paid the ultimate price with his death, the crushing of their souls.

Experience told him attempting to open the enclosed digital files would trip a safeguard and destroy any enclosed data. He'd have to see this bullshit farce to the end and then hand the evidence over to a cyber-nerd.

Lucky for him, they had one in the family, after a sort. No doubt, Callie could hack the files, if Nate agreed to it first. That argument could wait on the back burner.

Thunder rolled across the heavens and filled the sky with threats of torrential rain, the precursor of which plunked against the glass panes as more heavenly grumbles permeated the air.

Through the window, jagged bolts of heated light ripped through the clouds to strike in chaotic, indiscriminate glee, just like the current events attempting to destroy his equanimity.

Tales of Kendra sneaking into her older brother's room during severe storms and eventually kicking him out of bed declared her only known vulnerability. As much as he wanted to settle on the chair in her room to soothe any rising nightmares, she'd consider it an invasion of privacy and a weakness she wouldn't want dredged up for his consideration.

Sleep would not come to her tonight except through unconsciousness. Nevertheless, that wasn't what concerned him at the moment. Someone hunted her.

The envelope's contents mystified as much as shocked him shitless. The gems alone would be worth a fortune. How in the hell could Billy have obtained intel from Colonel Kenson to secure such items without anyone else's knowledge? As a team, they hadn't kept secrets. Or so he'd thought.

In the distance, simultaneous flashes of light signaled the storm's stalking advance. Maybe he should sleep on the couch, in case she came out. No. *Then she'd see me as a jailer.*

At least she wouldn't bolt with the storm in full swing. When the heavens quieted, that might be a different story.

Flicking the light switch in his bedroom, he realized tomorrow would be a tough day with her adjusting to a new life around people she hadn't seen in years. A few hours of rest would carry him through her trials. T-shirt and socks landed in a pile in the hamper as he devised a mental list of things needed and intended to do. Sleeping in jeans would allow a shorter response time if he needed to move fast.

His last thoughts before sleep claimed him were Billy's last words, *"Take care of Kendra."*

Yeah, I've done a standup job so far, buddy.

He'd do better starting tomorrow.

Muffled cries and Krystal's plaintive whine followed a loud crack of thunder that galvanized him into action. Instinct saw his Glock from the bedside drawer palmed before sitting up and pushing the covers back. The thick rug underfoot absorbed sounds of his passage as he listened to pinpoint the source.

He'd left his door open to listen for her footsteps.

Following Krystal's low vocalizations, he opened her door.

From her closet came another thin cry.

Shit.

Insight came with another barrage of celestial anger rattling the windows. He pushed open the door to the walk-in closet.

After flicking on the low light, he set his weapon on the nearby dresser. Damn. He should've seen this coming and sat outside her door.

Kendra huddled in the far corner under a row of casual shirts. Spiky tendrils of hair camouflaged her tear-streaked face. Her entire body shook. Krystal lay against her side.

"Kendra, why didn't you wake me?" Approaching as he would a cornered animal, he spoke low and soothing, then gently scooped her up to his chest, holding her snug.

"I-I didn't want you to think I was a baby. I just d-don't like storms."

"You've never liked them, sweetheart. Let's sit in the living room for a while. Grab that blanket to keep warm."

Her trembling morphed into violent shudders with each of the sky's successive detonations. Not wanting to take her closer to the thing which terrified her most but loath to release her, he padded to the window and pulled each drape's cord, enclosing them in a private space where the world outside could rage at will yet not visually touch them.

She settled in the nook of the sofa with Krystal leaning against her side.

He could do nothing for the noise but talk to her, hoping she'd use his words as a beacon, latching on and allowing him to bring her into his world, if only for a while. Leaving the light on low would help her gain her bearings when she next woke, though it'd be a good while before she slept.

In his mind, she should always remain the sister he'd rescued from the tree after reaching the top limbs to prove her prowess.

Soft, whispered words wove the framework of childhood pranks and how they'd included a young tomboy who'd wanted nothing more than to imitate her big brother. Family, always family.

Before long, her deep breathing settled something he hadn't recognized as off kilter, an edginess always present like radio static if one tuned in close enough to listen.

Each wisp of exhalation warmed his thoughts, mingling with her natural scent to encourage fantasies that shouldn't exist. The thick cushion molded about his head buffered the severity of his self-chastisement. It was a while before his personal demons exhausted their relentless arguments and let him sleep.

The next thing he knew, Krystal nudged his knee and startled him. The initial storm's passing left a quietness in its wake that comforted even as it lulled him into a dream-like state. Soft, blue illuminated numbers from the kitchen oven declared it'd be another hour before light coral and amethyst hues suffused the distant horizon, another hour to cherish the time and company.

"You can go out, Krystal. Go ahead." The transceiver on her collar would open the electronic door and allow her to pass back and forth without allowing access to other creatures. He wanted more sleep, more comfort, and more peace. More Kendra.

Kendra stirred and repositioned herself. "What time is it?"

The throaty intonation, thick from slumber, stirred fantasies he didn't need.

Jesus, she's family.

"Clock says after four. Go back to sleep." An inexplicable need to possess her held him in thrall. The storm had spent its rage. A thin snippet of silvery moonlight slipped past the drapery's edge to highlight the soft locks spilling over her cheek and holding him prisoner. Her soft scent filled his mind with whispers of unfulfilled promises. He craved just another hour of her relaxed presence despite the lustful fantasies ravaging his mind.

"I wanna sleep in bed. Will you hold me?" Innocent words formed of a childlike need for security. This was the Kendra he'd known and searched for, the one unafraid to open up.

Yes.

Then reality intervened.

Oh hell, no. All-too-vivid dreams over the past few hours reminded him just how much Kendra had grown in all the right places, leaving him with an uncomfortable physical reminder.

Contrary to her obvious poor self-image, her form embodied the quintessential mold of the perfect woman's shape. One he might not have responded to so fast if he'd accepted Cindy's offer.

Disparity between the two women proved as diverse in form as in their life's perceptions and characters. Memory of Kendra half-naked floated through his mind where lust for possession rooted out thoughts of any other woman.

"I—I don't think that's a good idea. It's not big enough. You can have the bed. I'll take the sofa."

"I want to cuddle." Soft, circular motions of her fingers rubbing his forearm constricted every fiber in his body, except the ones expanding with increased blood volume.

"That's not such a good idea, either, but I'll take you back. The storm's over." He scooped her up and cradled her against his chest while trying to resolve the predicament without offense, afraid of expanding the emotional wedge between them.

Sudden muscles bunching in her back and legs telegraphed her intent to move without advising specifics. Reflex tightened his right arm— which she used to push off and flip over backward to land with cat-like grace.

Damn. The speed of her maneuver caught him off guard, his arms flailing in midair like a madman. It was a ninja move, born of instinct but carried through with the grace derived from practice. No wonder she'd been able to protect herself at the club.

Double damn.

Life on the streets had toughened her in ways he hadn't considered.

Wild tresses in artful disarray, chest heaving under an oversized t-shirt, and the glimmer of some unnamed torment brought a new dimension to one he'd falsely labeled kid. She was all woman.

"I just don't like being alone after a storm. It's certainly not to knock boots with you. You're such a troglodyte." Anger seeped deeper into every word spoken. Her defensive stance remained tight as if expecting him to—do what?

"What did you do on the street during storms?" *Hell.* Why did his mind act like a sieve, a filter for the worst things to say?

"Fucked anything with a dick and pretended Nate was playing the drums. What d'ya think? Why would you think I'd want to screw you?"

Ahh, defensive armor up and the street rat resurfaces. The fact she'd needed such coping mechanisms in the first place shamed him.

"Trust me. You're the last woman on earth I'd want to screw." The guilt would destroy him.

At this point, he could pound nails. "I believe I've warned you about the best cure for a dirty mouth." Standing in front of his Icarus, he remained helpless to do anything but pray to not further exacerbate the situation.

"Aren't I pretty enough? Using your detective skills, you should know I've grown. Or maybe you're the type that can't tell if someone's turned on or not." The devilish gleam in her eye should've been all the warning necessary despite the seductive tone.

The arching of her back inched twin points of forbidden fruit forward. Closing the distance, she splayed her finely boned fingers against his chest before rubbing motions on his pecs that had his shaft bobbing in time.

He was powerless to move, fascinated by the play of light and shadows spilling from the kitchen window across her face. He didn't allow his gaze to travel south below the hem of her t-shirt. That was a slippery slope, which brought to mind other slopes, like the curve of her breast and the roundness of her bottom.

The lightest brush of her fingertips glided up his chest and swirled over the smattering of hair. When she circled his neck and pressed the soft fullness of her breasts against him, breath rushed out to leave him stunned and starved for air. She didn't seem daunted by his pulsing shaft pressing against the softness of her belly through two layers of cloth.

Her soft tug on his head obliterated the disparity in their sizes with her mouth inches from his own. Like an out-of-body experience, he watched the distance close, fascinated and horrified all at once.

Butterfly wings couldn't have compared to the tentative touch of her cupid-bow lips. Nor would a volcano have contained as much heat as she brushed them over his own.

He was defenseless, unable to stop his hands from circling her waist and pressing her lower back closer for full-body contact. His shaft

70

pulsed, embedded in the heat of her stomach. When he traced the sculpted arc down to cup her rounded, tight ass, her groan reciprocated in his chest.

The firm muscles under his fingers begged for testing with light clenching while his t-shirt bunched, shielding nothing. Sliding the cotton fabric upward, his rough touch encountered the smoothest, softest flesh ever imagined, cool under his fevered exploration. Her breathing quickened, expanding the soft mounds against his chest.

His throbbing member demanded attention as never before. A slight twist of his lower body rewarded him with her enthusiastic response, tilting her hips into his frame.

From the distant portion of his soul, the dark recess where forbidden fruit tasted of life-saving succor, his thoughts registered her response, testing him. Instant access to the warm haven of her mouth yielded a slice of paradise no man could disregard. Mating tongues, sliding, writhing the way he'd fantasized her body responding with shy and energetic curiosity flooded his mind with endorphins. Blood pounded in his ears while his lungs burned for air.

Sanity came in the form of Krystal's whine.

Holy shit.

That certainly wasn't like kissing a sister. Despite her age, the necessity of registering as a pervert came to mind. The girl was off limits. With a gentle nudge, he disentangled their bodies, each of their heaving breaths punching the air.

"No, Kendra. We're not doing this. Not now, not ever."

A narrowed gaze betrayed the tenacity of a badger. Smiling, she nodded toward his tented jeans. "I think part of you disagrees."

"Kendra, you don't even know who you are yet, much less what you want out of life. A physiological response does not equal commitment." Unable to bear her scrutiny, he strode to the window and opened the curtains for a momentary reprieve.

"Who said anything about commitment? Maybe I just wanted to see what all the fuss is about." Hurt, rejection, and anger boiled in her expression until she turned and bolted out of the house.

"Kendra. Come back here!"

* * * *

Small stones from the driveway burrowed into her right heel, recognized as a distant nuisance, something her mind filed away to dissect later when the pain and humiliation of rejection relaxed its grip on her heart.

The next storm brewing in the low-lying, heavy clouds didn't diminish her desperation to escape, but quick thinking served her well with the perfect temporary sanctuary popping into her thoughts.

Instinct guided her around the house to the back. The route to her nearest bolt-hole would incur too much danger in her near-naked state. The oaf thought her so backward to not think straight. He'd go looking for her, thereby giving her a chance to sneak back in the house and dress before taking off for good.

Navigating over the slippery fence earned her another scrape and some bruises, but she didn't hear Conner's thundering steps giving chase. The thought of foiling his best attempts to find her made enduring the cold and spitting rain bearable. Rare had been the times she'd outfoxed him.

Once inside her temporary crib and curling into a tight ball, she clenched her teeth together to keep them from chattering. If he let Krystal out, the shepherd would probably make a beeline for her. Otherwise, she'd be safe from his wrath.

Distant booming of thunder grew closer, prompting muffled whimpers with each terror-inducing assault on her senses. Squeezing her eyes shut enhanced her hearing, her ears latching on to every chest-vibrating rumble to set her whole body shaking. There was no way in hell she'd go back inside until the last distant grumble subsided.

The epitome of all distractions—conflicting emotions—roiled through her thoughts while lingering sensations in her lower belly anesthetized her to the worst of the approaching hell.

Her brazen behavior began as a challenge, wanting Conner to see her as a woman, before she rejected him. The need to wound him ran deep.

Instead, her body had betrayed her.

Memory of Conner's heat scorching her lips and the bitterness of his betrayal in allowing Billy to return for that final tour kept her in a state of flux. She'd dreamed of that first kiss, the essence of which would reside in her memory as a measure against others to come.

Nothing would ever compare. Calling her a kid was camouflage, for the heated length of his passion had burned her belly through the thin cotton of her shirt, belying the truth of his words.

He thought her immature, too young, but he didn't measure the difference in years. They weren't that far apart. To his credit. She lay there half-naked, huddled in the small shelter trying to stay warm.

Flashbacks of years past reminded her that his stubborn streak wasn't something one worked around. Regardless of the circumstances, and undeterred by the fact she'd protected herself on the streets for years, he would never see her as anything more than a kid in need of protection.

It didn't matter his body recognized the chemistry between them. Conner's iron will would never bend enough to complete her, not once. He would never belong to her, but in that one moment of insanity, she would've taken his offering, deified the encounter, and by it, judge other men.

Another boom accompanied the detonation of the heavy clouds releasing their burden. Jagged streaks of terrifying light forked across the sky to reinforce her fetal position even as the rough bedding in her enclosure muffled her thin cries.

Billy used to talk her through violent storms, telling her jokes about angels scoring strikes in heaven.

She hated bowling.

Chapter Ten

Going off half-cocked had never been his style. In yanking on his shirt and shoes, he realized no halfway measures existed where Kendra was concerned.

Distant slamming of the front door motivated him to hurry as he remembered how fast her feet could fly. Already in the wind and armored with only his oversized t-shirt and a foul mouth, she wouldn't go far.

Would she?

Recent memories of her soon amended that thought. She'd go as far as pride drove her, probably to one of her hidden stashes.

Half-naked, racing through dirty alleys and traveling back streets, she didn't stand a chance. Regardless of her bravado, her altered emotional state put her at risk.

A split-second of hesitation and he left Krystal in the house as he hit the floodlights. The command to search would result in a lot of excited barking, and he didn't want Kendra fleeing the one creature who'd given her comfort. "Sorry, girl. You gotta stay."

Out the back for a quick visual inspection, he thanked the moon glow aiding his search of the perimeter. She'd run so fast from Ambrosia, almost outdistancing his best effort. As luck would have it, fate chose that moment to dump a heavier deluge of cold tears, conspiring to decrease visibility and help its little lost urchin escape.

Silvered rain veiled his vision and sent a shiver through his chest. How could he have bungled the situation so thoroughly? The demon inside howled with possession even as self-disgust increased his pace. He'd allowed his weakness to endanger her.

The wrought iron fence encompassing his backyard drew a patchwork of shadow bars along one side, reminiscent of what he should see if he continued along his insane course of no self-control. She'd already been attacked once. She might not escape twice. No tracts of shadow concealed a diabolical, ink-haired sprite.

A maple tree planted for shade had starting to bud, reminding him of years ago in Billy's backyard, where she'd demanded a leg up to the first branch, always determined to show she could run with the big boys. Studying the bare limbs now revealed no telltale curves betraying her presence. Half-naked and cold, she should've had enough sense to not run out in the rain. He figured she'd run to the backyard.

He'd handled the situation wrong, and she paid the price. Again.

After raising his three brothers, he couldn't manage one girl? Slithering through the back of his mind came words unbidden. *She's no longer a little girl and you certainly were ready to handle her.*

His home stood on a point bordered by water on two sides. Heavy briar undergrowth covered the woods of the third side, beginning at the lawn's perimeter. Thick undergrowth would not yield easily to human invasion. Forty yards of cleared space cost little time to a person used to running on a regular basis. Considering her stubborn pride and bullish mind, she could've taken to the woods or the street.

Damn.

After racing back into the house, he grabbed two jackets and his keys. The search might take a while, and he wanted to get her warm as soon as possible. He'd be damned lucky if she didn't catch pneumonia. Maybe he should warm her ass with his hand.

Two hours later saw him cussing again while checking an abandoned warehouse near the outskirts of town, the last known secret stash. Who knew how many more condemned hangouts she'd called sanctuary? Though the skies were beginning to clear, the air remained chilly and biting.

Where in hell is she?

As much as he hated to admit defeat, it was time to call his brothers for help and use Krystal to track. There was no excuse and no defense for his behavior. Yes, she'd run away, during a storm, in cold weather, wearing a t-shirt and nothing else. Meantime, he'd sported the biggest boner of his life.

It would be a simple matter for his brother's girlfriend to hone in on Kendra's thoughts and find her. He'd deserve the humiliation. Kendra did not.

He wondered if the time would come when Dani and Callie would reveal their psychic talents. That would draw her into his world, but subject her to the inherent dangers. In counterpoint, shutting her out equaled ostracizing her from the family, equally unthinkable.

One step at a time. First, I have to find the little hellion and convince her to stay.

"Maybe she's holed up in the woods somewhere," he wondered aloud. Several caves and overhangs in the rolling, timbered hills could offer shelter. "She wouldn't know of them, and she's barefoot." Had she gone anyway and stumbled upon a grotto by coincidence?

Upon his return, Krystal whined, even the condemnation from his dog was very clear. Snagging Kendra's jeans, he let the shepherd sniff then opened his front door. "Krystal, *sook*. Let's find our girl."

Instead of trailing up the driveway, Krystal's snuffling gait led to the back yard. He followed as fast as he could, catching her hop over the fence. When she pushed aside the flap covering the lower half of the porch door, his thoughts exploded with rage. Krystal made a bee line to the doghouse in the corner.

"Son of a bitch! All this time and she never left home?" Which meant she'd spent hours, wet and cold, in a doghouse. Is that how she valued her worth?

Again, he approached with caution before kneeling a short distance away to peer in the dark interior. A distant rumble across the heavens induced a wave of convulsive shudders in the occupant.

The paralyzing sight burned the back of his eyes, imprinted foremost in his mind to numb his thoughts. Thick bedding stuffed with cedar chips kept Krystal warm yet wasn't intended for the one who'd captured his heart.

"Jesus, Kendra. Come here. You're soaked and shivering so hard I should've heard your teeth chattering from inside."

Curled on her side in a fetal position, she'd wrapped her thin, shaking arms around her knees. With silence broken only by the clattering of teeth, she broke his heart all over again. Had she been wearing her own clothes, she could've used her lock pick set to sneak into the kitchen, but she only wore a thin piece of cotton.

"No. I'm not going in there with you. 'Sides, isn't this where mongrels belong?"

The wad of bile churning in his chest bolted up, threatening his composure and sanity. He swallowed hard, the sour taste not a fraction of what he deserved.

Meanwhile, a darker emotion took root in his soul and gained momentum with each shudder racking her body. Anger that she'd risk her health with such a stupid stunt boiled inside, forcing his hand to necessary action and consider the emotional consequences later.

"You know damn well that's not what I think of you." But it's what he'd called her at first sight.

Ensuring her safety trumped coddling her feelings. Using the same tactic as if reaching for an Eastern Diamondback, he grabbed her feet and pulled her out, thrashing and screaming. Several well-placed strikes ensured he'd carry his own bruises.

On another day, he might've asked for instruction when her diatribe included sexual scenarios never contemplated.

"Settle down, damn it. We've got to get you warm and dry, for Christ's sake."

"I hate you. You think you're better than anyone else, leading girls on."

"What? What the hell, Kendra?"

Of course, pulling her out feet first meant her t-shirt slid up to her armpits and exposed every bit of cold, shivering flesh. His inner demon knew the best way to warm her from the inside. Any other man might've grabbed a breast or short hairs to ensure cooperation in quick order. The thought crossed his mind.

"Jesus. This is like wrestling a bucket of eels. I never had this much trouble with my brothers." And, of course, comparing her to boys and eels was so, so much better than a mongrel.

Jesus Christ.

He learned a few more words and could only assume their meanings damned his soul for eternity. How out of touch had he become?

When he maneuvered her cursing and squirming mass free of the small house and disentangled her hands from its edges, she focused on a new target.

Him.

He'd underestimated her strength when her fist planted a solid strike on his jaw. Without hesitation, he manhandled her over his shoulder while keeping her in place with a hand on her ass.

Her bare ass.

She pummeled his back and flailed her legs until he swatted her butt. An enraged scream preceded her redoubled efforts.

"Calm down!"

Good advice, maybe I should take it.

"Mackendra, I'll give you two minutes to settle."

Solid hinges protested the abuse as he threw the back screen door open. Snugging her legs to his chest prevented her flailing limbs from breaking the back door's glass inset.

Window curtains torn from their brackets tumbled to the floor under the onslaught of her fury as he pivoted to close the back door.

He'd never lost his temper with a woman. Until now. Slow, deep breaths helped calm the eruption of violent intentions keeping him in a state of obsessive wrath.

"You will not risk your health for the sake of pride." Thoughts of Kendra debilitated by pneumonia strengthened his resolve in bringing her to heel. He would keep her safe, despite the drastic measures required. Through the kitchen she continued to scream obscenities and pound his back, then changed focus to snag a cast iron skillet from the hanging pot rack.

He disengaged her fingers before she could knock him unconscious.

"I'll do what I damn well please! You don't own me. Nobody owns me."

"No. You. Won't. Not anymore. Not as long as I draw breath." Once in his bedroom, he set her down to take off his coat, shocked yet wary when she stopped fighting. "Take that soaking t-shirt off. You'll be damn lucky if you don't get sick." He slid his jacket off and tossed it on the bed, his gaze never leaving her face.

Stepping to his closet, he kept one eye on her while grabbing a thick robe, tossing it to her. "Put that on."

Some unnamed source declared a temporary standoff, holding each immobile, gauging the other's stockpile of deadly weapons, both physical and emotional.

"No." Quiet, simple, to the point.

He expected the retort.

As much as he liked that particular shirt on her, the quiet sound of it rending apart under his grip provided immense satisfaction until viewing the necklace underneath. Earlier, he'd thought she'd worn some type of choker. The object of present scrutiny must've dangled down her back.

Another piece of the puzzle fits. This was Billy's way of ensuring I kept Kendra in my sights.

Her jaw dropped. Very slowly, her gaze climbed his frame until meeting him eye to eye as if waiting for his reaction. A certain innocence glimmered in the swath of moonlight illuminating her face. He could never fulfill the hope tinging her gaze.

Another standoff.

Quiet reigned as puzzlement suffused her features. The muscle ticking in his jaw probably tipped her off.

She turned to run.

Snaking his hand out, he grabbed her arm and spun her into his grasp. If she fought with outrage before, now she was wild, as comprehension of his intent dawned.

"Let me go." She was a woman possessed of every hellish demon from the underworld.

The dog whimpered inside the doorway. A single word sent Krystal sidling out.

"No. You're gonna put this robe on. I won't have you strutting around my house in your birthday suit."

A strong moral code and solid integrity had always prohibited him from exploiting a woman's weakness. Now, he obliterated those boundaries and intended to force his will on another.

Kendra's piercing screams rent the air. "Motherfucker!" With all her strength, she tried to disengage his grip on her arms.

Acute pain in his forearm alerted him to her innovative and tenacious resolve. He'd carry the bite marks for quite a while even if he didn't need a tetanus shot. The only reason she didn't draw blood, his grip on her other arm pulled her away.

"Can't get a good scream on with your mouth closed, can you, sweetheart? Can't bite me with it open."

"Fuck you!"

"Not in this lifetime."

Not one to give up, she grabbed the fine hair on his chest and pulled until he was certain to sport a bald patch.

Damn, that hurt.

"*Ahhh*, you brat." Grabbing both of her elbows, he pulled her arms back until he held both hands against the small of her back.

"I hate you!"

"Maybe so, but I'm still going to protect your ass." Holding her tight to his body prevented her from kneeing him in the crotch. Minutes passed as she continued to vent her rage.

Blood roared through his veins to compete with her epithets of hate shouted at the top of her lungs.

It wasn't until Krystal barked he realized she'd traded screams for sobs.

Further humiliation came with the awareness of how his lower half had taken a sincere interest in the proceedings. Christ, he was pervert. *That* thought brought to mind what was so wrong.

Oh, shit.

She was still naked.

As harsh as he'd been, he converted the energy into a gentle touch, releasing her hands and dressing her in his robe. Plucking the cover off the bed, he wrapped it around her, for both their sakes.

"For the love of God, Kendra, please don't risk your health or safety again. Neither of us will survive."

Sob after sob furnished the salty moisture seeping through his shirt while minutes stretched out in an uncanny silence, his moral blender shredding his libido. She continued to cry, each broken breath heaping despair on his overburdened conscience.

"Your spirit is too bright. I won't allow anyone to tarnish it." His fingers shook in an attempt to corral her wild locks, smoothing them down. He kissed the top of her head.

"I don't know who I am anymore. When I look in the mirror…" More sobs filled the room.

"Identity lies within history and accomplishment, not your reflection, Kendra. I'll help you figure it out." The situation was deteriorating by the second.

A young woman struggling to define her existence didn't need the object of her infatuation shredding her self-image.

Conner needed the mindset of dealing with an innocent, not a full-grown woman his inner demons wanted to possess. Unfortunately, he couldn't *unsee*, and *unfeel* things now burned in his memory. The sight of her wrapped in his arms, the feel of her soft skin under his touch, the heaven of her mouth. It all added up to annihilation.

He pulled the blanket tighter around her before leading her into the bathroom.

"Here. Take a shower. You need to warm up. I'll set clothes on the bed, and we'll talk when you come out."

She didn't complain or defy him, simply followed his request. He'd never felt like a bigger ass.

When she emerged, he was sitting with Krystal and nodded to the table. "Drink that. It'll help."

"What good will that do? I'm lost. I've nowhere to go. Nowhere to call home and no future." Defeat emanated from the set of her shoulders, the tone of her voice, and the way she hung her head.

Rock bottom. The only direction now—sideways or up. He determined it would be the latter.

"Do you want to see your parents?" He wouldn't force the issue since it wasn't safe for her to stay with them, but perhaps a brief meeting with them would start the healing process. Obviously, something had happened to keep her away.

"No. I don't think I'll ever go back." Words barely audible, her confession was as much information as he'd get until she decided otherwise. Some things couldn't be forced or coerced.

"As long as I'm alive, you will have a home, Kendra. I promise you that. But swear to me you won't run away again. I can't take it. I just can't."

Minutes drew out while she quieted then snuggled against Krystal, who'd jumped up between them. He needed information in order to help her.

"Where'd you get this?" With the expectation of earning a black eye or more teeth marks, he reached over to touch the stone she wore about her neck. The soft skin grazed by his knuckles pebbled with goose bumps.

"Billy sent it with a note. Said to never take it off and never show it to anyone but you. Said you'd explain. I lost the note, the last thing he gave me."

"I will explain, but not today." No doubt, the stone in her necklace matched the gems in the envelope. Billy's gift could have signed her death warrant. Her brother had thought about her, sending one envelope to his lawyer, the other to his sister.

He groaned. "How did you survive? Out there all alone."

"A few weeks after I left home, I met Wes and Daeron. Daeron's lived on the streets longer than me. He taught me the ropes and how to fight." Intermittent sniffles muddled her words.

Christ, it was a miracle she hadn't end up in someone else's ropes, forced into the sex trade or selling drugs.

"Wes found us odd, cash-paying jobs. He offered us a roof over our heads, too, but that was too much. Something about him has always felt... wrong."

"So, is Daeron your boyfriend?" Though his first impression of the young man inspired respect, the thought of his hands on Kendra was repugnant.

"What? Hell, no. He's like a brother." Her voice broke on the last word. "He's helped me out of a lot of scrapes."

"When you got mouthy at the wrong time or with the wrong people?"

"Yeah, well. I'm still mouthy sometimes, but I've learned when to shut it down."

"You have? That's good to know." Conner covered his smile and snort with a fist.

"Well, I'll never cross a pimp again, especially one looking to add to his stable. I'm not anyone's whore."

* * * *

Muddling through her confused thoughts yielded no clarity to her situation or a path to winning Conner's heart, something she'd dreamed of yet now vacillated over on an hourly basis.

During her stint in Krystal's house, she realized Conner's earlier words rang true. Billy had made his own decision to return to the unit.

No one had ever handled her in such a way before. On the streets, she'd remained wary and kept her distance from others, except her pack. No doubt, Conner wouldn't hesitate to repeat his behavior as he saw fit. At the time, if she'd had access to a weapon, indecision would not have held her back. She would've hurt him.

Her body, on the other hand, had reacted differently. In between her screamed insults, she'd felt the brush of his hand down her back, stirring a completely different, and opposite, reaction. Even now, her belly registered the undercurrent of excitement flowing through her veins, energizing each nerve to leave her anxious and wanting—more.

Was she so far gone, so demented she craved confinement? Or was this what women, in general, came to like?

Sometimes the outcome of a standoff couldn't be changed. Regardless of his physical responses, Conner would continue to deny their attraction. All would perish when confronted with his stubborn idealism and sense of integrity.

She saw no choice but to run, leaving her heart and first love behind. Meanwhile, she'd bide her time and make him rue the day he'd ever crossed her. She'd prove herself a force of nature.

Chapter Eleven

A roller coaster of emotions constituted poor groundwork for any relationship. If he didn't get control of himself soon, they'd both lose.

Knowing Kendra, retaliation for his earlier manhandling would come as surely as he knew she'd eat every scrap of breakfast now sizzling in the pan. Problem was—he had no clue what form her vengeance would take. He'd stay on his toes considering her devious streak ran as wide as her vein of determination.

When she entered the kitchen, a quiet calm appeared to have filled her soul. A tentative smile graced her face, but her eyes, her eyes gave her away.

"Kendra, whatever devilment you're up to, rethink it. There are always consequences."

One of her old pranks consisted of offering the brothers homemade donuts, filled with soured mayonnaise.

"I'm not up to anything, Conn. Just hungry. Would you like some help? I don't really like charred food." A nod to the pan indicated the bacon currently burning.

"Crap. Sorry. How about pouring our drinks? Eggs are done." Nodding toward the coffee pot on the other counter, he added, "I like mine black. There's juice and milk in the fridge. I'll take juice, not vinegar with orange food coloring."

Remnants of yesterday's coffee remained in the carafe, thickened and cold. Without a word, she washed it before making a new pot, no complaints and no jokes.

Not good. What's she planning?

"No sugar? I seem to remember you used to have a sweet tooth."

But not for caramel-covered onions. "No, thanks. Black is good." After setting two plates on the oak table, he pulled out a chair and sat, watching her every move.

Difficulty came in the form of waiting for the other shoe to drop. She'd do something. The problem being he wouldn't figure it out until after she'd sprung the trap. Savoring the strong brew granted a few minutes to ponder her peculiar mood. "Coffee's good. Is that a bit of cinnamon?"

"Yeah. Just a pinch adds a subtle flavor."

Biting her upper lip advocated further questioning to determine what evil plan her darkening gaze shielded. Questioning it would undermine their fragile bond.

"First thing after breakfast, I'll show you how the alarm system works." Another disaster in the making, but he needed to extend trust in hope of earning like in kind.

"What type of cases do you accept in your private investigations firm?" Innocence dripped from her lips.

Jeez.

His gut rumbled.

"A little bit of everything. Fraud, location services, client protection, divorce, we're fairly diversified." He'd watched her scarf down everything on her plate, then several muffins from the tray on the lazy Susan in the table's center.

Throughout the meal, she remained polite yet distant, giving the appearance of cooperation—*if* he hadn't known her better. With the meal finished, she excused herself to the bathroom after clearing the table.

Marc's unannounced entry disrupted his contemplations in a rush of cool air bearing remnants of ozone. Perhaps he could help temper Kendra's coming storm before it got out of hand. The requested peace offering appeared even better than expected. *Thank God.*

"Does the band have...?" Unaware if Kendra was eavesdropping, he didn't give voice to the rest of his thought.

"After last night at the club? Of course. 'Sides, all mine have 'em." Marc set the extra items on the table along with several child safety locks for cabinets.

"Prick. There's less than seven years difference... I also want the necklace for her." Stoicism couldn't hide his soft spot for Kendra. His brother obviously realized feelings had evolved during their interaction last night. Marc's taunt with the child locks was just the beginning.

"Ready for jewelry already? That was faster than expected."

"Dumbass." Since Kendra's less-than-spectacular entrance at Ambrosia, each brother had bestowed knowing smirks and mumbled commentary referencing nursery rhymes, great walls, and shattered eggs. This wouldn't end until he'd ensured Kendra's safety and a place of her own.

"Hey, bro. You don't look so good. What's up?" Setting the present on the floor, Marc looked around. "One bundle of therapy delivered as promised."

"I'm fine. Thanks for this. How much do I owe you?"

"Seriously? She's as much my sister as wait—let me rephrase that since your brotherly feelings haven't resurfaced." Krystal sniffed and chuffed at the newest addition circling Marc's legs. "I'm surprised you look so comfortable in jeans," he added.

"Asshole. She's family."

Marc snorted before replying, "So, where is she?"

"Bathroom. She decided to run away last night. I found her in the doghouse, curled up on Krystal's bed." Conner's hands clenched at his sides. Nothing would ever banish the snapshot from his mind.

"Son of a bitch! Is that what she thinks of herself, how she's survived the last three years?"

"No. Ah, I don't know. I've found at least two abandoned buildings where I suspect she's squirreled away private stashes."

Marc whistled low after opening the fridge. "Looks like you need supplies. I'll help with that. What about the parents?" Marc eyed a small baggie of leftover lunchmeat suspiciously before tossing the fuzzy green ham in the trash.

Conner toyed with the special delivery. "She won't go back, at least not yet. She's probably trying to decide on how to roast my nuts at the moment."

"I called last night and gave them a heads-up on the situation. They didn't like it, but I convinced them to take an extended vacation with another couple until this blows over. If the shits from last night can't get to her, they'll probably go after her parents." Marc tossed the outdated mayo and sour cream in the trash.

"Jesus, this fridge should be condemned. So, what are we going to do with her? You want me to take her home? Dani could talk to her. You know she could help."

"No." Knowing the harshness of his voice gave him away despite trying to remain calm elicited a groan. "That's a whole new ball game. If the girls meet and I haven't explained Dani's ability, I'm a bastard for shutting her out. On the other hand, even if Dani and Callie agreed to it, Kendra's not ready for a revelation like that."

"Okay. I agree with that. I also know there's more to it than what you're saying." Marc's sharp glance morphing into a sly grin betrayed an understanding of Conner's deeper thoughts.

"Marc, she was wearing a necklace with one of the stones."

"Whoa. Didn't see that coming. Does she know how Billy got them?"

"I don't think so. And I don't intend to tell her for quite a while. First priority is get her settled then track down these dirtballs."

Everything concerning the young woman drove him nuts.

"I see. Gonna keep her after all." Marc's smirk was going to earn him a shiner.

"What? No, you don't see anything. Well, yeah, she's gonna be stuck here a while 'till we figure out this mess." Conner stood, galvanized by anxiety. The kitchen seemed to shrink under his restless steps before he absentmindedly kneeled to inspect Marc's present to Kendra. "Nice. Very nice."

"Conn, I remember that same agonized look on your face when we were kids. All these years, I figured it stemmed from punching Billy after he teased you about your overprotectiveness. Now, I realize it comes from not breaking his nose. And now you feel discombobulated because your feelings have changed. You see her as the adult she's grown into."

"Fuck. I used to help her climb trees and intervene when she got into school fights. She needs someone who can respect her boundaries."

"No, she used to be a kid, but just like you, she's grown up. Now you don't know how to handle the change. You've always been a sucker where she'd concerned. You're finally recognizing her as an adult. At least part of you—"

"Damn it. She's in danger, asshole." Pain radiated up Conner's forearm when his fist slammed against the granite countertop.

"Think about it man. The fact you can't control your temper should be your first clue." Marc held both hands up in front of him, placating even as he took a tentative step back. "Anything else you need? One of us will stop back later with food and goodies."

"Yeah, clothes. Lots and lots of clothes. She has nothing. Literally." Conner indicated the bloody jeans and shirt bagged in the corner. "Drop that by the lab and see if they can get a rush DNA off the blood on her shirt. I don't care who you have to sweet talk. We need to ID the creeps from the club, find the body, and deal with this shit."

"All right. I'll deal with the lab while Julien goes shopping." Marc picked through the clothes but stopped with the long rag, holding it at arm's length as he would a snake. His questioning glance signaled lack of understanding.

"In place of a bra."

"Jeez. Dude, you have a long way to go. Good luck."

"First, I need to make sure she's gonna stay. She has the crazy notion of running again. I can feel it."

"Yeah, Dani was the same way... at first." Marc's devious smile indicated how he'd cured that itch.

"Not the same here, Marc. Not even close."

"Conner, that girl has loved you since we were kids. She followed you everywhere and hung on your every word. From what I saw in Ambrosia last night, nothing's changed, except for the way you view her."

"Back then, she just wanted to be part of the gang, feel included. Hell, she doesn't even know who she is anymore," Conner argued.

"No, she wanted to be part of you. The sooner you realize *that*, the safer she'll be. Considering the level of frustration you're showing now—your subconscious reciprocates." Stuffing the clothes back in the bag, Marc offered a last bone on which to gnaw. "Dude, we all loved Billy and want to see her realize her dreams. Since you've offered the band a job at the club, how long do you think it'll be before another man snaps her up?"

Conner's growl filled the room.

"Just saying." Marc's grin widened. "Talk to you later when we drop off essentials. Think about it, bro. I saw her interaction with Jenkins on arrival. Wouldn't surprise me if he tries again once his ego relaxes. He's not too bad a sort despite being a mascot for the yuppie world, but I don't think he's quite right—"

Sudden rage carried Conner forward, his intent evidenced in his brother's back-pedaling steps to the door. "That arrogant, egotistical little shit better not touch her. I'll rip his fucking head off."

"Later, Conner." A decidedly knowing smirk accompanied his sibling's cocksure attitude.

By the time Conner returned to the bedroom, Kendra was sitting on the edge of the mattress, lost in thought. Despair had settled its mantle about her shoulders.

"Perfect timing." He deposited the furry bundle in her arms then smiled as her immediate low murmurs and soft encouragements signaled the pup's instant adoption.

Score one for stability. She'd always wanted a dog. Maybe the peace offering would tear down some barriers. Not that he'd stoop to bribing. She'd see through that. This was heart to heart. She'd figure that out, too.

He stepped out to let them bond.

Shuffling steps and puppy yips announced Kendra's hesitant entrance. Entertaining her squirming furball with nuzzles and cooing noises, she rested a brief gaze on his face. The mistiness in her eyes wasn't mistaken for anything but gratitude. "Thank you, Conn. He's the most beautiful pup I've ever seen. And... I'm sorry."

"Clean slate, Kendra. Now we start with a clean slate." She's apologizing for running away? Didn't sound like a Kendra thing to do.

The oversized shirt and sweats accentuated her urchin status, especially with cloth lapping the belt which held all in place. Even the thick, ill-fitting socks looked adorable as she padded forward.

"Ah, okay."

Nibbling her lower lip was a practice begun years ago and generally accompanied remorse over an undisclosed transgression. She stood still, indecision holding her hostage.

"He comes from Schutzhund stock, very good lines. His aptitude tests indicate he's quite amenable to training. What will you name him?"

"I don't know. It'll have to be special, like him. I've never seen a black-and-silver sable, long-haired shepherd before." When the pup wriggled for freedom, she set him on the hardwood floor. "Though, I don't know much about training. Will you help?"

"Of course."

The pup would provide great therapy on many levels, both physiological and psychological. When she met his gaze excitement danced in her eyes to breathe new hope in their future.

"I've got it." The sofa barely dipped under her slight weight.

The pup whined in protest when lifted but wiggled like a worm and snuggled in her lap. Although lacking the temperament of an official therapy dog, he was already worth his weight in gold.

It wasn't clear who comforted whom. Sitting beside her, Conner had never been jealous of a dog before. "And?"

"Thadeus. Thad for short." The smile gracing her lips held as much pain as joy.

"After your brother." Billy had instigated more than one fight over his middle name.

"It means gift from God." Moisture brimmed her eyes but resisted the pull of gravity from one too stubborn to grieve.

An odd gut discomfort began with a slight grumbling. Unusual, since his ironclad stomach could generally handle anything.

Kendra's mouth formed an O with its onset but said nothing. A slight flush of her face forewarned of trouble in one form or another, yet he didn't want to disturb their idyllic moment. It had been too long in coming.

With time's passage, the tinkling progressed to mild belly cramps.

Kendra's anxiety increased, betrayed by excited bursts of conversation as he walked her through the intricacies of raw feeding, discussed various training techniques, and the possibility of Schutzhund trials one day.

Mild cramps progressed to distressing discomfort with rumbling mini explosions forewarning of rectal Armageddon.

"I'm sorry, Conner."

"For what?"

"Uh, just everything."

His first trip to the bathroom provided enormous relief and enlightenment of her strange behavior and apology. On the sink's counter lay a small, torn foil wrapper. He'd purchased the over-the-counter drug several years ago but had failed to clear out his medicine cabinet since.

Thinking back, yeah, his coffee had tasted a little different. He hadn't finished the cup so perhaps hadn't ingested the full dose of laxative. His concern over Kendra had subverted his attention.

His steps back to the sofa were marked in contemplative silence. Dropping the small foil on the end table, he just waited until her hesitant gaze rose.

"Oh." Her face flushed before she nuzzled the pup's neck.

"Yeah, oh. Remember this, Kendra. Just because consequences aren't immediate, doesn't mean they won't happen." After the night they'd endured, he could no more chastise her now than banish the pup. Their thin filament of trust, already stressed to the breaking point, would shatter, sending slivers of doubt and defiance to topple their new beginning.

In retrospect, she'd probably given him what he deserved. Thank Heaven she didn't make a smoothie from the medicine cabinet's entire contents rather than seek a small vengeance. Over the years and from various situations, he did have a few prescription drugs which should be tossed. Something he'd address soon.

"I'm sorry, Conner. It was impulsive. I was mad. Are you gonna take him back?" Desperation etched her features as she clutched the pup tight to her chest, ensuring that nothing short of a pry bar would separate them.

"What? No, of course not. He's yours, end of story."

"Do you still want our band to play?"

"Absolutely, and where you go, Thad goes, meaning to the club and to the office. We'll take a crate with us. But you won't start tonight. You

91

need a day to regroup, and Thad needs time to acclimate to his new home."

Her childish retribution cleared his system in several trips. Each one accompanied imagined consequences to her firm ass, his conscience allowing the small indulgence in exchange for suffering the consequences of her iron will.

Julien's arrival brought out an interesting side of Kendra that incited new hope in his bid to keep her at hand, albeit temporarily. Years ago, she'd shared a comradery with all the brothers, but Julien was closest in age.

Even his brother kindled a shy smile and quick acceptance, the same thing he craved. Instead, he received the wariness of mental barriers erected for self-protection.

"Do you have all the items, Julien?" Conner accepted the heavy bags knowing his brother would read between the lines.

"Yes, Conner, I got everything you requested, plus a few extras." Impatience laced with deviltry infused his sibling's tone. A widened smile as he dropped several more bags to accept Kendra's quick hug seemed a little too bright. "Hey, kiddo. Glad you're in one piece. Welcome back to the fold."

Damn, Conner thought with a sigh as he threaded his fingers through his hair. *Everyone but me.*

"That's a lot of stuff." Kendra snatched one of Conner's bags. Pulling out a pair of jeans, she grabbed the label. "There's no price tag. Even without it, I know damn well I can't pay for all this." Turning to Conner, she admonished in a halting tone, "Regardless of how long I work for you, I'll never have the money to pay for this stuff. I can't accept these things." Stubbornness refused to release the tears pooling in her eyes.

"Nonsense, Kendra. Just try the stuff on and see how it fits, okay?"

With great reluctance, she gathered the bags and padded down the hall.

Conner retreated to the kitchen and held up two glasses. "Care for a Scotch?"

"That bad, huh. Maybe I should take her to my house."

Conner poured a double.

Afternoon light glimmered off the chain Julien pulled from his shirt pocket, the clear blue stone on its end fragmenting and refracting muted hues across the hardwood floor. "It has a different frequency than the one on the pup."

"Good, we can track them both, though I can't see them separating." Covering all the bases ensured a little peace of mind after the night he'd suffered. Not that he'd sleep well in the foreseeable future.

"Let me get the rest of the stuff and we'll fill in some of the blanks about what's happening. The rest of us have worked while you've been busy playing house."

As shadows crept along the kitchen floor, Conner switched to soda, knowing he'd need his wits about him after hearing his brother's report.

"How long can it take to try on some jeans and shirts?"

Julien ignored the comment. "Marc told me about her makeshift bra. Life must've been hard for her."

Julien's narrowed gaze betrayed the bifurcation of speech and apparent thoughts, a physical portent of some evil prank on its way.

"You think? Julien, what've you done? What did you buy?" His brother's shopping spree wouldn't have ignored anything, which meant... "I hope the clothes you brought are all appropriate." The sourness in his stomach converted simple reservations into a roaring premonition, dark and ominous.

Julien smiled as he stood with a sigh. Like his other brothers, he also enjoyed practical jokes. "They certainly are. She passed the twenty-one mile stone. Remember what that was like?"

His brother left on that ominous note. Whatever lay in the future, Conner would face it head on, with an empty gut.

A deep-cover operation took less time to plan than Kendra did in trying on clothes. When she came out, all traces of uncertainty had vanished. Such metamorphous should not have occurred due to a few garments.

"Great. I see Julien brought us groceries, too. Shall we see what we can scare up for dinner?" He needed to stick to safe topics until he figured out her angle. Something was up.

"Okay, have at it."

"I love to cook. It's been ages." Smoothing her hair behind her ears, she sighed.

Something about her demeanor, mild and accepting, didn't sit well, as if an alien presence had replaced her straightforward, no-nonsense approach with a more unassuming, moldable Kendra. He didn't like it, not one bit.

Determination still lurked deep in her gaze, festering, growing. Was this the start of a new revenge?

For a brief second, insecurity transformed her expression into the hesitant young woman lurking within. "Did Julien have any new information?"

"We don't have DNA results back yet."

Way to make her feel safe and remind her of the creep who tried to rape her.

"That'll take a couple of days, won't it?" Thad nestled against her chest before she eased him to the floor.

A short rewind to replay her last sentence in his mind allowed him to catch up. "At least. That's if we get a hit. Not everybody has prints in the system, but don't worry, we'll catch them." His gaze roamed her curves before snapping back to her face.

She smiled as his face heated, something he hadn't experienced in years.

"I'm not worried." When she stretched, the arching of her back declared her a woman, fully developed. "I'll get started cooking. Why don't you start a fire then have a seat at the island?"

Garments in the bags sure didn't look the same.

"I'll pour us a glass of wine while we wait for dinner." Not taking no for an answer, she searched the drawers for a corkscrew then retrieved the bottle of red Bordeaux from the fridge. "First, can you open this while I get the glasses?"

"You drink wine?" What happened to his little hellion? Something had switched gears in her head, turning her into an innocent seductress. He rewound prior conversations in his head to search for a clue.

Start a fire? Seriously?

If he didn't get control of the situation soon, she'd be leading him around by the short hairs, or he'd spend the rest of their time together in blue-ball hell.

Her pointed glance at the bottle and his inactive hands betrayed impatience. "C'mon. It's getting a bit chilly with the sun going down."

Curiosity dictated he allow her one glass. After all, it might take the edge off, at least for one of them. His need for relief was greater, judging by her smooth and effortless movements. In a vague, numb awareness, he opened the bottle, intrigued by her change in disposition.

Despite his better judgment, he found himself adding kindling then several logs from the rack before coaxing a small flame to blaze.

Another trip to the fridge and she pulled out a beef roast along with various vegetables.

"You really can cook? How? Where?" Three years on the streets might have taught proper methods of open-fire road kill kebabs, but little else.

Dawning struck with the speed of a bullet tearing into the flesh of a soft underbelly. Long ago, a one-sided conversation entailed listening to Billy brag about how hard she'd worked to learn the intricacies of the culinary delights he'd treasure once stateside. His little sister had wanted to appear grown up, a teenager testing her wings.

"Yep, Billy swore I could live with him after discharge, so I practiced. He couldn't cook, so I learned everything I could from Mom. My parents thought I'd be good for him."

"Your mom's a great cook." He left it at that, waiting to see if she'd continue, maybe ask about her parents, but she didn't.

She wasn't ready.

Dinner passed amid quiet conversation of times gone by. Sharing memories of Billy excavated old wounds for them both but was crucial in the healing process. Intermittent halting speech marked specific recollections, yet her face remained dry while bearing pain in quiet dignity. In time, the mood lightened with the reliving of childhood antics.

Her dubious pretense of geniality kept him on edge, recalling how this young woman ejected surrender from her vocabulary long before

95

puberty. So, if not a change of heart toward him, what was she planning?

The prior night, she'd run away. Now, she fancied the art of flirtation. *Coincidence? I think not.*

Her innocent, fumbling attempts at seduction created an effect which prevented him from standing for fear of exposing validation of her success.

Despite the nagging reservations, he enjoyed her easy company. They continued their chat in the living room, relaxing in front of the fire. She'd canted sideways to face him with Thad in the middle. He'd barely noticed the outside world had gone dark until she yawned. Firelight created a dance of light and shadows across her form that invited his visual exploration of each curve and recess. Restraining that compulsion exhausted him.

"About this mess, did Billy…" He hated to bring it up but the thought of her brother having sent something else, some clue as to what the hell he'd been working on, drove him to ask.

"I don't want to talk about that yet. I can't."

"We're going to have to, eventually."

"Tomorrow? Please?"

"All right, I'll take Thad and Krystal out while you brush your teeth." As he stood and called Krystal to his side, firelight caught a decidedly mischievous glint in her eyes.

Oh, hell.

"Come on, Thad, out we go." The pup had taken to Kendra better than anticipated, whining when taken away from his new mom.

Cool night air helped clear his mind over Kendra's change in attitude. In time, she'd reveal her intentions and motives. He prayed it wouldn't be too late for him to recover.

By the time he headed back inside, common sense reigned. In light of her softened perspective as a possible setup for taking off, he'd sleep on the sofa. She wouldn't escape him twice.

Yeah, the couch is exactly where he wanted to sleep.

Chapter Twelve

Because the sofa cushion kept sliding under his extensive frame, because he'd endured inappropriate dreams of Kendra all night, and because said tormentor strolled through the great room wearing half the scraps of cloth considered a negligee, Conner's mood headed south the moment he opened his eyes. Her walk into the kitchen was more appropriate for seduction than food prep.

The total of it cleared the prior evening's confusion in her change of behavior. With the types of purchases made, Julien had unofficially given his stamp of approval. Couple status.

It was going to be a long day.

"Kendra, go put on some clothes. Please." The please occurred as an afterthought. He was going to strangle his brother.

"I am wearing clothes. I really love the things Julien brought. Who would've guessed a man could shop?" When she sneezed several times, Thad, who'd nestled in her arms, licked at her face. "I'm going to take him outside, be back in a minute."

"Not like that, you're not." Conner lurched to his feet and rubbed his eyes while trying to reconcile remnants of sleep with a nearly naked Kendra. Brisk, cool air would help.

"I'll take him while you dress. No need for you to get sick." Having no neighbors within sight didn't quench the jealousy swelling from the blackest recesses of his mind, dark and dangerous.

He didn't bother with a jacket, needing the bracing chill. What the hell was Julien thinking, buying her such provocative shit? He dreaded to see what he'd bought for her to wear in Ambrosia.

"Damn, Thad, I knew I should have done the shopping myself, turtlenecks and nice slacks would suit her fine." Why couldn't his brothers see she was off limits?

Back inside, Kendra had done what he'd asked, almost. She now wore a thin, silky robe that fit her contours almost as well as his fingers.

"I'm making breakfast. How about an omelet?"

Why not? Everything else was scrambled. "No. I'll do breakfast. It's the one meal I can cook. You go hop in the shower." When he saw the denial in her eyes, her mouth ready to form the words that would obliterate his resolve, he cut her off. "Your hair's a mess. This is your first day at the firm. You'll want to make a good impression, don't you?"

He hadn't meant to hurt her, yet the resignation in her gaze belied his intent. Without a sound, she padded toward her bedroom.

God damn it!

Retrieving the present he'd asked Julien to fetch, he set it on the kitchen island. Maybe it would help smooth his blundering, disparaging comment.

Today's breakfast would call for extra protein, anything to keep his mouth busy a little longer. He wished he had the time to chop some wood out back to alleviate his growing frustration. Strong black coffee while sitting at the table and staring out the window helped soothe his mind. He waited until he heard the shower cut off to start food prep.

The newly acquired groceries weren't even appropriate—two cans of whipped cream, chocolate, and caramel toppings. He'd expected Julien to pick up fruits, vegetables, healthy foods. In the back of his mind, he heard his brother's arguments about her needing to gain weight amid smothered guffaws.

After setting out the eggs, cheese, and milk, he poured a cup of orange juice and sat, willing his thoughts to chill. The cool liquid brought sanity to his morning until he turned to see Kendra entering the kitchen.

A round of choking and gasping for breath didn't help either of their composures. Her prior cocky, self-assured manner disappeared in favor of hunched shoulders and a bright crimson expression. She buried her face in the pup's neck.

"You look very nice, Kendra. Julien chose well." In fact, the short pencil skirt displayed her legs to full advantage, the curve of her ass perfect as the fitted jacket stopped at its gentle slope. Though she didn't need the extra two inches of height, the heels were a perfect complement to both her legs and the suit.

"I figured I should look professional. I was wondering if you'd drop me off somewhere so I could get a proper haircut." She barely mumbled the words.

His blunder, his fix.

"Sure. You look great, but still missing a little something."

When her gaze lifted to show brow and parted lips, he held out a small box. "Julien picked this up, too. Said it reminded him of you."

As if it might jump out and bite, she carefully reached for the box, lifting it as she might approach a rabid animal.

"What is it?" Her small gasp upon opening the lid provided its own reward.

"Something your brother wanted you to have. We saw it that day we went to the boardwalk." He'd bought it in Billy's memory.

Giving jewelry to a young lady enduring a long-term crush wasn't his best move, but it would ease his mind if she ran.

"Oh, my God. It's beautiful. I've always loved dolphins and seahorses." Twin silver dolphins encircled a blue stone.

In fact, the brothers commissioned the covert tracking device after developing their private investigations firm, one of those things done in case the need arose. The dolphins originated from a memory of a young girl adoring them. Her dream to have a house by the sea where she could play her piano and watch the dolphins cavort, a fantasy.

"This is beautiful."

"Sapphire is your birthstone, isn't it?" The necklace having a GPS chip in it shouldn't stick in his craw like a festering wound, a necessary evil. He felt like a heel.

"It is." Tilting her neck to one side, she offered him the chain and turned her back.

When he circled her neck and fastened the tiny clasp, he couldn't resist a slight grazing of her neck, noticing the slight shiver under his touch.

Clearing his throat, he attempted some positive reinforcement. "You look great." The fact his voice remained gravelly reinforced his need to keep his thoughts above the beltline. A nice warning.

Breakfast passed in a corrupted vortex of silence, regret, and hope. Though his brothers might see it as backtracking, he had another gift for her, a decidedly unfeminine one, but one that might bring a smile or bit of comfort. Something familiar.

"I have something else for you, to replace the one you lost."

When she turned, he handed her a knife, a replica of the one Billy had given her years ago.

Her eyes lit up, accompanied by an excited breath. "It's exactly like the one I had."

"Yep. I'm sorry you lost the other, but keep this as a reminder."

The hug was spontaneous and heartfelt. A good beginning.

"Guess I'll have to buy a purse if I'm gonna be wearing skirts and such. Otherwise, it'll fit in the back pocket of my jeans, just like my other one did."

Upon entering the office, all eyes turned to her in appreciative speculation. Expectations of the pup taking center stage couldn't have landed further from reality.

After his own assistant left two weeks prior for maternity leave, he'd almost learned to manage without help. Kendra's presence offered a method to keep an eye on her.

His earlier conversation with Julien ensured proper groundwork for Kendra to work with the other assistants in learning the ropes. He'd never thought to ask if she could type. The only reason it mattered—he didn't want her catching flak from the other assistants.

Kudos to the female assistants who immediately took her under their collective wing. Getting her settled was easier than anticipated with everyone flocking around her and Thad. Her centered placement in the massive room ensured he could observe them both, telling himself he was ultimately responsible for the pup's training.

In the end, she added color to the office dynamic. The other assistants took it in stride when her typing skills lacked, giggled when she discussed the filing system, and in general accepted her on her own terms.

Appreciative glances from their two male investigators created a definite problem. One was too old and the other thought himself a playboy, of sorts. Neither was appropriate for one who'd been recently traumatized, which brought to mind her skill with a knife and the missing body. His solid glare sent them both back to work after introductions.

Each of the offices consisted of half-glass walls, while their assistants' spaces occupied the center of the room in a double row with hip-high filing cabinets running between, further promoting the sense of the open floor plan. Unfortunately, having her in plain sight proved a double-edged sword.

Equally lamentable, none of the investigators enjoyed any privacy. The design normally inspired a positive and bright work environment with light spilling in through each office window. Currently, it failed miserably.

Shaking his head, he focused on what needed sorting. Paperwork in the aftermath of finding Kendra included vital information since she'd inherited the legacy from hell. A call to John Masterson, attorney of record, began his inquiries.

Why Billy hadn't wanted her to collect her inheritance until in Conner's care still confused him. The reason for subterfuge remained unsolved.

Instead of stepping up to the plate, Conner had neglected his duty until Kendra turned twenty-one, which had left her homeless for three years. Good intentions wouldn't help him sleep at night.

Hanging up the phone, he'd barely filtered the significance of the information through his brain when his thoughts stuttered due to the commotion in the main office. Marc's girlfriend, Dani, breezed through the front door.

Oh, God. Please, no.

As if fate hadn't already kicked him in the teeth, a clear view of the open space yielded a warning of catastrophic carnage yet to come.

The slender psychic, escorted by her team of protectors, strode down the center aisle, smiling as if she couldn't derail his life in a heartbeat. Marc followed, a shit-eating grin sliding into place after catching his older brother's eye.

Due to their own trials with Dani and Callie, Marc and Nate spent less time at the office. The current situation smacked of collusion between brothers. Conner could feel the walls closing in.

I'm going to flatten his ass.

Marc strode to the open door way and smiled wide. "Hey, how's it going?"

His younger sibling's devious smile threatened to dislodge the wad of dread in his chest. No way could he catch his balance when those around him conspired to turn his world upside down.

He'd never considered himself a coward, but destiny picked that moment to freeze every muscle in his body. All he could do was stare, even lacking the ability to close his jaw.

Marc's smile widened. Being the polite bastard he was, his younger sibling sauntered in and sat across from Conner's desk while Dani strode over to sit with Kendra.

"Marc, stay out of this. She's involved in some serious shit, and Dani doesn't need to borrow trouble." Reminding his brother of the danger Dani could face might buy some time before the girls got too deeply involved.

"Hey, dude, we've always known you'd need a bit of a push when the time came. You can thank me later." Marc arched a brow then glanced out to the open area where Dani appeared to enjoy an animated conversation with Kendra. His grin morphed into a smirk. "I'd say they're gonna be fast friends. Looks like you're in trouble."

"Fuck it. Come on. Give me a break. Julien's already started. He brought her a ton of inappropriate clothes. She doesn't need that kind of encouragement."

"I think she looks fantastic. Can't wait to see her tonight." His sly profile radiated dire predictions.

The pencil in Conner's hand snapped in half, sending shards to litter his desktop.

His sibling turned abettor laughed outright. "God, we've all been waiting so long for this. It's gonna be sweet, so very sweet."

"Prick. You're just setting Kendra up for a fall, asshole." Conner brushed the pencil fragments from his desk. "I assume you're ready for our meeting? And Dani just happened to come at a time when I'm gonna be busy?"

Weekly conferences to discuss ongoing cases entailed an informal and relaxed affair. Today would be torture owing to Dani filling Kendra's head with all manner of crap. "You do realize karma's a bitch, right?"

"Which is why I love watching paybacks unfold. Lead the way, oh wise one." Marc's soft chuckle filled the air as Conner circled the desk.

"Is Dani going to tell her? I don't think Kendra's ready for that. If she waits..."

"Don't worry. That the beauty of living with a mind-reader. She'll handle it. And she probably won't say anything today, unless she deems it appropriate. Take a breath, man. You're worse than a little old lady holding fast to her coupons."

Dani's sweet smile was fodder for the devil. How in the hell had his family joined forces against him in less than twenty-four hours?

Solid walls, adorned with bookshelves and several large prints of the brothers and the firm's employees blocked his means of monitoring Kendra during Dani's visit.

Normally, the meetings included the assistants, but due to the nature of Kendra's circumstances, today it would be private, just between brothers. Any attempt to postpone it would incur endless jokes and mocking laughter.

"Are you sure Dani has thought this through?" His growled words to Marc ended with a sigh. He might have a lot of explaining to do in the afternoon. Kendra wasn't the type to hold back on her questions any more than her punches.

"She's more of the, fly-by-the-seat-of-her-pants type gal. It's her decision, and I trust her judgment." Marc sitting beside him at the conference table preceded the rest of his sibling tormentors entering. The wide grins pasted on Nate and Julien's faces forewarned of more trouble. Not long ago, he'd been in each of their shoes and had relished every minute.

"Gee, Conner, you appear a little vexed." Looking at Marc, Julien added, "You bring the fire extinguisher?" A calculating frown crossed his expression before adding, "Remember to always aim toward the base of a fire, in this case, Conner's ass."

"We should run a practice fire drill for the rest of the office. Let them know of the danger, even if Kendra's only as a temp." Marc's comment drew affirmative nods from the others.

"Maybe she could do a little re-decorating. Shades for his office, perhaps?" Julian's lips forced in a straight line didn't hide the laughter in his eyes.

"Nah, the half wall is enough, if they're discreet. 'Sides, the rest of us need entertainment," Marc added.

And so it began. "Not gonna happen," Conner warned.

"Ah, so we do need to bring in Kendra. Need a little thawing, do we?" Julien chuckled as he opened his laptop. "Nate always said your feelings would evolve once she grew up. I wasn't sure until now."

"And what a wonderful job she's done," Nate added.

"Do they make noise-canceling headphones for dogs? Wouldn't want to offend Krystal with Conner's, ah, activities," Julien added.

"What about the pup? Such an impressionable age." Nate sat on the other side of the large table, laughing.

Marc sniffed the air conspicuously, wrinkling his nose. "You all smell that? Conner has started wearing cologne again. Hell, we'll all need our sinuses scraped before long. You all realize a canine's sense of smell is so much stronger than ours?"

"Enough! Someone tried to rape Kendra, telling her to retrieve the envelope Billy posted before he died. Until we track the prick down, she won't be safe."

That narrowed everyone's attention. "In addition, Billy named me in his will concerning Kendra. I was to receive the envelope from his attorney on her twenty-first birthday. It went into effect when she stepped into the club. Smug bastard knew I'd take care of her."

"Dude, you're the only one surprised on that count," Nate added, sympathy evident in his gaze.

"Why didn't we know about all this before now? Why wait?" Marc's no-nonsense demeanor replicated in his brothers around the room. "And what's with the gemstones in the envelope?"

"I'm guessing when Billy retrieved the flash drive, he didn't want it turned over until Kendra was assured protection, in case they'd uncovered his identity. Maybe he suspected a traitor?"

"That would fit, since one of Kenson's men hopped in bed with the foreign bastards after Callie." Nate set his files on the table.

"Do you think Billy learned something about Callie or Dani from his 'off-the-books' mission?" Marc tapped a pencil against the table top, deep in thought. "That would explain him wanting Kendra within our group."

"Just to be clear, Kendra doesn't have any psychic talent, does she?" Nate turned a serious gaze to his older brother.

"Not unless you count defiance, abstinence, and getting under my skin." Conner ground his teeth when his brothers laughed. "Far as I can tell, her super talents include knife skills, which she's always had, and picking locks. I doubt there's a lock invented she couldn't defeat."

"I remember Billy teaching her to whittle blocks of wood."

"Yeah, she lost the knife on the street, I got her another, but what kind of man buys a knife for a girl?" Conner returned to his original thread of thought with, "The gems were probably in the safe with the drive, so I'm guessing he decided on a better use for them."

In short order, Conner described the envelope's contents sent to Kendra prior to his death.

"What a convoluted mess." Marc added. "It'd be nice if Callie could decipher what's on the flash drive. We'd know what cost Billy his life."

Chapter Thirteen

After the meeting, Conner hadn't been able to make his calls and wind up loose ends fast enough. Every minute the women spent together formed new and horrific scenarios for him to consider.

Now in the parking lot of Ambrosia, he took a deep breath before sliding out into the cool night air. As much as he'd wanted to keep Kendra home, she needed this, to be out, to socialize, and to be with her friends.

She halted mid-step in rounding the hood, studying him as a predator watched for its next meal. The change in her attitude since spending time with Dani unnerved him.

"What?" Kendra narrowed her eyes, assessing, calculating.

"Nothing. You look nice." His smile felt more like a grimace.

Instead of dressing up, she'd elected for jeans, cable-knit sweater, and light jacket along with tennis shoes, her old ones with a light squeak. If not for her attitude, he'd be wary of her running.

She was up to something—again.

"What did you talk to Dani about today at the office? You've been awful quiet, and frankly, that makes me nervous."

A quiet Kendra equated a panther preparing to leap.

Partial relief came from the fact organizational skills ranked low on her list of priorities. It would've taken days to find misplaced folders if not for Dani's help. The relayed, *"you're welcome,"* accompanied emoji's in his brother's text.

"Dani agreed that it was very likely that Billy's secret op is what got him killed. And that means the envelope and my necklace rolls into that. She's agreed to join me in talking with that damned Colonel."

"I think you two should leave that conversation to Marc and me."

"Because of the fact you're men? I don't think so, buddy. Oh, and she agrees its bullshit that I have to work at your firm for three months before you hand over the package." Her eyes narrowed, gauging his response as he escorted her through the lot.

Conner's gaze shifted to the back door of Ambrosia. The parking lot wasn't the place for this conversation, but he couldn't hold his tongue any longer. He needed her 'take' on those she called friends.

"She agrees with me. You're full of shit."

"We'll deal with that later. There's something more important to discuss... Kendra, I hate to do it, but I have to ask. Since it was dark when you were attacked, are you sure it couldn't have been one of your band?" Undermining her relationship with those she called friends concerned him less than keeping her alive.

"What? No! That's not possible. I've known them since I hit the streets." A slight panic edged her voice, complete with nibbles of her lower lip.

"Okay, just setting the record straight. You knew I'd have to ask. I'm sure you'd have detected any strange behavior in them."

She sidestepped to shift away from his touch. For an instant, it appeared she needed a target, something to vent her frustration.

This wasn't going as planned. Why was everything so screwed up when they were together?

"They're fine. If you don't trust them, then trust me. We should get going." Thick locks of ebony hair shifted across her forehead, partially concealing the hurt in her expression.

"Wait, Kendra. We've been at odds since you came back. We were never like this before. I hate it."

She looked up when he took her hand then tugged her closer until only mingled breath separated them.

"That was back when you could bear my presence and didn't see me as a gutter rat," she whispered, awkwardly skimming a lock of hair behind her ear.

A slight touch lifted her chin to meet his gaze. "No, Kendra. We've just been apart too long. Come here."

Wrapping his arms around her shoulders conveyed everything he couldn't say. To hold her tight allowed him to inhale the scent of her hair, his solid chest reforming the soft mounds of her breasts. Combined exhalations whispered along his skin to coil something deep inside like a phantom whip, waiting to lash him with his next misstep.

"You feel awfully warm, hon. You okay?"

"Yeah, I'm fine."

Her delicate hands on his back hardened his resolve. Her standard answer would soon be unacceptable.

"It'll never be like it used to." Muffled against his shirt and vest, her voice held the plaintive desire of the girl he once knew.

Current circumstances denied his mind access to those visual snapshots that had enriched their lives where everything was relaxed and natural.

"You're right. We can never go back in time, that's true. But it doesn't mean we can't move forward and evolve."

If he didn't take care, he'd lead them both down a dangerous path. He intended to curtail her world in small, slow degrees, careful of the slippery slope with the potential of leaving their emotions bloody and raw. He'd skate the edges in their relationship, and in the end, release her when the time was right.

If he could see them now, would Billy condone the plan in hopes of keeping Kendra alive or condemn Conner's restless spirit to hell? Either way, Conner's intentions just sentenced his filthy soul to an eternity of fire and brimstone. Until he found her a nice boy to love, her heart wouldn't fully heal.

"Your music is beautiful. I can see your hand in writing those songs."

"Daeron wrote the bass."

"I'm so sorry for all you've endured. It'll get better from here on out." He almost finished with, "Mongrel."

The instant her body began molding to his, the inevitable shifting of his own responses, psychological to physical, consigned him to a new private purgatory. After briefly tightening his hold, he put her at arm's length.

"We'll figure this out, little one. We'll do it together, one day at a time." The pounding of his heart affirmed he was in deep shit. "You really are warm. You sure you're feeling all right?" It didn't take a thermometer to tell she ran at least a low-grade fever. The evening was early, which meant it would go up as the night lengthened.

"Of course, I'm all right. We need to get inside."

Her look of confusion instigated a harsh round of self-recriminations. His intent to see her grow, finish school, and settle down, would require tact and setting limits. It would also require he never kiss her again, for that one simple action would destroy his best-laid plans.

Their current predicament suggested a rocky start to the undertaking.

Swirling of raven-black locks as she turned redirected his attention until sudden footsteps snapped his gaze to his brother's SUV, parked beside his own.

Faster than Conner could react, the masked thug yanked Kendra backward, against his chest, a gun to her temple. Clad in black, he stood a head taller, but bent to whisper in her ear.

"So good to see you again. Have to admit, smelling a bit better, too."

* * * *

Kendra stilled, letting her body relax and her mind take in everything around her. The voice belonged to the same bastard who'd attacked her before. She'd gone soft in 'rejoining' society. This was the price.

"Let her go, asshole. She doesn't have what you want." Conner sidestepped to give himself space.

If she reacted, Conner would die.

Not today.

Her assailant shifted so his back was to the vehicle. If he sought security in that position, he was indeed an idiot.

Kendra fisted her hands at her sides. Her conversation with Dani earlier helped complete the picture of her brother's demise. Though the data hadn't been deciphered, they knew its origin.

"On the contrary. She's exactly what I want at the moment. I love a good piece, willing or not, doesn't matter. In order to keep this short, give me the envelope, Conner, and I'll consider letting her live."

"Stupid asshat, kill me and your boss will end you in horrific ways even I wouldn't wanna contemplate. I hear Kyu-Chul has friends who are very inventive." Kendra felt the brief pause in her abductor's grip.

109

"And why would he care about a street rat like you?" The gunman's right hand loosened around her shoulder and dropped to squeeze her breast.

"Because I'm one of three he's searching for, idiot." Foul breath washed over Kendra's face in a whoosh. The second of distraction granted time to visualize her moves.

"Then maybe I'll just take you now. Hell, I could've saved myself a lot of trouble from the beginning." The gun barrel swung in Conner's direction.

"Shoot me, and you won't get the envelope. How happy would that make your boss?"

"Doesn't have to be a kill shot..."

"And you don't think the sound of a gunshot will bring tons of witnesses from inside? You don't hear music yet, asshole."

With no room between them, she couldn't snatch the knife from her back pocket. Helpless and under threat wasn't a good fit.

"Hmm, then I think I'll just take her with me. You can imagine the fun I'll have." Stroking the side of her face he added, "You'll come to think of me as good-time Charlie."

"You'll be dead before *we* can have any fun. Trust me, Charlie."

Charlie chuckled low in her ear. "I promise to turn you over to my boss once I get the envelope. That sounds fair. The sooner I get it, the less you suffer."

Kendra sidestepped in time with her attacker to prevent stumbling. Once beyond the plane of the vehicle, he swung the barrel away from Conner.

What she didn't count on—her aggressor had an accomplice, heard but not seen. In her mind's eye, thug two stood behind and to the right of her position.

"C'mon. Let's get out of here. This place gives me the creeps."

The minute the gun barrel swung away from Conner, Kendra elbowed her adversary in the gut and stomped his instep. Reaching for her knife in swinging around, she noted the open mouth, seen through one of three holes in the black mask.

"Fuck you both." The blade tearing through flesh and nerves of his wrist assured the gun dropped from his hand. It skittered under the rear of the SUV.

"You fucking bitch. I'll kill you for that." Charlie grabbed his wrist to stem bleeding and turned to his partner. "Shoot 'em both."

Conner engaged the second thug before a weapon appeared.

When Charlie knelt to retrieve his gun, Kendra sent him flying with a kick to his head. "Now is when the fun begins, good-time Charlie. Hope you don't mind if we start early."

Giving up on the gun, Charlie pulled a knife, similar to her own. Unlike her brother, she'd never trained to defend against such an attack, Billy's warning ringing in her ears. *Faced with a knife—run.*

"Oh, fucking hell." Kendra arched like a cat to avoid the swipe of the blade. Instead of her belly, the knife sliced through her jacket and across her upper arm.

Her exclamation drew Conner's attention and earned him solid punch to the gut. He stepped back to gather himself.

A scream pierced the night as the back door to Ambrosia opened.

Kendra glanced over to see Dani preceding Marc out the door.

"Marc, call Callie. We might need backup."

"Holy shit. That's one of 'em!" Charlie froze in place.

"C'mon Charlie. They've got the message. We can reach them anytime, anywhere." Conner's address spoken in the quiet confirmed the threat.

Both combatant's bolted toward the woods.

Conner's gaze flicked between Kendra's fingers seeping blood as she held pressure against the wound and the thugs racing for cover.

"No, Conner. It's not worth it. He left his gun. We can get prints." Marc assessed his brother in approaching Kendra.

"They both wore gloves, so probably not." Conner collected the gun.

"Yeah, but did they wear gloves when handling the bullets?" Kendra smiled when Conner shook his head.

"Um—" Dani stood by Kendra.

"That was rhetorical, Dani." Marc arched a brow as Dani hesitated.

"I'd rather have five minutes alone with them than their prints." Taking Kendra by the arm, Conner led her to the back door. "Let's see how bad this is and get you fixed up."

"Daeron taught me to do stitches. If you've got—"

Conner rounded on her in the next heartbeat. "You've had stitches? When?"

"Not what you're thinking. I cut myself on broken glass." She didn't bother telling him it occurred while she wielded it like a weapon.

"How'd you know about Kyu-Chul, Kendra?"

Kendra smiled at Dani, stepping beside her. "We had a very interesting conversation. Nate and Marc have amazing girlfriends." Kendra smiled, finally able to breach the topic foremost on her mind.

"What?" Conner's gaze bounced between Dani and Marc, then to Kendra.

"Psychics? Really? How cool is that. And you don't need to worry about me going too far. This is so freakin' fantastic I'd hang around just to talk with them."

Conner sighed. "Damn.

"Yeah, if you'd known it'd been that easy, huh?" Kendra laughed as Conner opened the back door. "Serves you right for not telling me."

"Kendra, it wasn't my secret to tell. And now that Dani has been recognized—"

"Yeah, I know. This isn't the place for her. But they won't be back tonight. I'm not the only one in need of stitches. I got one of those pricks good."

Inside, Nate and Callie greeted them, with Callie brushing Conner aside.

"We'll take care of her. Nate, can you grab the first aid kit? We'll meet you in Conner's office."

On stage, Daeron and Palmer both eyed him with suspicion as Kendra was bundled away between Callie and Dani.

From the side-stage stairway, Wes descended, animosity seething from every pore, his gaze never leaving Conner.

Chapter Fourteen

If the younger man intended to lay claim to Kendra's heart, he was in store for a swift and painful education. It was time to set him straight.

"Wes, what's up?" Conner hoped the band's manager took a swing. Even a weak attempt would be welcome.

"What's wrong with Kendra? Looks like she's seen a ghost."

"Two thugs attacked us in the back lot."

"What? This... It stops—now."

"I appreciate you looking out for her in the past, I'll take it from here. Kendra's my responsibility from now on."

"Because of what Billy sent you? That's bullshit. She's legally an adult. And she will be mine." Wes' hands fisted at his sides, murder in his gaze. "You've already proven you can't protect her. But I can."

"Like you did in the parking lot the other night?" Conner waited while Wes collected himself, flexing his neck and taking a deep breath.

"I've watched over her for three years, and I'll continue to do so. She doesn't belong in a place like this." Standing only a few inches shorter, Wes had a solid frame, one derived from structured, routine workouts.

"Then why'd you accept my offer on their behalf?" Conner held his own suspicions about Wes, none of them good.

"Because it was necessary." Without another word, he pivoted and headed into the main room, his bearing suggesting military background. A cooling-off time might do him some good.

Necessary for what? Some unclaimed motive had lain hidden in the younger man's gaze and the bitter twist of his lips, a suppressed violence waiting to be unleashed.

Their previous dealings had appeared honest and above board, yet this exchange involved Kendra on a personal level, and Conner would damn well uncover what lay beneath the band manager's lust.

For a second, he considered physical confrontation, but Wes was the type to hold secrets tight. A tangential approach would prove more effective.

No sooner had he pivoted toward his office, a new tangle of problems confronted him.

It wasn't his night.

"Hey, Conner. What's all the excitement about? Marc went running out of here like someone lit his tail on fire." Cindy's breathless greeting came at the cost of ample breasts straining the seams of an overworked bustier.

Did he ever perceive them as anything but grotesque? "Evening." He had no desire and no time to deal with the over-eager woman.

She'd never appeared happier.

"Are you busy tonight?" Excitement gleamed in her gaze wondering south along his frame.

He felt violated.

And guilty.

Despite the fact she'd practically begged him on many occasions and made it clear there'd be no strings attached, and regardless of how much she'd enjoyed herself, he'd used her. Plain and simple.

"Cindy. I made it clear on Friday we would never be a couple." His tone remained neutral but firm.

Disappointment lowered her gaze and the corners of her mouth while her hands fluttered helplessly as if wanting to yank him toward a dark corner.

Long blonde hair hung to her tiny waist, sifting over the navel ring with each deep breath. "Yeah, I know. You just looked kinda flustered. Thought I could help."

"Thank you for your consideration. I'm fine. Good evening." His frank dismissal received a quiet rumble from her chest.

On stage, Daeron was just leaning his guitar against the stage wall. The rest of the band prepared to take a break.

Great. Round two.

Conner had neither the time nor the inclination to confront the bass player, regardless of good intentions.

Dani and Marc stood near the hallway. She held her hand up to make whatever point was on her mind. When he neared, she snagged his arm.

"No, Conner, she needs to have this conversation for herself."

Looking beyond Dani, he found Kendra engaged in what looked like a heated discussion with Wes. The deep blush on her cheeks signified the exchange inappropriate. He caught the tail end.

"No strings attached Kendra, just a safe place to stay. Hell, nearly every man in this room has designs on you."

"I'm not sure—"

Daeron's appearance beside him took Conner up short. Street life had sharpened his considerable skills. He probably rivaled Marc in stealth.

Priorities.

Conner brushed Dani aside and spun Wes around in his tracks.

"You'll do nothing of the kind, damn it. She's here to play jazz, not become your play thing." Rage grated Conner's words into a low command.

As Wes swung, Daeron grabbed his arm, pulling him back. "Hey, Wes. No, man, not cool. We need this gig, and you're not gonna blow it for us." Daeron scowled at Wes before addressing Kendra. "You okay, kid?"

Kendra nodded, but the blush deepened.

"Let him go, Daeron. If he wants to take a swing, it's his prerogative." Conner wanted nothing more than to clock the presumptuous, smug bastard.

Palmer, on Daeron's heels, appeared ready to provide Daeron's backup if needed. They were a unit.

Security along with Nate and Marc joined them, Marc's words barely registering. "Hey, guys, this isn't necessary, I'm sure."

"Conner, Wes, no. Both of you, this isn't going to happen." Kendra stepped between the two men facing off, placing a hand on either chest until she sneezed, again.

"What the hell, Kendra? You coming down with something?" Daeron shoved Wes sideways to step closer, then pressed the back of his hand to her forehead. "Shit, Kendra. You're burning up. What the hell? You never get sick." Daeron looked around, indecision written in his frown.

The innocent contact with her face seemed too personal. Conner growled.

"Conner..." Marc's drawn-out warning held a tentative tone.

"It's all right, Daeron. I've got her. Come on Kendra. I'll take you home after we see to your arm." Conner turned her to face him, circled her waist, and pulled her close. "Nate, can you check my vehicle?"

"But they know where you live." Kendra swiped hair from her face with bloody fingers.

"They won't come after us tonight. One's badly wounded. I'll make some calls and get eyes on the house tonight."

"Same people. Same problem." His brother would understand and search for hidden electronic devices. "Dani will explain the rest."

During her short interaction, Marc's psychic better half would've collected whatever secrets she could latch onto then share them.

"This is bullshit. Kendra, come with me. I'll see to your care and safety. And I guarantee I don't have an empty-headed blonde waiting in the wings." Wes' belligerence hadn't ceased when Kendra reluctantly stepped into Conner's embrace.

Guided steps into his office led them away from Wes' grumbling, verbal abuse continuing until Conner closed the office door.

"Let's get the jacket off and see what we've got." Conner removed the coat and brushed her sleeve up.

"Damn. I like this jacket. Now it's ruined."

"I'll get you a new one. "This doesn't look too bad. Steri-strips will take care of it."

"Thank God for nice jackets. This could've been a lot worse." Kendra smiled and waited for Conner to clean and dress the wound.

"What was I ever thinking?" Conner scrubbed a hand over his jaw. He should never have brought her here.

"We're both fine. Let's leave it at that."

Daeron caught up as Conner escorted Kendra through the hallway. "Hold up, man. We need to have a meeting of the minds."

As if he didn't have enough to deal with. "Daeron, I need to get her out of here. You and the rest can finish out."

"Agreed. Take care of her, or you'll deal with me in a way you never imagined. I know where you live and will be checking on her." The threat, sincere in conviction, contained all the possessiveness of an older brother. A dangerous older brother who disregarded polite society's rules in favor of street justice.

"I sure as hell will." Conner murmured his address then glanced back, smiling at the murderous glare from Wes before escorting Kendra out the door.

A cold, brisk wind created small, leafy funnels at the edge of the parking lot. "Jesus, sweetheart, why didn't you tell me you didn't feel good? Nothing is worth risking your health."

"It's just a little cold, for heaven's sake." Frustration edged her tone as she settled in the passenger's seat and fastened her belt.

Circling the front of the vehicle, he berated himself for not acting sooner after noting her cough several times. At least it lacked the phlegmy congestion of bronchitis.

Hours in Krystal's doghouse had assisted whatever virus or bacteria now proliferated her system. Conner had no one to blame but himself.

A minute later, he turned on the heater. A quick stop at the all-night supermarket and he'd have a vaporizer.

"I won't call the doc unless it gets worse." No need to ruffle her feathers. That wasn't the biggest hurdle he'd need to deal with tonight. Since visually clashing with a certain conniving blonde, Kendra's outward show of confidence resembled that of a whipped dog.

* * * *

Life on the streets involved less mood swings and had proven easier to navigate than this new and substandard version of existence. If the stroke of fate's pendulum was inching toward normal, she couldn't reconcile it with the balanced and animated era before her brother's tragedy.

It all added up to her being safer on the streets.

Kendra still couldn't get her mind around the revelation at the office earlier. Even after proof, it still boggled the mind. Dani promised she didn't routinely invade others' thoughts except with safety concerns. She swore Kendra was safe with Conner and that persistence would see her goal achieved. Would Conner's iron will break?

Was it worth both their lives to find out? Logic dictated she leave.

How could she slip past someone who watched her every move? Not to mention the fact, it would break her heart to leave Thad behind.

Reminiscing over her idyllic existence before Billy's death didn't help the decision-making process. Childhood dreams belonged in the past.

No wonder her brother claimed Conner off limits when they were teens. The world dished out less agony when she guarded her heart with sarcasm, anger, and distance.

"Soon as the motor warms up, we'll have heat." He leaned over and briefly linked their hands before kissing her brow.

Should she smack him?

After grabbing a soft blanket from the back seat, he spread it across her lap before pulling onto the highway.

His smile was sad and filled with unnamed secrets she'd like to explore—if she stayed around. For the moment, she wanted to close her eyes and let the gentle sway of the vehicle lull her to a sleep where her biggest concern equaled which pair of jeans to wear or what food on her plate to eat first.

When she'd first taken to the streets, survival approximated a surreal possibility with the outcome insignificant. When a vicious pimp cornered her, intent on acquisition, Daeron's intervention had saved her life.

Subsequently, he'd befriended and taught her what areas and people to avoid. He'd continued teaching her street-style self-defense. She'd found a rhythm that made sense of her seemingly unpredictable and fickle environment.

Readjustment entailed a steeper learning curve than anticipated. Her headache intensified. Even women on the streets were kinder than the blonde bitch. That stare had personified a hatred never experienced, as if she'd have Kendra drawn, quartered, and chucked in the ocean.

Absolute confusion came with Conner's overprotective concern and leading her away from the band manager. Even though he didn't want her, he didn't want anyone else to have her either.

Wes, who'd always been like a brother, wanted to protect her, but now he wanted her heart.

Conner, the special someone she'd always loved but who saw her as a kid. He reminded her of warm summer nights, safety while watching a storm, and spicy confidence.

Conner promised to take care of her one minute then issued orders like a dictator in the next. She had no clue how to handle either side.

Rubbing her temples, she finally decided the entire sordid mystery was best left for another day. Daeron seemed her only rock, a true friend. Constant, kind, and emotionally steady, he never wavered or asked for anything but companionship.

"Headache?" Ambient light from the dashboard cast a play of shadows across Conner's face. "We'll be home soon."

"Just a bit. It's a lot to take in, from all sides."

Though the bite of cold hadn't touched her when a brisk wind blew under her coat's lapels, now she shivered within the SUV's shelter.

Two small ticks of a knob preceded the rush of warm air through the vehicle's foot and hand vents. The rest of the ride remained quiet despite the waves of undefined emotion radiating from her protector.

When Billy had returned between tours, she'd immediately sensed a difference in him—an edge in his voice, how he carried himself, and the way he thought. Now, looking at Conner and understanding the fact change was inevitable, she still wondered. How could this be the same man who'd buried her cat with such care or made a small wooden cross for its grave and dared Billy to say a word?

Soft light poured from the home's windows when they stopped in front. "Stay put, Kendra."

"All right." As exhausted as she was, she didn't have the strength to argue. A burst of cold air encased her frame when Conner opened his door, his dark gaze pinning her in place as he circled around to her side.

She opened her door.

With a low growl, he stopped her from stepping out, instead choosing to carry her, this time cuddled to his chest and not like a sack of potatoes.

"What have you done with the man who buried Zena?" She was too exhausted to sort out his inconsistent and migraine-worthy emotional toggling.

"I will always care for you. Get used to it, scrub jay."

"Hmm, I always liked that nickname better."

Inside, he settled her on her bed and removed his jacket from her shoulders. "I'm gonna draw a warm bath for you. Stay put."

"First, we talk. What are we gonna do about the Korean bastards after us?"

"I'm going to call a meeting, one no one can refuse."

"With Kenson?"

"Him too."

"Why didn't he tell you before about what went down with Billy?"

"Probably didn't think Billy was successful. Kenson doesn't know I have the envelope."

"What are we gonna do?"

"Work out a plan and see it through."

Inside, the mattress felt too good to resist the lure, soft as a cloud enfolding her outstretched frame. The blanket he pulled to her chin was as fluffy as the soft fur on Thad's belly.

She hadn't realized the extent of her exhaustion until Conner nudged her awake. Scented steam billowed from the bathroom with an enticing aroma that made her smile with memories of years gone by.

"Come on. A good soak will help."

In the end, it didn't matter. All the energy expended in hopes and dreams dissolved into wasted effort with one look of a woman whose breasts appeared in a doorway long before the rest of her frame crossed the threshold.

His conscience appeared to eat him alive, relegating a street rat to pain-in-the-ass status.

"You steady enough on your own?" Conner reached for her jacket.

"Try it and I'll cut your hand off."

"All right. Call me if you have a problem." He kissed her forehead turning to leave, just like a parent would.

At the door, he advised, "Your fever's spiking, so the water's gonna feel a bit lukewarm. I don't want you shivering and driving your temp up, so adjust it accordingly, okay?"

From her position, she could see the deep soaking tub. "I haven't forgotten how to clean myself. But since when does a man like you draw a bubble bath?"

"Since a mouthy little tomboy loved lavender bubbles."

"Why do you have... never mind." She didn't want to know.

A grateful sigh escaped at the lack of blonde hairs on the brush sitting on the counter as she stepped inside the steamy space.

Warm, sudsy water encasing her body felt wonderful despite outside threats.

"I'll gonna grab some Aspirin and something to wash 'em down with. Holler when you're ready. I'll leave my robe on the hook by the door. It's heavier and warmer."

Ancient dreams of resting in Conner's arms resurfaced in the periphery of her musings. Years ago, she'd seen them as a course guided by destiny. Now, she realized the path wasn't safe to contemplate, much less travel.

He'd changed so much. Wasn't she a different person, too? He'd always valued her mind and talent, told her she could be a doctor, Wall Street whiz, or concert pianist.

The water was divine, soaking away her frustrations. By the time she pulled the plug, every muscle in her frame felt like jelly.

After she'd stepped out, he was there in an instant, sitting on the bed.

"Here you go. Take these. They'll help."

Reaching her hand out to accept his offering, her vision swam, necessitating she grab his forearm to keep her balance.

"Kendra?"

Her legs gave way, but she didn't hit the floor.

Strong arms swooped her up high against a muscled frame, his heat overwhelming even as it comforted. Shifting her slightly, he nuzzled her neck. Shivers and gooseflesh covered her body as his lips grazed her forehead.

"Let's find you something to sleep in."

"I prefer to sleep naked." He'd know if for a lie, but she couldn't help herself.

Halting briefly with a stony expression, he gave nothing away.

Near naked in his arms and heading to bed, this had to be her final victory. Dani had given good advice and deserved a hearty thanks on their next visit.

If only her head were clear. Her whimper echoed in a mind filled with images of his large, magnificent body covering her, taking her to new levels of understanding, and yes, loving her.

Krystal whined as he maneuvered to pull the covers of her bed down. What?

"I thought I was sleeping in your bed…" At this point, confusion desiccated her hopes of a magical night. It wasn't the first time he'd pumped up the tire but refused the ride.

"Not tonight. You're sick and need to rest."

Not tonight? Yeah, and that made it all better. "What if it storms again?" A sudden chill induced a slight tremor.

"Then I'll sleep in the chair by your bed."

Depositing her on the mattress drove another nail in the coffin containing her hopes for a night of ecstasy. She shot up, determined to hold onto the shreds of remaining dignity. "I don't want to get chilly during the night. I'll pick out my own clothes, thank you very much."

The heat of his gaze affirmed his desire and fortified her resolve. The unwritten rules of his game may have been a mystery just now, but she'd always been a quick study. She'd learn.

Selecting a see-through, lacy baby doll, she turned from the dresser to find him standing stock still in the middle of the room. Slowly, she shrugged her shoulders to remove the robe.

By the time she raised her arms to let the material drift over her head and down her torso, he'd left the room amid unidentified grumbled ramblings.

"Fucking tease." She slipped under the covers, exhausted as much from the long evening as from Conner's dithering.

Through the closed door, Conner's voice held a smile. "That oxymoron is one of the reasons you need to go back to school."

With a harrumph, she rolled over and settled in. What in the hell just happened? Hard evidence supported the fact he found her desirable.

Minutes later, an excited, yipping Thad scrambled across the bed to her chest. Conner's smile now encompassed the benign half of his Jekyll and Hyde personality.

"Good night, Kendra. I'll get Thad early and let you sleep in tomorrow morning. We have a lot to discuss." The buss to her forehead had nothing to do with a grown man kissing a woman and everything to do with a parent tucking his child into bed.

Wonderful. Maybe he'd like to hear the results of her taking care of her own needs.

Unfortunately, she was too damn tired. She'd save that adventure for another day.

Chapter Fifteen

Krystal's growl preceded the doorbell ringing. Even an unwelcome visitor would be appreciated. Conner needed a distraction. At this point, anything would suffice.

Tomorrow, he'd temper Kendra's infatuation with education, though not the kind for which she obviously hungered.

Her friend's influence wasn't helping. If he hadn't intervened tonight, she might've ended up in bed with Wes and changed the course of her life. Along that vein, he'd have to have another talk with his brothers about encouraging a situation that wasn't going to happen.

In the end, he owed it to her to see her settled with a young man who nurtured her dreams and her heart. He owed her that much. A young, corporate type who kept normal work hours and whose family gathered at the parents' house for Sunday dinners was what she needed.

"Krystal, *sitz*." Despite the late hour, the likelihood for either of two visitors on his doorstep had kept him awake. *Might as well get past the first hurdle.*

Opening the door granted a view of his front porch, and the dead animal strung from its soffit. A northerly breeze carried away the bulk of the stench as it swung back and forth.

"Can't say as I approve of your decorations, man." Grim awareness saturated Daren's tone as he moved closer to examine the intended threat.

"Damn it. She can't get a break, but maybe forensics can find something useful."

"Left by the bastards after Kendra tonight or stemming from your PI work?"

"Probably from tonight's visitors... You recognize it, Daeron?" Kendra's befriending a stray animal or three while on the street would come natural. "Is—was it a companion to her?"

The enemy's knowledge of Kendra's habits declared the threat closer than previously known or expected.

"Can't tell. She took in two stray cats, along with several other critters." Daeron retrieved a knife from his back pocket and cut it down. "It's a warning she doesn't need to see."

Conner noted Daeron's disgust and reluctant handling of the scorched remains.

"Set it on the step. Its evidence. I'll ask one of my brothers to pick it up." Conner gestured to the living room. "Come in. I'll get you something to drink while we talk." This was the person he'd hoped to see first.

"I don't drink alcohol." Curiosity mixed with indecisiveness warred for dominance in the young man's expression. "Your dog bite?"

"Only when necessary, and I have tea, soda, and water." Conner signaled Krystal to greet his young guest.

"Surprised she didn't kick up a ruckus when someone hung that thing." Daeron gestured to the evidence.

"She was upstairs with Kendra for a bit."

Both dog and visitor cocked their heads to the side in judging the other's character. Little surprise came with mutual acceptance.

Approval and nonverbal speculation preceded the offered paw before Daeron amended. "Water's great. Nice dog. Bet Kendra loves her."

Hundreds of studies analyzed personalities based on the nature and quality of man's interactions with animals. Daeron's kneeling to eye level and petting Krystal revealed a nice slice of character. In his mind, Conner reviewed the few known facts about the guitarist en route to the kitchen.

"Yeah, she does." Conner used his body to block Daeron's view of his covert actions. The telltale squeak went unchallenged as he wiped the glass's exterior before filling it with ice and water. "You've been outside for a while." Offered as an assumption more than accusation, the statement accorded Kendra's friend respect and acceptance.

"I wanted to make sure she was all right. Took me a while to get here." After visually contemplating the sofa and recliner, Daeron sat in the overstuffed easy chair. "I don't trust Wes. And I don't want her alone with him until I've figured out his motives, besides his desire for horizontal refreshment."

"You see her more as a sister." Conner offered the glass of water, studying his guest.

At just an inch or so shorter, Daeron held close to equal mass and kept his body in shape. Though his garments had seen better days, they were clean and neat with a slight scent of soap, earning another measure of respect. Like Kendra, in Daeron's world, being homeless didn't equate to being dirty.

The sofa's upholstered cushions gave way to Conner's bulk. Daeron obviously had something else on his mind. It seemed unlikely Kendra had shared Dani's secret, but it'd be nice to know for sure.

The final objective included helping the younger man who'd protected Kendra on the streets.

"Unlike you." Daeron's gaze narrowed. "She trusts you, said you all grew up together, thick as thieves. Doesn't mean *I* trust you." After a sip of water, he met his host's gaze while delivering some insight and an ultimatum.

"She was a kid when we first met. Didn't know up from down, much less how to survive on the street. All I've heard for three years is Conner this and Conner that. Fine. But if you cross the line of friendship, you'd better be damned sure you're gonna keep her. She's not disposable. I'm the reason Wes and Palmer have maintained their distance."

"Tell me about them." For that alone, Conner owed the young man a great debt.

"Why?" Daeron demanded equal footing at every turn.

"Someone is hunting her. I need all the information I can get to find the motherfuckers. I'm sure by now you know I hold a private investigator's license." Without a doubt, Daeron meant her no harm but lacked the experience and training to take necessary action.

"All right. Guess I could use the help." Taking a sip of water allotted time to gauge his host's measure. "I met Wes right after taking Kendra under my wing. He found us odd jobs, offered a place to stay, the latter refused." A careless hand gesture intimated he'd discarded the offer and had never suffered regrets.

"Cliff was a street rat before I met him. Nice enough sort, friendly, if a little on the odd side. Palmer's a different story. I pulled him out of the gutter 'bout a month after I met Kendra. He doesn't trust anyone or anything, won't let anyone close, but it's a little more than that."

Pot meet kettle.

Conner nodded, assessing for signs of deception but found no telltale twitch, avoidance, or expression indicating duplicity. "Has she told you Billy asked me to look out for her?"

"Then where've you been for three years while she's barely scraped by and stayed out of the gutters? Looks like you have plenty of room..." Disgust laced his tone just as his wrinkled nose and lowered eyebrows defined Conner's existence on the lowest rung of any social ladder.

A long road lay ahead in a bid to gain the young man's trust. "I didn't know she'd run away after the funeral." Conner rubbed his eyes, trying to blot out the images of Kendra, alone and terrified, huddling in the corner of some abandoned, filthy basement during a storm.

"Now that she's here, I'll keep her safe and deal with Wes. As far as Cliff and Palmer are concerned, I'll do my best to help them. You're welcome to stay here. Like you said, there's plenty of room, and I can help you get on your feet."

"My feet are just fine and not for you to worry about." Daeron relaxed back in his seat after setting his half-empty glass next to the coaster on the side table.

"I don't want to see her separated from her friends, as long as they mean her no harm."

"Thanks, but no. I'm safer on my own." Again, Daeron looked around, this time nodding a grudging approval.

Dispossessed of all worldly goods, he embodied a wisdom unknown to those who enjoyed lifelong stability. Through undisclosed trials, he'd developed a strong moral code and a sense of honor evidenced in his protectiveness of Kendra.

Before Conner had reached puberty, he'd lost both parents and adopted a caregiver role for his siblings. He and Daeron could easily have exchanged paths while retaining many similarities.

Listening to the young man describe Kendra's various situations honed the black cloud of culpability engulfing him until bile burned his throat. Through the accounting of hardships and small triumphs, Daeron exemplified courage and integrity, compassion, and an uncanny hardness developed over an extended period of self-sufficiency. Emotional distance allowed him to focus on the facts of the past without seeds of bitterness taking root in his tone and flourishing into hardened cynicism.

It didn't take a genius to realize his guest shared information in order to gain like in kind. By unspoken agreement, Conner answered questions, avoiding references to Dani, Callie, and psychics.

"All right then, time for me to head out." Daeron stood, glancing at the hallway before adding, "I'll be back to check on her."

"Good. She needs you in her life. Feel free to drop in any time." Krystal followed when Conner pushed to his feet and headed into the kitchen.

A show of good faith could go a long way. From the drawer containing odds and ends, Conner secured a cell phone and charger, intending it for Daeron. Unfortunately, it contained just enough battery life to program in his cell and landline numbers. Shadows preceded his return to the great room.

"What's that for? I don't do charity." He held the items as if they contained enough germs to desiccate several third-world countries.

"It's not charity. Borrow it for Kendra's sake. She's sick, and I assume you'll want to talk to her if you're not going to stay. Plus, if you run into any trouble, you can call me. I *will* help. Whoever attacked her might go for her friends next if they can't get to her directly."

"I'll be fine."

Rare was the young man who inspired admiration within minutes of a first one-on-one meeting. He thanked whatever vagaries of fate that put Daeron's path on a collision course with Kendra.

Integrity as well as a code of honor established a good base on which to build. The fact Daeron held no obvious sexual designs for her allowed easier breaths. What if that situation changed? Hunger radiating from her other male friends had declared it open season on Kendra.

Contemplating the general homeless situation long after the young man left, he bagged Daeron's empty glass in hopes of learning more about Kendra's friend.

With time, Daeron's trust would grow on the fragile thread established, hopefully accompanied by the grace to accept help. After confirmation of identification, Conner would run discreet inquiries to identify any roadblocks in need of navigating or smoothing.

Soon, the background check on Wes should shed some light on the band manager's motivations and business dealings. Years of reading people identified ulterior motives. Something was definitely there. The *what* needed identification.

ID on Cliff and Palmer should also be forthcoming through the prints left on the instruments at the club, if in fact either young man existed in the system.

Before turning in for the night, he checked on his guest, noting her fever was down. She appeared to rest comfortably.

Kendra's phlegmy cough startled him awake as early-morning sunshine spilled across his bed. He'd overslept. As the eldest of four brothers, age-related and iron-building vitamin jokes rang in his ears while motivating him to move faster in caring for the dogs. Kendra hadn't stirred when he'd scooped up the pup.

Thad's ear tips flopping forward and the quirking of his head side to side in response to Conner fumbling the med kit from the kitchen cabinet gave the pup a comical appearance. The furball was better medicine than anything concocted in a lab.

They re-entered her room just as quietly, taking a minute to drink in the angelic rendering—innocence delineated in the curve of her jaw, beauty sketched in the soft fan of eyelashes over silky skin, and honesty radiating from her very pores.

How could extreme deviltry exist in such an ethereal package? Manipulative methods to negate her inclination to bolt would take a toll on both their hearts and souls. Where did he draw the line?

He could use her obvious infatuation to hold her interest until he'd sorted out the mess and helped her rejoin society.

He understood her hesitation with Wes as a romantic interest, since she'd set her cap years ago on capturing Conner's heart, not realizing she'd always held it prisoner.

As soon as he assessed her condition, he'd let her go back to sleep.

In the black silky baby doll.

Made of lace.

That left nothing to the imagination.

Damn.

Just as when he woke in the middle of the night for no other reason than the weight of Krystal's three a.m. stare, Kendra's eyelids fluttered open before a smile curved her lips.

"Hey, thanks for taking him out." Curling up and sitting cross-legged with the covers pulled to her waist, the black lacy cups of her outfit hid nothing from view, yet her enthrallment with Thad took center stage.

The pup scrambled to her outstretched arms then huddled down in the nook of her legs, nipping at her fingers.

"No problem. How're you feeling?" The med kit's tinny click piqued the pup's interest when the lid flipped open.

Thad's eagerness to escape his mom's grasp mimicked running in place on a revolving conveyer belt. Several failed attempts to gain solid footing resulted in scattered covers exposing more of Kendra's creamy flesh.

Focusing on his med kit after sitting, Conner tightened his jaw as beads of sweat covered his brow. Deep cleansing breaths proved useless. "Hold still a sec." The thermometer's probe against her temple beeped almost immediately, again drawing the curious pup's attention.

"You have a thermometer? What else is in there?" Her leaning forward exposed a wonderful view of perfect mounds, her nipples poking innocently at the lace.

He groaned. "We're all more than the sum of our parts, sweetheart." Keeping his gaze on her face took a heroic act of willpower. In his mind, he knew what each sweet palm full would feel like with those sensitive nubs pebbled and begging for his touch.

Her grin detailed knowledge of devious intent as she straightened then arched her back with arms in a sensuous stretch.

The stethoscope's binaural metal spring was as cold as its diaphragm, giving him ideas to curb her devious mind.

"You know what you're doing with that thing?" A quirked brow designated him a cartoon character playing doctor despite being game for exploration.

"In the military, I was a medic among other things." The molded earpieces weren't as cold as the bell he placed at the base of her lung.

"Fuck!"

He smiled at her reaction. Not the same as a cold shower, but it did adjust her attitude. "Deep breaths, in through your nose and out through your mouth."

Her lung bases were clear. "Again." After working his way up each side, he added, "Now say the letter E each time I place the diaphragm against your back."

"Diaphragms are used to keep men from slipping one past the goalie."

Conner sighed.

With successive parts of the exam completed, his own breath came a little easier. Even at this age, her condition could devolve into something worse, especially considering previous nutritional choices. "All right, no E to A changes, dullness with percussion or crackling, all signs I wouldn't want to hear. Why didn't you tell me you weren't feeling good last night?"

"What? I'm fine." As if just noticing her exposure, she pulled the covers back to her waist, adjusting Thad in the process.

His jeans could use an adjustment.

"I have a doctor friend who owes me a favor. I'm gonna give him a call."

"But it's Sunday, and I don't feel that bad."

"Because you're young and strong. I don't like the sound of your cough. And as I said, he's a friend. Be back in a few minutes. Stay put." He smiled at the mumbled references to tyrants and dictators.

Several hours later, she sat on his couch, wrapped in a light blanket and watching the distant waves breaking on the shoreline. "I don't understand why I'm taking a prescription drug when all I have is a cold."

"Maybe because you're undernourished and he doesn't want you developing pneumonia. Besides, you have fluid in your right ear, and that has a fifty-fifty chance of evolving into an infection."

Despite her slight fever and cough, she'd eaten every scrap of breakfast, prompting images of how and what she'd eaten over the last three years. The backwash of shame for prior failures tallied far more sins for which any mortal could atone, all worthwhile if she forgave him in the end.

For the moment, all seemed content as Kendra snuggled close with her pup and watched clouds gather and darken, framed by floor-to-ceiling windows. Dressed in snug jeans and a clingy top, she rested her head against his shoulder and tunneled her fingers through Thad's fur. If only she were someone other than Billy's little sister.

His self-control stretched thinner than a spider web but not as strong.

"The approaching storm doesn't seem so scary now." Her drawn-out sigh furrowed the pup's long hair and elicited the fur ball's squirm. "I think the rest has done me a lot of good. Didn't think I would, but last night I slept like a log. What time are we leaving tonight?"

"Seriously? You're not going anywhere." He'd waited for this all morning, wondering what form her own storm clouds would take with his dictate. His decision had nothing to do with the fact that at least four men were mentally salivating at the thought of seeing her in Ambrosia again.

"But we need to work. Daeron—"

"Will receive sick pay like the rest of the band. And by the way, he stopped by last night. Wanted to check on you. Why don't you give him a call? He can fill you in on what your friends are doing. I lent him a cell phone, though it didn't have much of a charge."

"Like he's not gonna find a place to plug it in?" Her indignant attitude paralleled that of her younger years.

"All right. Give him a try. Invite him over." Though he'd formed a tentative trust with Daeron based on a mutual need of protecting Kendra, Palmer and Cliff weren't as accepting of a tentative friendship.

"Palmer's not like us. Cliff definitely wouldn't come."

"All right, how well do you know Wes?" Though Wes's initial intentions were clear, he'd made no long-term declarations. Observation of last night's interaction proved Kendra was uncomfortable with his advances. Not that he'd get another chance.

She shrugged a shoulder. "Daeron knows him better. Why?"

"Just curious about your life and everyone in it. I don't want you separated from your friends, and I'll help them if I can."

Krystal alerted to a visitor's approach with a deep-throated bark. In keeping with his pup standing, Thad's puppy growls portrayed an enthusiastic apprentice status. The chimes sounded many times in succession as if the caller could advance time at his dictated pace through mere dint of will.

Conner tucked the blanket around her shoulders before striding to the door. Krystal's tail wagging indicated acceptance before the rush of cold wind brought the familiar woodsy scent inside.

"Daeron? What the hell's going on?"

Blood spatters smeared Daeron's worn hand-me-down shirt and threadbare jacket. Both hands trembled slightly, stained with the telltale crimson of someone's life essence. Standing upright, he held his hands out to show he wasn't seriously injured.

"Jesus, come in." Conner grabbed the younger man's arm and led him inside, visually inspecting for sources of the caked blood while urging him to the kitchen.

Kendra's gasp preceded a hoarse cough. "Daeron, what happened?"

A small, steady rivulet of crimson dripped from Daeron's fingertips with the jacket's descent down injured forearms. Reluctant acceptance of the handling was evidence of his distraction. In the expected manner of stoic men, he apologized for blood splattering the floor.

"Palmer and I went to one of your bolt-holes, Kendra. I was gonna bring your stuff. We got jumped. Palmer's dead."

"Did you see who attacked you?" In rolling up the tattered flannel sleeve, Conner found defensive cuts needing more than gauze bandages. Applied pressure stemmed the blood flow.

"No. They wore masks. Two of 'em. Palmer was in front of me. One of the bastards stabbed him as soon as we entered. Never asked for money or nothing. Just said they'd be contacting me soon with a time and place."

"These need stitches." Conner gently probed at the wounds, shallow enough to avoid nerve damage but deep enough to warrant artificial closure. "Let's take care of these before I make some calls."

"No police." Daeron's intense stare flashed a silent message to Kendra.

"Got a record?" As the oldest of four, Conner knew when his younger siblings kept secrets. Yet without greater insight of Daeron's life, ferreting them out would take time. Time they might not have. "Come on, I can sew these."

"Of course your first thought is that I'm a criminal." Derision colored his tone as the injured man hesitated before sitting at the kitchen counter.

"I need to get out of here," Kendra whispered as she tossed the flannel shirt aside and checked for other wounds.

"No," said by both males in unison. At least that verdict was something on which they agreed.

History bore the evidence of her ideas evolving into reality once she worked up a head of steam. The most successful time to divert her from a misguided path was immediately after conception.

"Kendra, can you go to my bedroom closet and grab a warm shirt? No need for Daeron to freeze." Time alone with the younger man would allow them to form a united front.

As soon as she turned the corner to his room, he met Daeron's gaze, stare for stare.

"Look, you know as well as I do, if she leaves here, they *will* find her. They knew the location of at least one hideout. How many people do?" Conner needed Daeron's support in keeping them all intact.

"How do I know you're not a closet psycho and orchestrating this behind the scenes?"

"Daeron, I was in the club when she was first attacked. Listen, I just want to help you both. I can't do that if she runs, and you know as well as I do, she has every intention of bolting. You don't trust me? Fine, stay here with her." Further conversation halted as Kendra returned with a black corduroy shirt in hand.

"Hey, can I borrow a pair of socks, too?" Daeron asked. "My feet are wet."

"Yeah. Kendra, you mind?" Conner took out the necessary items from his med kit and began cleaning the worst of the wounds.

"Not at all, which drawer? I don't want to go pawing through your stuff. God only knows what's in there." Fear and anger balanced the scales in her expression. "Who would do this?"

"Top drawer, Kendra." Conner's awareness of her mental state surpassed the surface flurry of activity. With directed motions, her mind would search for a center where rationalization provided relief from terror and the inexplicable.

For the moment, he could provide a short reprieve. The shirt fluttered in her hands as if she couldn't decide where to place it. He gently took it and set it aside. "Kendra, we're going to be fine. We'll figure this out."

"But..." Her gaze searched Daeron's face, looking for—absolution?

"Mongrel, we'll get through this. I promise." Daeron's use of her pet name stirred only mild irritation as she turned away.

Once alone, each man again took the other's measure. "At least she didn't know which drawer for the socks." His begrudging acceptance was a start. "But if you hurt her, these wounds won't compare to what I'll do to you."

"Got the memo. Now, how did he hold the knife?" Conner drew up medication in a syringe to prep the wounds for stitches.

"What?"

"How. Did. Your attacker. Hold his knife? Describe the blade. How much of it could you see?"

"Only about an inch was showing," Daeron replied.

"Damn. That reeks of professional status, and they let you go, only wanted to scare you. Where was Palmer stabbed?"

"Shit. Neck sliced. He'd turned away at the last second, but it was too late." Daeron winced as Lidocaine spread under the edges of the deepest laceration.

"All right, location. Which building? While this numbing medication is taking effect, I'm gonna place a call to my brother. Keep Kendra's mind occupied when she returns. I don't want her leaving."

Chapter Sixteen

Dark clouds boiled across the sky, burdened with the cleansing rain that would wash away tracks and scent trails. On the back porch, a stiff wind blew one of the chair cushions off its perch, its tumble-roll across the tiled floor much like Kendra's path, at the whim of something stronger and out of control.

With timing crucial, Conner sighed when his sibling answered on the first ring. "Marc. Trouble. Palmer got a red necktie. I'm stitching minor wounds on Daeron now. Need you to track and don't go alone. I'll text the location. Professionals involved. Have Julien check on Kendra's parents, their cell number's on my desk at Ambrosia." After giving the few other particulars, he hung up and reinstituted his stoic mask before stepping back inside.

Kendra's alternating sobs and halting questions camouflaged Daeron's low speech. She'd slung her arms around his shoulders, sobbing against his neck. As soon as Conner entered, she moved back, allowing space to work.

"This is all because of me."

"No, Kendra. This is because some psycho desperately needs a mental and physical adjustment." Conner's words drew Daeron's attention as he opened the sterile towel then pulled on the pack's gloves. Military experience and three younger brothers had shaped him into a fairly decent tailor of the flesh.

"Kendra said you're ex-military and have a bunch of like-minded friends." Muscles tightened, yet Daeron didn't move when Conner inserted the curved, sterile needle at the largest wound's middle edge.

"I have no reason to hurt any of you. Think about it, Daeron." Time was of the essence. The most productive time during an investigation occurred within hours of the incident.

"Unless you wanted us out of her life."

"Daeron, Conner didn't do this. He wouldn't. He's not like that. Look. This has to be about the envelope, and he already has that locked up in his safe at Ambrosia."

"Actually, it's not in Ambrosia," Conner continued as Daeron hashed the facts over in his mind.

"All right. So let's say you're not orchestrating this shit. How do we find these bastards? You're the investigator." A small wince provided Daeron's only evidence of aversion as Conner pulled thread through both edges of the deepest cut.

"Marc and Nate are on their way with their dogs to track what they can. Julien's looking into some other angles."

"You mean Wes?" Daeron asked.

"Among other things, yes," Conner noted but didn't expound.

"But Wes wouldn't..." Exhaustion, confusion, fear, and frustration formed swirling eddies of complex heterogeneous veins in her varying expressions to demonstrate Kendra nearing her breaking point.

"We're not jumping to conclusions. We don't have much to go on, so we're gathering information." A pointed stare warned his injured guest not to argue. "Kendra, why don't you get us all something to drink? Preferably something without caffeine."

Her flitting about the kitchen entailed a lot of wasted movements, opening one door after another until she found glasses. "Green tea doesn't have much caffeine, right?"

"That's fine, sweetheart. Thank you," Conner replied, thinking of other inane ways to occupy her mind and body.

By unspoken agreement, Daeron helped with that detail while Conner sewed and bandaged lacerations on both arms. By the time they all settled in the great room, early afternoon sunlight had chased away lingering shadows and darkened clouds.

Satisfaction unfurled in his chest when she'd sat next to him and cuddled Thad close, validating his attempts to reestablish a good rapport.

Time proved well spent as Kendra relaxed against him. Yet in plying his guest with innocuous questions, Conner failed to find order amid the insanity surrounding them. Prepping a late lunch provided mindless, busy work while mentally sifting through the gathered information. Through it all, they gained no further insight.

"This all stems from Billy's overseas mission." A scalpel's edge of mistrust sliced through Daeron's calm façade. "With your team."

"Whatever hornet's nest he delved into, my team had no knowledge and nothing to do with it." Guilt tainted his heart with doubt and taunted the soul with endless possibilities of what ifs.

Billy had been part of his team, thereby making Conner responsible for his actions. Over time, his mind had rejected culpability but not the outcome, relegating it to the darkest recesses of his spirit where it festered and spread the faintest tendrils of shame to tinge his viewpoint in shades of grief and repentance.

"Hey, Daeron. Back off. Billy and Conner were as close as brothers could ever be. We all grew up together. Billy trusted Conner enough to put me under his wing." With one hand pointing to each man's chest, Kendra reinforced her point.

"So, what's in the envelope?" Daeron's deceptively calm voice held all the patience of a man who'd learned to navigate and manipulate emotions to his advantage.

"Something for Kendra when this is all settled. If she wants to share that information, that'll be her decision."

The macabre jingle emanating from his cell fit his current mood, the ringtone indicating Nate's timely intrusion. "I'll be back in a sec. I'm gonna take this call and get my laptop." He needed information to form a plan.

"Conner? What the hell?" Nate's lack of ribbing signified the depth of shit into which they all waded. "How many bodies did Daeron claim were here?"

"Shit. They slit Palmer's throat before letting Daeron escape with minor injuries. What'd you find?"

"Two bodies. I'm guessing one is the drummer since he had one of your business cards in hand. I'll let you know when I get ID on them. On the back of your card was also a note. Just says to hand over the envelope."

"What do you mean you're guessing one is Palmer? You met him."

"Bodies are burned beyond recognition. Card was placed on the charred skeleton."

"Hell, let's not let our women in on that detail, for fuck's sake. Have you called it in yet?" Conner's mind worked furiously in trying to piece known facts together.

"No, first I'm gonna see if I can pull any prints off the card. Oh, and about the dead animal left on your porch? Nothing usable found. How's our girl?"

"As well as you might expect. Did Dani pick up anything from those bastards last night?"

"Nothing we didn't already suspect." After divulging further details, Nate paused. A bad sign.

"Nate?" Conner wondered how much worse it could get.

"I'd asked Julien to check on her parents staying with some friends upstate. Late yesterday, the friend's house blew up, supposedly a gas leak. Fire took everything and everyone. No DNA confirmation on the bodies yet."

"Oh, God." Conner sat on the bed, wondering in what twilight world fate deemed fit to drop him. "Keep me posted. I won't tell her until we know for sure. Why go after her parents? They've had no contact for three years."

"Dunno. Police will wanna talk to her once they start connecting the dots." A short pause and deep sigh followed. "Darius tracked someone to a dead end. They got in a vehicle. Considering we started in an abandoned building, I've no idea what or who we tracked."

"Which means we'd better hurry. Contact Colonel Kenson. Press him this time. See what extracurricular activities he assigned Billy."

"Got it. You're gonna sit tight on Kendra and Daeron." Nate's statement declared it a fact.

"Daeron's iffy. Did Julien dig up anything on Wes?" Finding a way to keep Kendra in his home now might prove difficult if not impossible, considering the body count.

"Squeaky clean. Too damn clean. Found nothing prior to three years ago. I don't trust him," Nate replied.

"Neither does anyone else, apparently." Conner intended to have a detailed conversation with the band's manager as soon as possible. They hadn't yet obtained his prints. "Thanks, Nate. Later."

Deep breaths didn't clear the virtual pollution cluttering his thoughts. In reviewing the situation, lack of information stifled them all. Of note, Kendra and Daeron had used some nonverbal earlier he intended to dissect and exploit.

Silent footfalls permitted the revelation of the tail end of Kendra's conversation upon re-entering the great room. "I'll have it soon."

"Who's on the boner phone?" Daeron's sarcasm channeled suspicion and wariness.

"Did the dogs find anything?" Kendra's hope was short-lived when he shook his head.

"Not exactly. Palmer wasn't the only one at the scene. There was another body. We don't have ID yet. We're reaching out to an old commanding officer to see if he knew what Billy was doing."

"Son of a bitch, this is a nightmare. Was it Wes?" Kendra paced through the great room and back, hands crossed over her chest.

"Don't know yet," Conner replied.

"It all started when she met up with you, Conner." Daeron's thinly veiled accusation stirred instant anger in Kendra.

"And if I hadn't gone to him, how well do you think my parents could figure all this out by themselves? By running away, I delayed the inevitable and brought the trouble to Conner and his brothers."

"All right, all right. Sorry, dude. I just can't wrap my head around why anyone would kill Palmer. If they wanted information, then torture, yes, but to kill? That doesn't make sense."

"It's a message to scare you into submission." Conner wondered again what Kendra was hiding. "Daeron, do you know why Palmer would have one of my business cards on him?"

"No, but he wasn't the same kind of street rat, not like Kendra and me, so I didn't know him as well." Daeron shook his head. "Damn senseless waste."

"It was found in his hand." Conner reached over to scratch behind Thad's ears, thankful when Kendra didn't pull away.

"Then it was put there after the fact. Someone is targeting you too, but in a different way." Daeron stood and slid his borrowed shirt over the bandages.

"Yeah, as a conduit to Kendra," Conner confirmed.

"Well, I'm no good to anyone sitting here. I can get more information on the street. I'm gonna find Cliff and get him out of the city for now." Daeron eyed Conner once more. "Watch over her while I'm gone."

"No, Daeron. You can't go back out there. They'll kill you." Kendra's desperate grip of Daeron's shoulder betrayed the strength of their friendship.

"Kid, I've lived on the streets a whole lot longer than you. I'll be careful now that I know they're playing for keeps. I'll be back when I find something we can use."

Conner held his hand out as Daeron stood. "You're obviously over eighteen, so I can't tell you to stay, though I sure would advise it."

"No thanks, but I'll come back tonight. We'll compare notes."

Though nighttime temperatures no longer dipped below freezing, apparently Conner's comfortable couch outranked a concrete floor where pillows consisted of bags stuffed with garbage and hair fished from a drain.

"Still got the cell?" Conner knew better than to offer food or money. The money earned from past performances would suffice for a while.

Daeron replied, "Yeah, it's charged up." A contemplative expression broadcast the doubt he'd radiated since arrival. "Which means I can be tracked."

There was nothing Conner could say since that was his intention.

Chapter Seventeen

"Kendra, let's sit and talk." Conner guided her to the sofa with a light touch.

"You're just gonna let Daeron go out there, all alone like that?" Disbelief bled to anger. How could he be so callous?

Allowing Conner to tug her to the couch seemed like a betrayal to Daeron. Wrong on so many levels.

"Daeron is an adult, not to mention he's lived on the streets for eight years. If anyone can survive out there, he can. When he's ready to come in, I'll help him. The men who killed Palmer *let* Daeron go to deliver a message."

"How'd you know how long he's been alone?" Keeping up with Conner Crofton had always proved an impossible feat, but this surpassed prior levels of information mongering.

"We talked a bit last night while you slept. He has solid judgment, strong character, and common sense, an incredible combination. It's a good thing he didn't stay and fight his attacker. He would've died with Palmer."

"Street smarts." Not only had Daeron lived by them, he'd tried to teach her the same skills.

"You two are close. What do you think he'll do now that you're off the streets?"

"Who says I'm off the streets? I'm twenty-one." Realization struck— the defensive note in her voice just confirmed her status as prey.

Conner just gave her the look, the one with half-lidded eyes and a wry twist of his lips, the combination advising, *yeah, go ahead and try it. See how far you get.*

She sighed. History proved her deficiency with bluffing or denying him, and she saw no need to repeat her mistakes—best to pick her battles.

"We'd talked about opening a little café near the edge of town. A place where folks could sit, have a cup of coffee, talk with friends, that sort of thing." Belly up and grumbling, Thad clamped both paws around her hand as she stroked his chest. "The band wasn't my idea, just a way to make money. But now, Cliff and Daeron..."

"Are going to be all right. Cliff will be out of town soon, and I trust Daeron's instincts. The café sounds like an interesting idea. I can help you guys get started." Krystal nudged his knee before licking the pup's face.

"How come he and I never argue, yet it seems that's most of what you and I do?"

"You two think of each other as siblings. There's no sexual tension."

"But we've never..." Embarrassment prevented her from finishing the sentence but not the thought. With Dani's help, she'd wear him down eventually.

"No. We haven't. And we won't."

"What? But last night... because you see me as a child?" Anger forced her words through clenched teeth.

"I see you as a young woman without a clear path for her life. The mere fact you couldn't complete that sentence, supports my viewpoint."

"Oh, I know exactly what I want. I'm going to the club. I'll find myself a boyfriend, and I will have sex. If not with you, then..." Her declaration brought about more of his teeth grinding, something he did a lot around her.

Her inner brat continued the happy dance, knowing Conner wouldn't allow another man near her.

"No—you're not. Number one, we've already proven it's not safe for you to go out, and now you're sick. On top of that, well, just no. End of story. This situation is not a game you play on a whim."

"I'm not a kid. In addition, I can promise you that by the end of next week, I'll be dating someone. I've had several offers at the club."

In the next heartbeat, Thad lay on the floor and Kendra struggled to breathe as Conner lifted her to his lap.

"If you're referring to Jenkins, the guy you were ready to knock unconscious your first night at the club, he is not the man for you." The sotto voice scared her as nothing ever had and in a way that made her hunger for more.

144

Her resolve to hold his stare faltered with the intensity of his feral gaze boring through muscle and nerve, through the invisible shell that encased her heart. The fact he would never bring her harm made the angry lines furrowing his brow less intimidating.

With each frantic crash of her heart, trepidation mutated into an all-consuming heat that seared the breath in her throat. Her quiet breaths marked time as she waited for him to answer her silent challenge.

Slowly, his mouth descended, as if hesitant to test the substance of her flesh and discover if in fact she was real. One hand trapped her jaw and urged her mouth open. When his tongue invaded, stroked, and prohibited anything but surrender, she moaned, taking in his breath and beseeching him for mercy with her capitulation.

His growl affirmed his assurance as much as the arms holding her snug. He fisted one hand in her tumbled locks, positioning her head for better access while the other slid up her thigh.

She couldn't help but twine her fingers in his hair, begging for more, for it all.

When he pulled back, both their chests heaved for breath as his gaze drilled to the center of her heart. "Sweetheart, you'd better be damn sure of what you want, because I'll never let you go. Say you want me again and there's no take-back and no retreat. I'll overhaul your mind and tune your body to a beat that will test your sanity." A twist of his hips sent frissons of current from her core to disseminate throughout her body. "And then I'll demand even more. I'll have no mercy where your safety is concerned."

Words refused to form, failing to slip past the images he projected with his harsh words. Excitement flared to a poignant ache. The thought of him filling her body and soul rent her mind speechless.

She could only nod.

"You have to say the words, sweetheart. And then we start."

"I want you, Conner. I always have. There has never been anyone else and there never could be." Her words must have penetrated the fog of lust engulfing them both. His hands gentled in her hair, smoothing the strands back and behind her ear.

Resting his forehead against her own, he inhaled deep as if shoring up his self-control. "Jesus, Kendra. I've wanted you since the moment you stepped in Ambrosia. I keep trying to resurrect the brotherly feeling I've always had—but I can't. It's gone."

Closing his eyes denied the advantage of her gaze piercing the invisible thinness of his steely armor. Victory brought a smile she couldn't deny. A slight twist of her hips snapped his gaze to hers, narrowing as they took in everything, claiming her for all time.

"This isn't what I'd planned for you. I'm a hard man, babe. I'm afraid I won't control myself and we'll go too far. I'd rather set you free than hurt you."

The evening shadow on his jaw scraped her palm as she held him. "I trust you. I know you. I'm ready for this."

"You don't even understand what my life—it's harsh. I'm demanding and controlling, but I'll always put your welfare first, both body and mind."

"Conn, you've always been controlling. It's been your nature since we were kids. That's nothing new. Yes, I do know you, your heart, and your soul."

Closing his eyes, Conner groaned. "This isn't the way this should've gone. I pray I'm worthy. Sweetheart, you are so far from ready. This if for keeps."

* * * *

Conner marked her lip nibbling and restless gaze as the onset of a deeper awareness of the possibilities to come. His conscience rode him hard for scaring her, for underneath the false bravado, he saw the frightened girl cowering in a woman's body.

After the manipulation forcing a southern plunge in his moral code, he had no right to feel this excited, this alive. He hadn't felt this energized since joining the military.

Damned if she'd be with the likes of Wes or Jenkins. She deserved better. The fact he'd lost control meant she deserved better than himself. At least he'd taken other proposals off the table and held her welfare as his highest priority.

The new development in their relationship would allow him to iron out many uncertainties within her wavering emotions.

First things first.

He refused to begin a relationship built on less than solid foundation. Certain truths had to come to light.

If she fully entered his world, he could draw out her insecurities and instill the confidence she deserved, then set her on a path of her choosing.

"Tell me why you didn't come to me, Kendra, three years ago." The lightest of grazes over her silken locks induced a shiver. Never had he touched anything so soft. He smiled at her uncertainty. "Tell me, sweetheart."

"I—I was angry." Her growl combined the pain of a young girl's broken heart with a badass street rat.

"Why?" The seed of her anger, sprouted in abandonment and nurtured by homeless, dark and troubled times, required exposure to light in order to release the toxins contaminating her soul.

Tears seeped from the corners of her expressive eyes. "Why do you fucking care?"

And there's my little warrior. "I've always cared for you, Kendra. I always will." Soul deep, he knew she needed the security of trusting he would always be there for her. She was no longer alone and never would be again.

The silkiness of her skin contradicted the filthy mouth and screw-you attitude, the dichotomy the biggest aphrodisiac this side of heaven. Each set him on fire. Methods of curing them blasted through his mind and hardened him to painful proportions.

"You made him go back there to—" A plaintiff sob prevented her from finishing the sentence.

"No, Kendra. We believed he had come home to you. That's all he talked about. We didn't know he'd planned on re-enlisting."

"I-I..."

"Why, Kendra? Why didn't you come to me?" Setting her off kilter by grazing the swells of her breasts was a necessary evil he shouldn't enjoy.

"Conner, no. Please, I don't want to talk about this." Spoken through gritted teeth, she clamped her body tight, as if attempting to hold onto a pain that if released would rip her apart.

"Talk to me, sweetheart." Each second and each panted breath tore another piece of his soul, now tattered and spilling a flood of guilt to fill his chest.

A distinctly unladylike growl filled the room.

"Billy left and didn't return. All because he wanted to follow you instead of taking care of me. I wasn't important." Her voice broke on the last word.

The confession had cost her dearly, for woven between the threads of loyalty, stubbornness, and courage, fate's insertion of resentment pulled at the one thing she'd treasured above all, love for her brother. In time, he'd see that faith restored so that she understood Billy had loved her above all else.

"I appreciate your honesty, but you are so incredibly wrong."

And now we'll get to the heart of the matter and start to heal.

"He sent you that necklace, what else?" Using his left hand, he brushed across her back and down her arm, his fingertips grazing the side of her breast.

"Please, Conner, I don't want to talk about it."

Silence drew out, the air pregnant with swelling tension like a grenade with its pin pulled, waiting to explode.

"We can have no secrets between us."

This time when he pulled back, she growled a threat obviously learned from the streets. *Thank God she can't see my sad smile.* The fact one part sorrow and two parts heartache composed his motivation shamed him.

"The necklace, sweetheart, tell me about it."

"Okay, okay. Three days after—after some colonel came and talked to us, it arrived in a battered yellow envelope."

Harsh pants filled his mind. Open, exposed, and vulnerable, emotionally and physically, her entire body shook, needing the

148

confession he knew would come. He'd spent hours thinking about the why of her running.

"Please, Conner." Thin cries and filled him with crushing guilt.

"Tell me." He used a grazing touch over first one breast then the other, thumbing her nipples through her shirt and bra.

She trembled as he continued his sensual assault, his fingers drifting down to feather across her tight belly then brush the seam of her jeans.

Her hips tilted into his touch, keeping time with his back and forth motion. Her eyes glazed and breath quickened.

"And with it a note?"

Her legs shook. A fine sheen of perspiration covered her body.

"Yes. A letter, too. He said to come see you and don't let anyone else see the damn necklace." Tears leaked from the corner of her eyes

"Why didn't you?" This was what he'd been waiting to hear. The confession that would rip her apart, then allow him to help bind her heart, soothe her spirit, and work together to find a new path, a new way of life. Only with her body strung tight and her mind in a maelstrom of confused lust would she tear it free.

"Because he loved you more than me!" The sob tearing from her throat must've shredded the tattered remains of her most precious organ, the one he wanted to claim for eternity.

"Oh, love, never believe that." Though he needed further information, he couldn't take her pain.

Increasing speed and pressure, he sent her over the edge, her scream filling his mind.

Damn, her first orgasm with a man who'd used it to gain information. When she relived this in her thoughts, and no doubt she would, maybe in time she'd forgive him the manipulation.

Perhaps not.

With one arm around her shoulders, he held her tight until the contractions ceased racking her core. For now, he needed to bring her down and help her through the tide of emotions yet to come. Warm, breathy pants contorted to harsher broken whimpers.

Physical relief eased her sexual tension while overwhelming the chokepoint holding her grief in check. Her soul now lay as naked as her mind as sob after sob shook her thin frame. Releasing the physical and mental bonds was the only place he knew to start.

Expelling the toxic contagions poisoning her mind ripped off her layers of armor in one fell swoop while leaving her open to bond with him, expectations he'd never fulfill if she didn't forgive him for the calculated maneuver. God, he was a fucking heel.

Never in his life had his spirit appeared blacker than the deepest pit of hell. Her words would echo in his head until his spirit met up with Billy's, and regardless of where that took place, Billy would pummel his old friend into the next phase of existence.

"Kendra, around that time, the team was dealing with a very difficult situation, and Billy wanted to see it through, which is what we did. That's why he re-joined. It was about finishing what he'd started, not abandoning you. You know how he was." Smoothing her hair from her face, kissing her forehead, and gently rubbing her arms was all he could offer in comfort. That, plus his words probably meant very little in the grand scheme of things.

"About the gemstone, weren't your parents curious about it?" Her folks were likely dead and buried under a ton of explosive debris. For now, that was too much to thrust on her shoulders.

"They never saw it. They blamed me for so much…" Convulsive waves of shudders overwhelmed her capacity to speak.

"You've never cried for him, have you?"

"No." Hiccups prevented further speech.

Conner held her tighter, rocking slightly, comforting both souls, both overcome with grief. The healing process always proved long and arduous, taken a step at a time, sometimes forward, sometimes back, and occasionally sideways down tangent paths that circumvented the end goal.

"What are you and Daeron planning, sweetheart? I know you're up to something." To his knowledge, she'd never offered an outright lie. She didn't have it in her moral repertoire.

In the monotone of one exhausted, she said, "He's gonna find out who they are, tell them we have the envelope, and draw them out in the open."

If fate had reversed the situation, he'd probably have done the same thing. His respect for Daeron grew exponentially. Despite his determination, the young man had too little information and lacked the experience to navigate a world of assassins and spies. Effectively dealing with the tangled scenario required tact and time. He had very little of the latter, virtually none of the former.

"Kendra, I will not allow you to place yourself in jeopardy. My brothers and I will deal with this. That stone came from overseas and some very powerful men are looking to reacquire it." Its value is probably nil compared to the other item now residing in my safe. The other stones, a sizable fortune in gems, had accompanied the sought-after item. Billy's orders to secure the flash drive surely didn't include taking the jewels. Remorse over leaving his sister explained the stones' presence—a small indulgence.

"Yeah, figures." Slumping posture combined with the resignation in her voice multiplied the sins of his subjecting her mind and body to such extreme lengths to obtain facts.

He'd just consigned his soul to hell, which he would bear. However, in doing so, he'd also condemned her. A young woman coming into her own had a lot to learn before setting permanent sights on one particular man.

Guilt was something he could survive. Kendra was someone he couldn't live without. He'd already accepted her mind and body into his keeping. He would do just that and keep them regardless of anyone's objections. If she ever turned away from him, it would destroy him but he'd set her free.

"Daeron's gonna find out who their contact is. No one can stop him once he sets his mind to something." Whispered words carried fear for her friend.

"I suppose you're right. However, let's convince him to be smart about this and accept help. Once we get the middle man, I know someone who can root out the source, regardless of its country's origin."

"Colonel Kenson? The guy who came to the house that day? Dani talked a little about him."

"Yeah, I believe he owes us both a world of information. Plus, he can run interference with the local PD and give us the time to sort this out."

With the truth of her feelings in the open, the venom of Billy's abandonment lost its sting, evidenced when their low murmurs reminisced about one they'd both loved and lost, Conner as a teammate and brother-in-arms, Kendra as a sister. The why of it all still eluded them.

As the long minutes passed, Conner drew her fully into his world, fleshing out plans for the future. "So you and Daeron want to own and run a café."

"Yeah, it's what I've wanted to do. Billy said he'd help with startup money once I graduated."

"I don't see why you can't."

Billy's sending the gemstones equaled a cozy little café.

"Conn, no bank is gonna lend a high school dropout a hundred thousand dollars."

He smiled against her hair, the plan forming in his mind amid soothing murmurs and silken locks. Billy's death would not be in vain, and Kendra would have a lasting physical reminder of her brother after the hellish nightmare ended.

"And what would you name it, this café?" Curiosity burned, given she'd obviously spent time thinking about it.

"Dunno, maybe The Sleepy Mongrel Café, or Blue Jay's Café. I like that better than scrub jay."

"Nice. Billy would approve of either."

Silence drew out in a comfort rarely known despite Kendra existing as a walking contradiction. She'd lived on the streets, yet gave what she could to Father McKinley's church, helping frequently with feeding other homeless victims of circumstance.

She'd held onto her privacy and kept many secrets close to the chest yet didn't mind invading Ambrosia to learn his. Her character was tough as nails, yet in her eyes lay an aching vulnerability that broke him, drew him into her world and ensured he'd slay any and all dragons in her path.

When her breathing evened out in sleep, the time had come to set events in motion. No force on earth could make him set her anywhere other than his bed, for even if his logical mind hadn't read the memo, his heart had already taken up residence with her soul.

With her warm exhalations soft on his cheek, he kissed her after settling the covers under her chin. The image of her in his bed trailed him to the kitchen like an insistent pup yapping for attention.

Chapter Eighteen

"Come on, Thad, back in the house."

A phone call to his brothers helped clear erotic fantasies running forefront in Conner's mind on a continuous cycle. Exchanging carnal bliss for the image of some dirtball slicing Kendra's throat provided a wakeup call. He would protect her at all costs.

Instinct advised he could eventually win Daeron's trust, essential for the plan forming in his mind to work, but time was not on their side. The boy's courage and loyalty to Kendra made him not only a valuable asset but also a big risk if used as leverage.

Sitting at the table, he waited for the mocking that would accompany each of his brothers' arrival.

It didn't take long.

"**W**ow, you actually have food in the fridge. Damn, bro, we knew Kendra would be good for you." The whisper of cool air from the closing fridge sent tiny dust motes scurrying past Marc's head. "This is better than expected. Where is she?"

Conner groaned inwardly. This wasn't going to be easy. "Sleeping."

Chortles morphed into hearty chuckles.

"Please note, guys, this is my cooking you're about to enjoy." Julien accepted the pie from Marc and set it beside the large bottle of soda on the table. "Better grab Conner some of the pink stuff, his guts can't take much concentrated sugar."

"Sleeping, huh? She must be exhausted to nap during the day. I remember her overabundance of energy as a kid." Nate's comment elicited a round of guffaws before he slapped Conner on the back. "Way to go, Conn. About fucking time. Looks like your brooding days are over."

Several thuds denoted cabinet and drawer closings after Nate grabbed paper plates and silverware, then toed out a chair to straddle.

The Crofton brothers did their best planning in the kitchen amid food and banter.

"Yeah, but I'd expected to see a bigger smile on his face. Damn," Julien added. "It's been a while. Maybe he needs a manual."

"Focus, guys. This isn't good news. We have to involve Colonel Kenson." Conner's declaration halted all activity. "And you know damn well it's gonna be hell trying to keep Callie and Dani apart from this."

Shifting behavior at the table mimicked the tortuous shadows created by the living room windows.

"Shit." Nate scooped a piece of pie and dumped it unceremoniously on his plate. "I thought we'd settled things down after finding Ray and dealing with the colonel's traitor."

"Apparently not. One of the thugs last night knew about psychics. They want both the women *and* the flash drive. We can't contain this any longer. We have to bring in the colonel." Conner understood his brothers' wariness.

"You know he's a hazard to Callie and Dani. All he wants is to get either in an uninhibited conversation." Nate took a swig of his soda. "Callie hasn't finished decrypting the flash drive yet."

"Billy stepped into something that got him killed. I believe Kenson sent him out solo that day to relay sensitive data about other prodigies." The vivid memory of Billy gasping his last breath in their hut burned in Conner's mind.

"Why does life keep circling around to this?" Marc stabbed his piece of pie with his fork.

"It's leading to Kendra and me now. Billy's post contained a note to never show the drive to anyone. It said to come straight to me."

"Then why didn't she? You think it contains the location of other facilities like the one that held Callie?" Marc's fork stopped halfway to his mouth, waiting for an explanation.

"Kendra was pissed off at the world, and scared. If I'd checked on her after the funeral, I'd have known she'd run away." The sour taste of regret filled his mind and heart. He'd broken off communication with her father and mother, unable to bear recriminations in their eyes. His brothers, who generally followed his lead, had done the same.

"Why didn't her folks call you, or—they blame you for Billy's death." Nate's mind was as quick as any, but there were too many missing pieces to form a picture. "By the way, the remains in the explosion? Not her family. Must've been their friends, the homeowners.

"All the more reason to contact the colonel. GPD will think I had something to do with Palmer's death. Do we have an ID on the other guy?" Conner asked.

"Doubt they'll be looking in our direction," Julien shrugged a shoulder. "The card in Palmer's hand got misplaced."

"Blood at the scene matches that on Kendra's clothes from the attack at Ambrosia. Hopefully, we'll have ID on at least one of them." Marc leaned back in his chair, balancing on the back two legs, a practice begun as a teenager not deterred by one of his brothers occasionally swiping the legs out from under him.

"Anything on the manager, Wes?" Conner asked. "If he's acting as someone's intermediary to obtain Billy's package, why not approach me directly?"

"Nothing new, but he's involved somehow. Prior to Kendra's life on the streets, I've found no records on him. I'd be glad to pay him a visit tonight." The nature of Marc's visits always ensured a result, even if it wasn't the one expected.

"Not yet. Wes doesn't strike me as any smarter than middle management, and we want the top dog, whoever's pulling the strings in the background." Conner shoved his plate aside, no longer able to tolerate one of his favorite dishes. "That bastard's kinda like a mole that starts out harmless but darkens as it grows. Not wise to ignore him."

"We won't. I'll dig some more. If I don't find anything significant, we'll stop by one night while he's sleeping." Deviant thoughts usually hid behind Marc's humorless smile.

"Daeron is in the wind again, snooping. I hate to say it, but he's our best chance at wrapping this up quickly."

"You trust him with her life?" Julien's question was a gauge of not only Daeron's motives but also Conner's insight.

"Yeah, my gut tells me he's a good kid. I'd like to help him when this is all over."

"Okay. I'll contact Colonel Kenson tonight. When he hears someone's hunting for psychics, he'll be all the hell over it." Julien's smile lacked the humor so common to his nature. "Which is why I'll be the one to make contact. I'll also loop him into the local PD and the burned bodies."

"Press him about Billy's last assignment. Be prepared for a big response when you mention the envelope. Tell him I've secured it but won't turn it over until Kendra's safe. I'm thinking he'll have to send a team overseas to finish this."

"Damn Kenson anyway." Julien's chair squeaked across the hardwood as he pushed back to stand.

"Without his involvement, Nate wouldn't have Callie and Marc wouldn't have Dani." Threadbare logic could only sustain Conner for so long. He needed to put an end to the bullshit. "As far as Daeron's concerned, I'd really like to have someone on him but considering he's an eight-year veteran of the streets, that's out of the question. Anything on his background check?"

"Not yet, no record found for his fingerprints," Nate replied, rubbing his chin in thought.

"Hey, does he like dogs? I can chip the collar." Marc's idea held merit. "We'd at least have a twice-a-day check and could feed them both."

"He doesn't strike me as the type..." Nate started.

"He probably won't accept responsibility for an animal, but I'll talk to him about it." Conner explained Daeron's intention involving a phony package. "When it comes to delivery, he's not going alone."

"Perhaps Kenson has a young enough recruit or three that could fit into the street crowd." Marc stood, the fork screeching against his plate as he headed toward the sink. "Let me know if I need to bring my dog over later. Unless you'll be busy."

Each of the brothers smirked.

"Not funny, assholes. It hasn't been like that," Conner retorted.

"Dude, you're wrung so damned tight, you need to either shed the carnal fascination or take a trip to pound town."

"Working on it. Now, you guys need to vacate. Daeron won't come near this place with all of us together. He doesn't like crowds."

"Well, if anyone can get through to him, it'd be you. Look how well you did with us." Julien slapped Conner on the back after clearing his dishes.

Marc's good-natured shoving preceded them all leaving.

With their intentions set, only fate, nameless participants, or several hundred unknown variables stood to ruin the plan. Regardless, life's puzzles were completed a piece at a time. Occasionally two happened at once yet without intel and countermeasures, their best defenses were weak against a well-organized enemy.

After taking Krystal and Thad outside, his deliberations remained undisturbed while sitting in the great room and watching the repetitive violence of the ocean waves crashing along the beach.

Kendra's silent steps brought her to stand before him, her expression indicating a contemplative spirit in need of strengthening. Without hesitation, she scooped the pup into her arms and sat beside him, nestling like a small animal against the storm.

"Your brothers were here." Her statement lacked emotion, suspicion, or uncertainty, and demanded he answer the unspoken question.

"Yes, I've caught them up to speed on everything. Julien's going to contact Colonel Kenson and enlist his help since this clusterfuck originated overseas."

"What about Daeron?"

"I have a plan and could use your help." Without going into the finer details of GPS-chipped collars, he described Marc's work in training protection dogs. "If the offer comes strictly from me—"

"Daeron will refuse. But if I help, maybe he won't."

"That's what I'm figuring. This would be good for Daeron, too. I'm hoping he'll come back tonight and mull it over till morning."

"I don't know that he'll spend the night. He's never gone into detail and never stayed at Wes' house, but I know he's had it rough."

"I believe the fact you trust me will go a long way. How're you feeling, sweetheart?"

"Better. Lots."

So much rested on things they couldn't control. So many lives at stake. The calamity of errors combined to threaten them all.

Chapter Nineteen

Gently rolling hills teamed with the first flush of spring to fill the frame of the firm's office window. Instead of the normal serenity-inducing vista, he only saw Kendra's face as it'd been the first night in Ambrosia, sprayed with blood.

Damn her reckless determination.

Now, he realized she'd persisted, doggedly determined as ever to help her street friend solve their mystery. Daeron had shown up and refused a dog's company or a spare bed but claimed the couch, which meant little Conner remained frustrated and chafed.

Dani and Callie arrived along with their protective details to be present for the group meeting. The combination would end in trouble. He felt it soul deep.

Conner shook his head. Kenson was due any minute. Glancing through the glass at his brother, he noted the words *'you're fucked'* mouthed from his sibling, which inspired thoughts of a good knockdown, drag-out fight despite his collision with destiny sliding down a slippery slope.

From the central area, Dani waved, innocence personified concealing a devious mind. Callie smiled his way before introductions with Kendra.

"Hey, Conn, isn't it great our girls get to hang for a bit while we talk? I told them to have lunch in the conference room." Nate strode through his office doorway, grinning like a fool. The corner leather chair whooshed under his settling weight.

"As if I need them all together, conspiring. Hell, Nate, give me a break. Kenson'll be here within the hour."

"Man, the sooner you stop fighting this, the better for us all. We're tired of hearing you growl and grumble all the time."

As the three girls passed en route to the meeting room and out of sight, Conner rubbed a hand over his eyes before pinching the bridge of his nose.

"Take it easy Conn, half the team is outside for perimeter guard. They're fine. Hell, you're worse than we ever were."

The vibration of Conner's cell phone halted his intended lecture. "Text from Lightning."

Nate shot to his feet, drawing Marc's attention in the next office. Simultaneously, his phone rang and Julien appeared in the doorway.

"Colonel's here early. Look alive." Conner hustled to stand. The office's central area revealed their visitor striding forward with purpose written in each step. The only room not visible was the conference room where they held weekly meetings to discuss ongoing investigations.

"And there goes the day. He's gonna want to see Kendra, who's with Dani and Callie," Nate said after a groan.

"It's all right, Dani and Callie will run interference if needed." Conner headed to his office door, meeting the colonel face to face. "Afternoon, Colonel. I expect you have news for us?"

"Damn, you boys band together fast. It's like trying to sneak up on a coalition of lions. I take it with both teams here the girls are in your conference room?" A certain shrewdness about his eyes suggested hidden motives. "I need to talk with Kendra." Without hesitation, Kenson headed toward the meeting room.

"Please, be my guest, as if you didn't know the girls arrived minutes ago." Conner's sarcasm, lost on his ex-commanding officer, brought a nervous chuckle from his brothers.

As Kenson reached the door, Dani pushed it open to block his entrance, a wide smile gracing her lips. Sincerity appeared to radiate from her open expression if one didn't know of her incredible mind. "Hello, Colonel, so nice to see you again."

Shrewd turned predatory as Kenson held out his hand. "Well hello, Danielle, what a pleasant surprise."

"And why do I get the feeling it's no surprise at all?" This time, Dani's smile reached her eyes, the devilish gleam hiding secrets many would kill to know.

"The details of which I'd love to discuss on another day." Nudging her aside, Kenson entered, followed by Conner, Nate, Julien, and Marc.

Conner lacked the gentle tact of Marc's girlfriend. In his reality, an unseen second hand ticked away the minutes before someone else attacked Kendra.

161

Knowing they'd have to give information to receive like in kind, he contemplated the least threatening facts to reveal.

"Shall we all have a seat?" Kenson gave no mobile manifestations of the age shown in his graying temples. His movements, like the workings of his mind were quick, efficient, and carried little waste. His social armor of blue jeans and denim shirt appeared as casual as a well-brushed hunting blind in the middle of a post-harvest corn field.

All three girls wore virtual targets for one reason or another, and the colonel had long been trying to discover their secrets.

Conner also knew the tricks of the trade, having learned from the best, Kenson himself. Gentle interrogation began long before either party walked into the room.

Nate tensed when the colonel offered his hand to Callie before pulling out a chair. After the obligatory greeting, she padded to Nate, cupping his cheeks in her palms then urging him to sit beside her, opposite Kenson.

Simultaneously, Dani prompted Kendra to sit near the end of the conference table, cattycorner to Conner, who took the remaining seat. The fact Dani manipulated each so she could sit by the colonel brought chuckles from each brother. Marc, her better half, grinned wide.

"I see the girls have already united, and damned if I wouldn't love to know what these grins held back." Kenson grunted before laying his briefcase flat and taking his seat. Julien secured the door.

Kenson's calculative contemplation settled on each girl in turn as if he could delve into their minds and separate the secrets he longed to acquire. "Some of this documentation is classified, but I'll hit the highlights."

The snap of the locks releasing echoed his crisp, economical movements. The attempt to incur favor and credence by including the women was lost on no one, judging by suppressed smiles and furtive glances.

Conner began the meeting with a question of his own. "Anything on Palmer's autopsy?" Three years of loose comradery on the street could equal a decade of close friendship under normal circumstances. Painful as it might be, Kendra deserved to know about her companion.

"No, we can't match DNA yet."

"Why not?" Kendra asked.

"Because they burned his body." Dani's answer drew the colonel's intense regard.

"And how would you know that, young lady?" Colonel Kenson pivoted in his seat to give Dani the considerable weight of his full attention.

"How else would there be no DNA?" Dani nibbled at her lower lip.

"I didn't say we had no DNA. I said we couldn't *match* it." Kenson' stare turned predatory, a hawk who'd found his next meal, surveying the area to determine the best approach.

"Oh, I misunderstood. Sorry," Dani replied, her gaze sliding to Marc.

"I doubt that on both counts." Kenson's declaration and unrelenting study elicited a grumbled warning from Marc.

"Back on point, Colonel. What about the other body?" Conner, out of sheer determination, stayed focused.

"That's a different story and where we get into classified information." Kenson pulled several photos from his briefcase. "Unlike Palmer, who we're trying to identify through a dental forensics specialist, we've identified the other man through his medical history. A prior leg injury required surgical pins, which as you know are easily traced."

The photo's quiet slide across the table was disproportionate to the ominous apprehension rooting in Conner's thoughts. He passed the eight-by-ten glossy around the table. "I don't recognize him. Should I?"

"Not likely. He's a foreign national, which is all I can say in present company."

"Colonel—" Conner began, remembering Callie's clash with foreign agents.

"No, son. You have your secrets, so do I."

"Which means you're not going to tell us about the wild goose chase that got Billy killed." Years of working for Kenson had enlightened Conner to the inner workings of the older man's mind.

"Not yet, but I can tell you he tried to relay data from a foreign government. If I'm correct, it concerns both Callie and Dani."

Marc sat straighter in his chair. "Explain."

"Don't know for sure or the extent at this point. It was supposed to be a simple relay. I thought Billy had failed. Now I know he didn't, not if your envelope contains a specific flash disc." Kenson again speculated as he visually dissected Conner then Kendra, before settling on Callie, their ultimate hacker. "Have you tried to open the files?"

"So, some foreign asshole thinks Kendra has a valuable item." Conner redirected Kenson's attention and outlined the basics of their plan in hopes Kenson would fall in line. "Billy's attorney sent me something a month ago, intended for Kendra on her twenty-first birthday. When I received it, I'd assumed it contained facts about his will, et cetera. I didn't open it until I found Kendra recently."

Kenson shook his head, not to be dissuaded. "Even with the computer skills your firm possesses, I assume you didn't try to open the files. I'll be taking that today, thank you." Kenson nodded his thanks.

"Not so fast," Marc spoke up.

"Agreed. We need to catch them and annihilate the source. One of Kendra's friends—" Conner was hesitant to involve Daeron.

"Daeron, Cliff, or Wes?" The colonel smiled.

"Huh. Figures you'd already know." Conner shook his head.

"Made it my business."

"Daeron's poking around, trying to find out who's new on the street. We want to set up a sting." Kendra's voice betrayed the uncertainty in her mind. She looked to Conner.

"Excellent idea, Kendra. I have just the men for the job. I get the information I want. You step out from under the thumb of foreign watch dogs."

Kenson denied further details as to the mission costing Billy's life, though his understanding of Kendra's years on the street shouldn't have surprised them.

"Men, I want you to stay out of this. I'm looking into it and won't have these women placed in jeopardy. I have someone undercover. You each have much to lose, and there's been too much loss already." His sympathetic glance at Kendra broadcasted a regret he would never voice.

When the meeting adjourned and the colonel left, the women took Kendra into Conner's office for some quiet conversation while the men discussed how they'd modify Kenson's plan, once decided.

Chapter Twenty

A slow westerly slide marked the sun's path below the horizon amid pink and purple hues. After the rinsed dinner dishes were tucked in the dishwasher, Conner sat with Kendra and watched the ocean waves' perpetual crash and retreat while awaiting Daeron's arrival. Long ago, he'd given up on knowing such incredible peace.

Now he wondered if he could survive without it.

Kendra's contented sigh stirred the long wisps of hair surrounding Thad's ears, instigating a shake that sent them flopping back and forth. "Why are they waiting to contact us? It's been almost a week since Palmer..."

"I don't know, sweetheart. None of us are gaining headway."

"Daeron should be here soon. Think we can convince him the spare bed would be more comfortable than the couch?" The innocent concern in her tone belied the scheming devilry in her mind. "Sure wish he'd keep one of Marc's dogs with him."

"No, babe. You're not taking the couch and you're not sleeping in my bed, yet. That's a step we're not ready to take until we're clear."

Kendra's unique and perceptive empathy manifested in various techniques to increase his suffering, perpetuating his constant and painful consequences.

Her guileless voice dripped innocence while her actions revealed a sharp wit. She'd spent too much time with Dani and Callie.

When the familiar notes of the doorbell announced Daeron's arrival, Conner shifted Kendra in favor of a little space and some deep breaths of cool night air. Krystal dogged his heels while Thad remained cuddled in her lap. Though expected in one version or another, the sight greeting him took all the strength and experience of an older caregiver to hold his tongue. "Damn."

Daeron's condition, a bruise marring his right eye, a split lip, and blood smears below his nose, detailed his recent activity.

"How bad, Daeron? Ribs, belly?" Conner led him through to the kitchen, gesturing to a stool. "You should have called me. Damn it, at least take a dog with you."

"Couple of ribs I think, but I've got a time and place for the exchange."

Kendra's thin cry incited Thad's whining as she quickly extricated herself to hover over her friend. "Why'd they do this?"

"Because they're pricks." Daeron rasped out.

With Kendra's help, Conner managed to remove the torn shirt, revealing bruises already forming over two lower left ribs.

"Should we tape them?" Tears graced her lashes.

"No, that would prevent him from taking deep breaths and promote lung infection." Conner placed one palm on Daeron's lower chest in front and the other on the middle of his back, pressing in slightly with each. "Damn it, I should've been the one out there."

Daeron gasped at the pressure applied. "Yeah, and you'd have killed them, breaking the link to the source. Then we'd have to start this shit all over."

"Looks like a broken rib. Any trouble breathing?"

"Nah, I'll be okay. Had worse. At least now we'll end this shit and get back to life."

Not life as you've known it. Conner's plan to help the young man had formed during their evening conversations, shaded by restrained anxiety and waiting for the inevitable showdown.

"They want to meet tomorrow night in town during the block party on Jefferson Street." Another groan and frown accompanied Daeron's weak cough. "I told 'em Kendra's not coming. It'll have to be me or no deal. They accepted, with a penalty."

"What? No, Daeron, I won't let you take that risk for me."

"Now we know why they waited to contact us. They want it local and public. However this plays out, we'll have enough backup to catch whoever is responsible," Conner murmured, turning to Kendra. "Sweetheart, can you grab a wet washcloth for Daeron?" Her concern was heartfelt, but damned if she'd take any part in the exchange.

Several backward glances marked her pace until she disappeared down the hall.

Conner laid out the plan before adding, "When this is over, I'd like you to help Kendra get on her feet."

"She's always been there. You just can't see it."

"Kendra's plan to open a café sounds plausible, but she needs someone else she trusts beside her. I've already got a business taking a good chunk of my time and have no interest in running a chat and chew."

The young man would see through Conner's ruse, but perhaps he'd take the well-deserved helping hand.

"Don't s'pose you'd agree to see a doctor." He spilled two Aspirin tablets into Daeron's palm before retrieving a soda from the fridge.

"Don't need a doc but thanks for these. I'll be fine. And we'll see about the other."

Having planted the seed in Daeron's mind, Conner hoped he'd think it over. His friendship with Kendra would thrive, strengthened through years of ups and downs.

Kendra nudged Conner aside to visually inspect her friend's injuries. "Come on, Daeron, let's get you comfortable. You're sleeping in my bed tonight."

Her obvious brain filter malfunction resulted in Daeron's sputtering cough.

"Oh, you goof, I'll sleep on the couch."

"I'll call Kenson, give him an update." Conner shook his head as he swiped his cell.

After relaying the information through a conference call, he took both dogs out before getting some sleep.

It wasn't the first time Conner slept on the couch, but at least he didn't worry about either guest slipping out the back door. Sensual images of her splayed on his mattress kept his mind whirling until faint edges of gray poured through the window.

In reviewing possible scenarios for the coming night's op and potential glitches, too many existed to count and counter considering

Daeron's lack of training. On the other hand, he'd never met a better strategic planner than Kenson. They'd make the best of the situation.

Callie and Dani would monitor the operation as it unfolded, safe in the second story of a well-protected home.

Krystal and Thad greeted the latest arrival with threatening barks until Conner's hand signal silenced his shepherd. "Morning, Colonel. Come on in. You know your way around."

The open floor plan granted a view from front door to kitchen, allowing Kendra to watch the military man's approach. His greeting each Crofton with a stiff nod halted mid-step as his befuddled frown roamed over first Callie, then Dani, each garbed in black BDUs. The resultant shock was priceless. "These girls are not going to participate—"

Except for the short meeting at Conner's firm, Kendra's only interaction with Kenson occurred three years ago. Now, as she watched the other women tense in his presence again, she wondered what bleak and stygian circumstances warranted the degree of wariness. She hadn't wanted to pry earlier, but they were taking a risk on her behalf.

"Of course not, Colonel, but we're not leaving them alone, either. They'll be with their protective details a safe distance away while Julien stays here with Kendra." Conner stood his ground, his resolve unshakable. "Would you care to join us for breakfast?" He gestured to the countertop covered with all manner of food.

Kenson shook his head then fixed his gaze on Daeron, assessing character, strength, and determination. "Young man, there's a hell of a lot riding on this night's work. I appreciate your willingness to help. I don't forget those to whom I owe a favor."

Daeron's response held equal resolve. "I don't give a damn about you or this country since neither ever did a thing for me. I'm doing this for Kendra. And if you use her as a pawn in your scheme, better watch your back. One day you'll turn around to find me there when you least expect it. And I don't play fair."

Kenson grinned, unfazed, and took a seat beside Daeron. "Loyalty and determination are two qualities I admire most. I think when this is said and done, we should sit down for a chat."

Clinking dishes protested their sweep aside as the colonel made room for his briefcase. From its contents, he pulled a manila envelope. "I assume this is similar to the one Billy sent?" After receiving a nod in return, he continued, "I have duplicate items that you, Daeron, are going to give to the contact. Looks like they got a few good licks in. Sure you're up for it?"

"Hell, yeah."

"Remember, we need the contact alive. A corpse can't give us the details to end this hellish reverie." Kenson extracted a street map of the city. "As far as weapons..."

"Got it covered," Daeron replied.

As the women stood and cleared the table, Kenson' glance flicked between each as if trying to discern some unfathomable secret.

"Give it up, Colonel. Not gonna happen." Nate smiled in the face of the colonel's grumble.

"Hmm, I'd love to know why you're including them here in the planning."

"They're safer with us and right where they need to be." Nate's reply came quick and sure.

"Damn it. All right. Here's the agenda." Defining each man's area on the map, Kenson laid out the intended scenario. With only a few minor adjustments, each assignment coincided with Crofton plans.

"Now, how about you turn over the real thing, Conner," Kenson suggested.

"Sure, soon as we have the middleman secured." Conner's thoroughness would dictate they eliminate all threats before releasing the leverage.

The last rays of light had vanished below the horizon hours before, leaving the future up to the shadows and all they concealed.

Kendra understood the Crofton brothers always watched each other's backs. Daeron's presence equaled a wild card. The newest and most important member was untrained, untried, and injured, variables no one could control.

"I've never worn any kind of mic before." The twinge of mistrust creeping into Daeron's voice echoed through the transmitter in his ball cap.

"Daeron, you don't have to do this." Kendra looked around helplessly. Conner had promised to protect her friend, yet she'd learned firsthand how life transformed the expected into tragedy. Things beyond human control decimated lives. Each man checked his weapon in preparation for moving out.

"You may trust these guys, Kendra, but I don't know them. This is the only way I know to keep you safe." Daeron pulled her in for a quick hug before considering Conner. "If this goes south—"

"Nothing's gonna happen to you, Daeron. We're all going to be close, and Kenson has three teams surrounding the blocked-off area along with key personnel that'll mingle with the crowd. Together, we've got this covered. Not to mention, a little extra insurance." Conner's glance flicked to Nate and Marc, each nodding agreement.

"But Palmer was one of us and..." Imminent departure brought a flood of doubts to Kendra's mind. "And we haven't found Wes. Do you think he's involved?" The safety of Conner's arms stifled the rest of her thoughts.

"Everybody's going to get through this, Kendra. Krystal and Julien will stay here with you. We'll be back soon."

Seizing the duplicate envelope, Conner led the men out to their waiting SUVs.

After closing and locking the door behind them, Julien retraced his steps to the kitchen. "How about I fix us a drink while we wait? I think you could use it."

"I'm not a drinker."

"Yep, I figure there're a lot of things you haven't done yet. Time to surge forward, Kendra. Conner's a good man."

* * * *

Conner watched the grin spreading across Daeron's face. For once, the handoff went as planned, with a little help. "Well, young man. You kept your cool and everything went almost like clockwork." No doubt, any offer by Colonel Kenson now would receive a hearty acceptance, therein breaking Kendra's heart.

"Daeron, you're a natural." From the back seat, Nate unfastened the Velcro of his vest.

"I think we should all sit down and have a chat, get to know each other better." Conner stepped on the gas in heading home, catching his brother's eye in the rearview mirror.

"Agreed. How about a cookout tomorrow afternoon? My cabin," Nate added, his acceptance of their youngest team member clear.

"Would one of you like to explain how that punk fumbled his knife? According to you, Conner, he held it like a pro. Yet he just dropped it. Then, he stood there with his mouth gaping like a fish on dry land. Someone explain that, please."

"Hey, we were behind you, Daeron." Marc shrugged his shoulders. "How would we know?"

"After cuffing him, you both look toward the closest home's second story window. What's that all about?"

"Kismet, Daeron. It so happens that we knew the homeowner. Dani and Callie were up there, watching." Conner smiled with the knowledge of both Callie and Dani's help.

"Whatever. But the colonel's man said the same. I know there's more to the story."

"Hey, at least it's over, for now. Let's all get together." Nate redirected the conversation.

"What do you mean, for now?" Daeron swiveled in the passenger seat to address Marc.

"Meaning, Callie and Dani are special..." Conner's leading question was meant to draw out what Daeron knew about the women.

"Yeah, Kendra told me the same thing, but wouldn't explain, just blew it off—like they're both super geniuses."

"They are. We've learned there's a group, international, with locations in several countries that are imprisoning prodigies and trying to harness their talents for their own use." Conner divulged as much as comfortable while still protecting sacred trusts.

"Well, I'd sure as hell like to be part of the team busting them up."

"We'll keep you in mind," Nate advised, "if we have to face them again."

Daeron removed his ball cap and let out a deep sigh. "Sounds great. Damn. Did you see the look on that bastard's face when Kenson's men closed in? That went smoother than I'd expected, but I would've liked to return the favor of some broken ribs." Daeron leaned back against the front passenger seat, closed his eyes, and took a deep, halting breath. "I didn't suspect that couple of being part of our team. When Kenson had said I'd hand over the envelope and that would be the end of it, I had my doubts."

Regardless of the colonel's ignorance concerning Callie's help, the takedown avoided collateral damage.

Yet Conner's sixth sense alerted him to a threat, insidious, hidden among the shadows like quicksand slowly devouring its prey. That same instinct had carried his team through countless missions in all types of terrains and undercover scenarios. Never in his life had sudden fear driven him so hard.

He couldn't hit the speed dial fast enough, the numbers blurring before his eyes. When Julien's phone went straight to voicemail, he stomped the accelerator and caught Nate's eye in the rearview mirror. "Call Kenson. Tell him we need a team at the house. I'll call Marc, he and Lightning will secure the women even if they have to knock 'em out. No mistakes."

"What the hell, Conner?" Daeron's hands fisted at his sides. "Did Kenson double-cross us and take the original envelope?"

"No. I believe we have another player, one we didn't see coming. Julien knows better than to not answer his phone." Two wheels left the ribbon of blacktop as their vehicle slewed around the curve merging onto Route 13. "How in the hell could anyone get the drop on Julien?" In their line of work, it always paid to expect the worst.

The business district passed in a stroboscopic blur of streetlights and dimly lit storefronts. How many times had Kendra walked similar barren streets, wondering what horrors the shadows withheld?

Small stones and dirt flew as he navigated the sharp turn into his driveway. A hundred yards ahead, light shone from the windows and wide-open front door. "Shit. Those motherfuckers."

Nate's voice in the background held equal frustration, more than blood bound the brothers. The adversities of their lives beginning long before their father murdered their mother in a drunken rage also harbored the normal angst of growing pains. Afterward, four brothers stayed together through foster care, managed by and accountable to the oldest, Conner.

"Colonel's men will be here in a few minutes." Nate refastened his Kevlar vest as Conner skidded to a stop in front of the house.

"Damn it." The front door hung by one hinge, mocking, disdainful. Conner rounded the SUV as Daeron and Nate slid out. Never had his heart pounded so hard, fear gripping his soul, squeezing until he focused by the thinnest of threads that if broken would condemn his mind to eternal hell.

Krystal's hoarse breathing just inside the door, raspy with congestion, stemmed from the bloody wound of her right shoulder.

A low groan tagged Julien's location as Conner made sense of the scene. "They blew the door? Nate, check the rest of the house. Julien, how bad?" Conner snatched the blanket from the sofa to stem the flow of blood from his brother's shoulder. "Lungs?"

"No. I can breathe okay. They took her. Cindy and two men, faces covered. Go. Get her." Pain clouded his eyes as he tried to get up. "Sorry."

"Help is on the way. We'll get Kendra back. You hang in there." A haze of rage veiled Conner's vision as he looked around helplessly.

"House is clear, ambulance and the colonel's men are en route." Silent as in all missions, Nate approached his side.

"Daeron, c'mere and hold pressure. I'll check the computer. I can track Kendra as long as she's still wearing the necklace I gave her."

Conner shoved a footstool out of his path as he stood and stalked to the kitchen for his laptop.

A raucous clanging from pots and pans skidding across the floor overshadowed the low hum of the computer's fans whirring into action. Conner's swift and reckless movements granted access to his hidden safe while creating a racket worthy of any gourmet cook's temper tantrum. "This God damned envelope will not cost another life!"

"You keep a safe under your kitchen counter—smart." Daeron's grudging respect resonated among the background noise.

Returning to his laptop, Conner opened the tracking program. "Got her. Let's go, Nate."

"No. I'm going." Daeron's voice rang with determination. "I have no medical training, so I'm useless here. I know the streets better than either of you."

"Damn it." Nate looked to Conner then added, "He's got a point, Conn. I'll take care of Julien."

Seconds later, Conner swerved the SUV back onto blacktop, fear for Kendra taking the curve on two wheels. Calling the colonel, he updated their situation. As he clipped the phone to his belt again, the vibration alerted of an incoming call. "Hello."

Chapter Twenty-One

"Since we haven't heard from our third man in the town square, I thought I'd call and deliver the ultimatum myself."

"What do you want, Cindy, and what the hell?"

"Oh, Conner, I would've preferred things turn out differently, but when you picked this street rat over me, I figured I'd accept a generous offer and take the money instead. I assume you have the items with you and are on your way? Or do I need to give you directions?"

"I'll be there in thirty minutes—"

"Make it sooner, I'm bored. On second thought, take your time. I think I'll show your little whore just what a fierce beating feels like. Never thought I'd enjoy a human punching bag, but I've proven I can learn."

The call disconnected before Conner could begin his verbal assault.

"How in the hell did your ex get involved in this?" Daeron's accusation, though well deserved, failed to enlighten or counsel.

"Damned if I saw it coming. If it'd been Wes, then yeah. There's been something off with that guy from the beginning."

"I've never fully trusted him. Maybe he's there with your jilted freak. Either way, I'll kill whoever's taken her." Daeron's declaration confirmed a determination rarely seen in one so young.

No doubt the younger man would do exactly as he warned. "Considering the risks you've taken, okay, but if you hesitate, we all die."

Daeron snorted. "Not a problem."

A pair of gloves retrieved from the center console conveyed their own meaning. "Put these on. If you shoot, shoot to kill, not wound. Then ditch your gloves and jacket, which you need to zip up now. I'll take responsibility."

The SUV sailed north on the coastal highway through seemingly endless stretches of straight road. Patched moonlight gilded the highway and sprinkled black diamonds on the restless sea to his left as the fickle wind carried the pre-storm scent.

"How much farther?" Daeron pulled back the slide to check the chamber of his Glock.

"About fifteen minutes. They're holed up in a warehouse by the docks. Probably waiting for transport." A rush of adrenaline compelled his fingers to crush the steering wheel while the oppressive silence charged and found him incompetent. His bottled scream roared in his head, finally emitted as a low growl.

"We may have company." Conner nodded toward his rearview. "We don't have time for confrontation." With his luck, Dani and Callie would soon follow.

Daeron described the docks as best he could in the allotted time, supplemented by Conner's dim familiarity and devising likely scenarios. "This'll have to be an evolving plan since we don't have time to assess."

"Not a problem. That's the way I live. I know the docks well enough even though I prefer to keep my distance. You'll have to follow my lead."

"Whatever happens, we take care of Kendra first. Everything else is secondary." Conner's declaration, though unnecessary, brought a little sanity to his thoughts.

"Already there, man."

Narrow exits soon bisected the highway leading to small businesses while the scent of saltwater prodded his memories of Billy and Kendra joining his brothers for a scuba dive during leave. The water's sharp tang combined with the sweet, pungent zing of ozone bit into his memories with teeth that ripped through his spirit.

"Looks like we lost our tail." Daeron inhaled deep as if to clear his mind for the job ahead.

"Maybe."

Conner patted his jacket pocket, aware that he may have to hand over sensitive information to secure Kendra's release. He didn't intend to lose either one.

Inner demons castigated him for another failure.

She should have been home dreaming of picket fences and gourmet recipes. "He might be lagging back after cutting his lights."

The engine quieted before the tires ground to a halt behind the warehouse neighboring his target building. No sliver of light or small squeak betrayed their presence when the vehicles' doors opened, then closed.

There existed no sign of a posted sentry, nor the time for proper recon. By now, the colonel would be on his way, but that didn't mean Kendra's life would be top priority.

"Stay behind me, Daeron."

Two security lights bathed the asphalt littered with fast-food wrappers and other detritus detailing human negligence. Reflected starbursts from the hoods of two SUVs pierced the darkness with stabbing beams. Technically one story, the warehouses provided substantial storage space where high windows foiled his intent to view the interior. He'd have to go in blind.

A rustling off to his right signaled another presence. A second later, Callie and Dani trailed Marc, Nate, and Lightning.

"What the fuck are you doing here with them?" Conner's harsh whisper didn't faze either woman.

"You know we can help, just as well as you should've known Callie's been in your computer since day one and knew where you were going." Dani grinned at Daeron, then Conner. "We've decided to let him in. He's as much family as Kendra now."

"This is bad timing," Conner countered with a shake of his head. Before Daeron could voice his opinion, Conner continued, "This is a crash course in what we can do. If you ever spill a word, you'll end up at GTMO, understand?"

"Sure. This'll explain the weirdness occurring at the drop earlier?" The first note of uncertainty entered Daeron's voice.

Dani closed her eyes and dropped chin to chest. "Okay. Inside are two women and two men. One—Kendra is hurt, but I don't think too bad."

"Positions relative to the door?" Callie asked, taking a stick and sketching a rough outline of the structure in the dirt.

Dani took the stick and drew a smaller rectangle. "Here's the personnel door..."

Each X marked the position of one of the kidnappers relative to walls and contents inside.

With the mental template in place, Conner listened to the offshore wind stirring mini debris-laden dust devils in preparation of heaven's physical rant. Either way, this would prove one hell of a night for the woman he'd sworn to protect.

"They'll expect us to come in through the personnel door. There's no way to approach from two different directions... But Callie, if you could provide a distraction around the loading dock, it would help." Conner squeezed closer to the building, daring a glance around the edge and surveying the side parking lot. From there on, they'd be visible and vulnerable to anyone rounding the front corner.

"Any sentries outside, Dani?" Marc asked, pointing to Lightning then the structure's left side where the industrial size door slid on tracks.

"No. Everybody's in, but they're expecting us, meaning more than one."

"Whoa," Daeron took a step back then halted. "You really can—"

"Yes, now keep up." Conner admonished, then turned to Callie and Marc.

"I'll go in first. They're expecting me. Once I pull out the flash drive, that'll be your signal, Callie. Okay?"

"But she won't be able to see you," Daeron palmed his weapon in preparing to follow Conner.

"Daeron, you should probably wait here. Kendra will kill us if you get hurt... "

"Fuck that. I don't care what crazy things you all can do. I'm going in there," Daeron challenged.

"All right, but follow my lead." Conner understood the young man's loyalty. He'd make a good addition to any team.

The stillness stretched out like the silence of an indrawn breath— before an earsplitting scream rent the air. Kendra.

It was time to reach inside for the soldier, the stone-cold killer respected and trusted by his team. Gone now were the flashbacks of Kendra's breathtaking responses, his thoughts resolute, engrossed with the intent to kill. His whisper to Daeron, "Only one of them survives to give information," received a sharp nod.

It was too quiet.

For the past twenty minutes, visions of Kendra, bloody from Cindy's revenge, had invaded his soul. Her pain twisted in his gut.

He heard no murmurs or signs of movement. Regardless, they had to move forward.

Thirty yards to the building's front corner closed fast as a gut-wrenching scream followed the thud of flesh on flesh. Kendra's agony raised bile in his throat. This time when he got hold of Cindy, there'd be no security, and no stopping until she could never hurt another soul. He'd never harmed a woman before, but every rule had an exception.

One hand held up stayed his team before he spread his fingers then cupped his ear to indicate they wait and listen.

Daeron nodded. In the dim light, not one bead of sweat painted his furrowed brow. Narrowed eyes and firmed jaw dictated him as battle ready as any soldier from Conner's old unit.

Unbroken floor-to-eaves sheet metal denied light to seep from the building's front. Even the large rolling door, closed against the night, rebuffed any attempt of interior light escaping.

One small personnel door on his side lent little hope for reconnaissance as Kendra's muffled scream shredded caution and good intention of taking anyone alive. Testing the doorknob, he found it unlocked. There'd be no benefit in hindering his entrance.

The slight crack through which he glimpsed Kendra gagged with hands bound and secured to a rope straddling a rough-hewn rafter almost drove him to his knees. The smell of spilled diesel fuel and unidentified chemicals drifted from inside.

Kendra stood balanced on her bare toes, sobs shaking her body. Blood splattered her shirt.

Several containment platforms lined one wall while numerous aisles of stacked barrels straddled the width of a forklift's circumference.

On Kendra's right, ski masks denied identification of two men, exposing only eyes and mouth. Widened gazes revealed extra white that contrasted their hoods while clenching fists, lip licking, and shifting weight foot to foot inspired thoughts of unique torture techniques. He could take out one, but the bastard whose gun was trained on Kendra might get off a shot. Not a risk he could tolerate.

On the left, the bitch he'd once considered with pity now held up her fist, part of the brass knuckles she wore reflecting light.

Cindy's movement halted the wheels of his deliberation. Action vs. inaction. Neither option would end with an acceptable resolution. Conner holstered his weapon under his arm.

"Stop." Throwing the door wide, he stepped inside and to the left, his arms held wide to draw attention to himself. Chipped cement shavings littered the floor along with dirt and smears of blood. Kendra's blood.

Approaching with both hands up, he gave them no reason to shoot. His body tensed, teeth ground, fantasies of murder filling his mind until Kendra's body bucked under the onslaught of another punch.

The groan soured his stomach. Her legs visibly trembled. A thin line of crimson dripped from her split lip."

"Ahh, so the lover finally shows." A certain diabolical delight brightened Cindy's gaze to feverish intensity.

Not closing his eyes on the female viper, he gnashed his teeth until the filthy words threatening to erupt and send the bitch in a fit of rage crumbled like so much dust.

The taller man nearest the wall of barrels refocused his weapon, marking Conner the recipient. The gun in his hand weaved slightly, his clenched fingers tightening rhythmically on its handle as if his mind whispered seductive, forbidden commands. A certain stillness held the other man captive, his eyes never leaving Kendra's body while his gun remained holstered under his shoulder.

"Let her go, or you don't get the envelope." Bile ripped up his throat.

Pulling his mask off, the taller thug smirked. "Not hardly. You can tell Daeron to come in now or I'll shoot his little friend just for fun. I've been waiting so long for this. You can deposit your gun on the floor, Conner, very slowly."

"Palmer. Further words failed to spit forth as Conner removed his gun as ordered using thumb and index finger.

"Huh, you dicks thought I was just another homeless idiot. When that Korean prick approached me with an offer of money, a clean digital slate, and Kendra's body, in exchange for a little snooping, I couldn't pass it up." Victory puffed out his chest.

Cindy's calculated smile coincided with raising her arm for another brutal strike against Kendra's bound form.

"Stop or you'll get nothing." Panic edged Conner's voice, seeping from an ever-growing endless well. Behind him, Daeron's quiet gasp revealed his shock.

Cindy's hesitation accompanied a challenging gaze filled with contempt and superiority until a single glare from Palmer elicited a frustrated whine. She dropped her arm to her side.

Once again a victim of circumstance, Kendra pivoted on wobbling legs, her anguish scalding his mind. His step forward ended with Daeron's grip on his arm.

"No, Conner. Keep your head." Daeron nodded toward his one time, band member. "Palmer? What the hell are you doing? We—" Words died off when the single muzzle swung his way.

"Cut her down, Cindy." A half-grin tilted one side of the drummer's mouth, his words issued with a challenging blandness common to cold-blooded killers. "So you liked my little sleight of hand, Daeron?"

"You faked your own death. Whose body—" Daeron began, clearly confused.

"A homeless vagrant. Since you'll find no records of my existence, no prints, it was a simple matter to accomplish. I like things tidy. The other prick was a man who'd failed one too many times. I have to say, the ploy made my boss very happy."

"Not tidy. Sociopathic." Perplexing agitation gave way to disgust, a kaleidoscope of emotions sliding across Daeron's face with his weight shifting foot to foot.

"So where is this boss? Why isn't he here?" Conner reached for the glacial cold that allowed him to strategize. He wanted to stall long enough to meet the ring's organizer. Palmer couldn't be more than the lowest rungs and likely didn't know those in the higher ranks.

"Doesn't like to get his hands dirty. We'll see him soon enough. Then I'll exchange the flash drive for a tidy sum and enjoy Kendra as my personal plaything. Before morning comes, she'll be begging to suck my cock. And when I tire of her, I'll make another profit selling her to foreign businessmen." Flushed skin and febrific gaze merged tinges of delusions with insanity.

"But you promised I could make the little whore pay for stealing what's mine if I helped. She... I'll cut her down." Cindy's petulance died a quick death with Palmer's raised brow. Dropping her gaze, she accepted a switchblade from thug number two.

Conner's gut tightened when the blade hovered near Kendra's throat for a few extra heartbeats. Everything in life existed as cause and effect. Sometimes the finer nuances of distinguishing one from the other eluded the best and brightest. His rejection of Cindy had caused Kendra immeasurable pain. The hunger for blood now shone in the deviant's unstable gaze.

Though he didn't pull his gun, the second stockier gunman's thirst for violence echoed in his tightly coiled body, thrumming in fists which repeatedly clenched. Under his mask, the outline of his jaw displaced the knit fabric side to side as if contemplating the probability of whose blood would spill first.

"Cindy..." Palmer's threat was clear. "Let's be gracious."

How long had Kendra been standing there, stretched with toes barely touching the floor? When freed, she dropped hard, her bound hands scraping the cement before falling on her side. Stark terror filled her visage with the realization of her destined future. Low whimpers and halting sobs hindered her breathing.

"Easy, Mongrel, I don't want you damaged too much. We have an exciting adventure planned. Now that the gang's all here, it's time to take a trip." Palmer's hatred rippled outward, his smile the stone in a pond covered with scum, the wavelets radiating outward to spread the malevolent odor.

"What about me? You said I could have her. You bastard." Cindy's body bucked backward when Palmer's first bullet pierced her chest. Its barking echo reverberated in the metallic confines.

A prismatic range of emotions flashed across Cindy's face—surprise, pain, hatred, and then acceptance—while her crumpling form made little noise. A steady dribble of blood splashed the cement, mixing with dirt and debris before forming indistinct shapes seeping into and flowing along the concrete cracks.

Kendra's garbled scream pierced the quiet night, her struggle to stand hindered by racking sobs. Less than a yard separated her from the murderer. Dry heaves shaking her frame hindered balance in trying to stand.

As if sensing things to come and wanting his turn early, the accomplice reached for Kendra, his arm banding her chest, his other hand stroking her cheek, neck, and collarbone, in anticipatory glee.

Her response included an elbow to his ribs and a half step to the side.

"Stop, or I won't tell you where I've hidden the flash drive." Conner didn't like the odds of everyone surviving the encounter.

"Oh, you'll give it to me, but first, for the bastard who has proved a thorn in my side by watching this chit like a hawk." Without hesitation, Palmer turned to Daeron. "I've been waiting years to do this." His smile twisted to form a malevolence unseen and not expected.

Another loud crack, another cartridge spent, another projectile hit its mark, below the bottom of his vest.

Daeron dropped to his knees under the force of the shot. With clenching fingers unable to contain the flow of blood from his belly, he groaned before collapsing to the floor. Fetal position denied further assessment of his wound.

Kendra vomited. When she straightened, her raven's hair swung back to reveal unadulterated hatred and rage, wresting rational thought from her gaze. Pain and fear subverted by her mentor's downfall outstripped her ability to focus.

Obvious intent, though futile, radiated outward in tensing muscles, baring teeth, and flaring nostrils, forewarning the obliteration of her sanity. Silent steps and murder in her eyes as she rushed Palmer resulted in his Sig Sauer swinging in her direction.

"Kendra, no!" Conner lunged into action. The ten-foot separation equated miles to the extent he couldn't stop the bullet. He should've seen this coming.

Blood roaring in his ears muted the detonation filling his mind. Kendra bucked backward into her second kidnapper as Conner latched on to Palmer's wrist, fighting for the upper hand.

The scuffle for control ended quickly. Palmer's size, though formidable, lacked the brute strength and experience of countless missions, not to mention the adrenaline flooding a mind filled with rage.

One last shot. Strings of blood and other matter covered Conner's face and chest as he retreated a step. The ex-drummer jerked backward, dead before his breached skull cracked on the concrete.

A gun barrel pressed to his temple froze mind and body. *Shit.* Thug number two.

"Where's the envelope, Mr. PI?" The thick accent registered somewhere in the back of his mind.

"You're—"

The weapon flew from the gunman's hand, then hovered in midair several feet away. He started to reach for it, his jaw slack. The wheel gun hovered another foot back, but the click of it cocking froze him in place.

Callie, in the doorway stood beside Dani.

Marc rushed forward and knelt by Daeron's side. "Hang in there, man. Help's on the way." Ripping his shirt, he used it for a makeshift bandage.

Only the thug paid attention to the gun still hovering two feet away. "How is that happening?"

Another voice entered the fray as Conner rushed to Kendra.

"Damn. Seems I'm always a bit late. Backup's on the way." Wes tried to edge around Lightning, now blocking his path.

The gun Callie held with telekinesis lowered back and clanked on the cement as Lightning secured the stocky kidnapper.

Conner's mind refused to assimilate the cold, hard fact of Kendra's impending death, evidenced in each gasping breath. He wouldn't survive it, wouldn't try.

His thoughts centered on her as Wes studied the scene. "Anyone care to fill me in on what happened here? Like—specifics?"

"Not now, Wes," Dani said.

On the filthy floor, Conner's worst nightmare unfolded, Kendra bleeding, fighting for each inhalation. "No, no, no. Kendra."

Blood oozed in a widening arc from the wound in her upper chest, gravity pulling the stain to an elongated crimson mandolin whose soundboard rested on the floor.

Using his jacket as a pressure bandage stemmed the flow of blood, Conner pleaded, "Please, baby, open your eyes for me." The flush was gone from her cheeks, replaced with a paleness rivaling moon glow.

Each gasp marked a unit of time in a way nothing else could. Still, her life's essence colored his bandage. He wanted to beg her to stop bleeding but afraid she'd stop the coarse, ragged breathing too.

"How bad?" Wes knelt by Kendra's side, examining the wound. "Kenson is here, ambulance on the way, again complements of Kenson."

"We need an airlift." In the back of his mind, Conner attempted to piece the elements of the elaborate goat-fuck together, assembling one disaster after another. The only surety was that this woman owned his mind, heart, and soul.

Her breathing remained shallow, eyes closed, the injury keeping her thoughts in some unconscious realm he could neither fathom nor join. Gathering her semi-upright in his arms with her head against his shoulder eased the crepitation with each inhale but also decreased the blood flow to her brain. *Fuck!*

Kissing her hair amid soothing noises, he whispered, "Sweetheart, if you survive this, I'll scold you endlessly for pulling such a stupid stunt. If not, I'll follow wherever you lead and pull you from the very jaws of hell itself." The former could only transpire in a nightmare, the latter was based in reality, for he would not walk the earth without her. The toxic inferno festering in his soul, carried for so long, purged in fear and yoked by undisciplined sins, damned his spirit to the deepest pits in Hades.

Minutes passed in helpless rage.

Kenson strode in, flanked by a squad of soldiers dressed in black. "Chopper in less than five." At seeing Dani and Callie partially hidden by Marc and Lightning, he sighed. "And why shouldn't I be surprised to find you two in the thick of things? Sure as hell wish we had time to talk."

Other words passed over Conner, meaningless in a world where Kendra's future lay between the probability of death and the certainty of disfigurement. He'd once thought nothing could snuff out a light so brilliant, so loving and sweet. Now, he realized without her, light wouldn't exist in his universe.

He would follow wherever she led.

Chapter Twenty-Two

The chopper ride passed in a blur of meaningless sights and sounds while medics worked on Kendra and Daeron. Vaguely, he remembered someone blocking his path to the aircraft. Several punches later, he'd not been asked again to move from her side.

Once attendants rushed the injured into the OR, Conner holed up with Marc in the surgical waiting room, met soon after by Nate, Callie, and Dani.

Two teams of military protective detail surrounding the women had drawn inquisitive stares and conjectures to which he paid little heed. The next time he'd circled the room, only two strangers remained. Sudden exhaustion saw him seated and drawing concerned stares from family and friends.

"Conner, any news yet, son?" Colonel Kenson surveyed his surroundings upon entering, nodding to the women.

"No. Well, yeah. Julien's in recovery, he'll be fine. Daeron and Kendra are touch and go. Don't know anything else, yet." Conner stood again to tread the small room's perimeter.

"If you'd like to sit for a minute, I have news." Kenson pulled one of the plastic chairs to face the utilitarian couch where Marc and Nate sat. "Or...you can continue pacing."

"What's up, Colonel?" Marc tugged Dani to sit beside him. His brothers preferred to keep their better halves close.

"Thought you might like to know how this freaking puzzle fit."

"Who is Wes?" Conner glanced out the window, not sure whether he could distinguish between the colonel's white noise and the metronomic throb of blood rushing in his head.

"Wes was hired by Billy's attorney three years ago. Billy's will stipulated funds left to ensure Kendra's safety. The attorney hired an investigator, Wes, to keep tabs on her until she came of age and took control of her inheritance. Billy obviously had some convoluted thinking about her receiving the information you safeguarded."

"Son of a bitch! Why didn't the bastard tell me he'd hired someone? I've known Masterson for years!"

"Apparently, Wes has looked out for her, finding odd jobs, etc. but could never get closer with Daeron's presence. Hence, he tried to help them all. He intervened at your club yet couldn't find the body when he returned. We assume whoever hired the thugs left them in Kendra's hideout to keep you involved."

"Why the fuck didn't Wes get her off the streets?" Conner's fists clenched repeatedly, needing a target, any target on which to unleash his wrath. Wes would do nicely.

"From what I gather, and I haven't seen Billy's letter to the attorney yet, Wes assumed she'd be safer where she was unless accepting his protection. If not for the attorney's long-standing friendship with her family, Wes wouldn't have located her on the street. Moving targets are harder to hit, and street kids are hard to locate, especially if they've adapted to their environment." Kenson's words made little sense. "As long as she remained homeless and not connected to you, the stalkers would know she didn't have the envelope, which would then make her a direct target."

Wes would get his comeuppance for a piss-poor plan.

"I understand that look, son, and I advise against it. Wes has taken an extended leave of absence," Kenson added.

"What about Billy? What was he working on that last day?" Conner asked, wondering how forthcoming his ex-boss would be. Little did Kenson know, Callie recovered the information on the small disc. They now had the general whereabouts of another facility near the Texas-Louisiana border.

"It was s'posed to be an in-and-out information relay but ran into complications. I didn't know anything about the jewels until your brother described the envelope's contents. My only interest is the flash drive."

"So, do you know who's behind all this?" Marc asked.

"We've traced Palmer's associate to a foreign national from North Korea, no longer a guest. According to the man you captured, his boss was listening and knew what transpired in the warehouse. He took off when things went south."

189

Kenson continued, "I understand he and the few cronies left are due to have very unfortunate and extremely prejudicial accidents this evening. They won't be bothering you again. As for the intermediary you captured from the scene, he's headed for black-site seclusion."

"Good riddance." Conner yanked the envelope from his jacket's inner liner. "Here, you've been looking for this. I assume the gems were taken as a matter of convenience. For that matter, why didn't Billy send this directly to you?"

"It was a joint effort with another agency. Not all intelligence is time-sensitive. His partner didn't make it, but must have suspected a leak in one of our departments. As it stood, he was correct, but his hesitation bought Billy time to escape." Colonel Kenson scrubbed a hand over his jaw before continuing. "I guess Billy thought he was protecting his sister. We'll never know for sure."

Kenson accepted the package and opened it. After retrieving the small thumb drive, he slipped in a note before handing the envelope back to Conner. "Billy died for this. If I'd suspected the specifics of the data, I would've sent the entire team." His jaw tightened as he shook his head. "I think the other items here could find a better use with you and Kendra. I assume you'll see she gets these? Looks to me like one of those would make a nice setting in a ring, or whatever you guys use these days."

"You said earlier that this could concern Dani and Callie."

"I'll have to decode these files. I'll let you know."

"I'll see Kendra gets these." Conner accepted the package as if it might bite. "Colonel, her parents, ever since the explosion, we've been unable to locate them."

"They're in one piece. I moved them to a safe house. Their address and phone numbers are on the slip in that package. I understand you and Kendra haven't visited since Billy's death."

"Yeah, I'll pay 'em a visit. Kendra needs to make amends." Conner tucked the envelope in his jacket pocket. A sideways glance at his brothers earned him three pointed stares.

An approving gleam entered Kenson's gaze. "Yes, I suppose she does... also."

Each morning for two days, Conner rose before the crack of dawn after three to four hours of sleep. Changing Krystal's bandage had become routine before setting off for the hospital. The quick stop at his younger brother's house kept his siblings updated with her progress while dropping off a list detailing a few requests.

"So, what's it today, Conner, moving Mount Everest or draining the Black Sea?" Marc asked, opening Julien's front door as Conner raised his fist to knock.

"I wrote it down so your soggy brain wouldn't forget. After taking care of you guys all these years, I don't feel bad making a few minor requests." Conner smiled as he handed the folded list to his younger brother and received a squirming Thad in return.

The specific changes made in his home carried out by Marc and Nate would kick start Kendra's new life. Julien, already home after acquiring his discharge papers the day before, no doubt reveled in the doting care.

Chuckles softened Marc's expletives, but approval widened his gaze. "Nice. She'll love it."

"Thanks, Marc. I'll let you know how things go." His mind settled incrementally with the threat to their lives ended. The new lease on life permitted his spirit to relax with the image of Kendra accepting his terms.

However, the biggest step, one he'd never before contemplated, weighed heavily on his mind. What if she refused?

Picking up Thad took precious time but the attachment they'd formed was good for both displaced souls. Yesterday, they'd entered her private room silently and debated on the timing of his declaration until she'd awakened. The quiet had allowed for a unique introspection while contemplating his plan and making another list in preparation for her discharge.

Hospital security would've tossed the pup out immediately if not for Kenson' insistence Thad was a service dog in training and smoothed the path. The nurses had smiled while shaking their heads but ultimately had a soft spot for both the pup and Kendra.

Since the military assumed financial responsibility and Kenson visited daily, in uniform, no one questioned his authority. He'd sat with them the first evening until Kendra and Daeron slept off the anesthesia from respective three and four-hour surgeries.

With her discharge today, they'd finally be able to rest. No longer debilitated with indecision, he measured each stride along the hospital's brick walkway in increments of his intended verbal approach, dissected and measured for sincerity and acceptability.

The monumental step could've been timed better, but the weight of his anxiety declared today ground zero for their new beginning. He hadn't told anyone for fear of appearing foolish, but inside, his body hummed with the nervous energy of a man facing a judge's sentencing. Sweat beaded his brow while his jerky movements felt awkward and uncoordinated.

What if she declared it all too much? Bruises were healing, but the scar proved a permanent reminder, however it faded and dimmed with time.

Walking down the bustling corridor, he stopped for aides and nurses alike to greet Thad, now a well-known canine celebrity. Stress, excitement, and fatigue, contributed to the facial tic that probably likened him to a mindless idiot winking at everyone in passing.

After everything he'd survived, it was ridiculous for his palms to sweat and mouth to rival the Gobi Desert. One way or another it would all be over soon.

The lights were off when he entered her room, the vertical shades allowing thin streams of sunshine to stripe the floor by her bed and remind him of the bars he'd recently believed he deserved. One obstacle overcome.

Stillness reigned while he sat in the low-slung chair to watch her sleep. Thad protested his restriction with squirms and grumbles, accustomed by now to nestling in the crook of her elbow.

Her innocence, balanced and roughened during her street time, remained intact despite her past and present traumas and struggles to survive. During their talks, she'd described details of how both Wes and Daeron had guided her in a world gone cold and uncaring. With time, perhaps he could forgive himself for her suffering. Regardless, he'd do whatever it took to make amends.

"Hmm, you're here early. I thought you were gonna sleep in this morning." Wiping remnants of sleep away, Kendra chuckled as Thad scrambled on her bed and proceeded to cover her face in pup kisses.

"I've slept enough. I have good news. They're starting Daeron on solid food today. If all goes well, he'll be home day after tomorrow."

"Wow. Fantastic. Do you think...?" The hope emanating from her eyes paralleled the same look she'd bestowed when wearing a ponytail and freckles as a teenager seeking his approval.

She was no longer a kid, and her freckles had faded with time. Through extensive conversations, he'd come to see her in a new light, maturity on many levels occurring faster because of her experiences, but a young woman who knew her mind just the same.

"I've already asked him to stay with us. He's thinking it over." He didn't miss the sheen in her eyes, but she needed to know the rest. "Colonel Kenson made a counter offer I believe he's also considering."

"I don't like the sound of that, not at all."

"I told him, if he took Kenson's path, our firm would have a place for him when he's discharged. I think he needs to find his own way, sweetheart." Conner smiled as Kendra absentmindedly fingered Chad's collar.

Snuggling the pup closer, she froze after a quick inhalation. "What's this on his collar?"

"Don't know. Better take a look." Conner moved to sit on the side of her bed.

"No. Really?" Pushing the strip of leather through the buckle, she freed the collar, then removed the ring.

Taking it from her hand, he slid it on her left ring finger. "Marry me, Kendra. I love you as no one else ever could."

Through tears and a half sob, she choked out, "Yes. Yes. I've always loved you, you big oaf. Took you long enough to realize it."

Taking possession of her mouth sealed their fates, regardless of what transpired in the upcoming and long-awaited meeting. She'd said yes and so belonged to him, now and forever. Letting her go would never be an option.

"How in the world did you get this done so quickly?" Multiple diamonds formed the shape of a seahorse in profile with the largest diamond shining as its eye. "It's the most beautiful ring I've ever seen. And it's huge."

"A friend owed me a favor." With the biggest hurdle of his life behind him, time held less significance. The next few hours gave voice to hopes and plans, sorting prospects and possibilities. Little by little, a sense of calm took residence in his spirit.

Still, there was another matter to discuss, another elephant they'd avoided far too long.

"We'll solidify the plans after we get home and comfortable. For now there's something else."

Regardless of life's longevity, there would never be a right time for what came next. She needed to know the rest, and he couldn't in good conscience, hold back any longer. From his inside coat pocket, the sealed note held a message written in her brother's scrawl. "Billy wrote this letter to you, held by his attorney who contacted me again yesterday, one for you and one for me. We all knew there was a chance we wouldn't return..." His hand shook. "Wes informed the lawyer that the threat against you is over after Colonel Kenson confirmed the source was eliminated."

"What about the threat to Dani and Callie?"

"Remains to be seen."

With reverence and trembling fingers, she slipped the letter from its envelope, her eyes misting. Nothing could bring Billy back, and many things would rekindle the pain of loss. Eventually, they'd share bittersweet memories.

"He's apologizing for not keeping his promise to come home, asking for forgiveness. He couldn't leave his brothers in danger." Tears streamed from her eyes, lifted by the rough pad of Thad's tongue as he whined.

194

"He knew I've always loved you and says to not let your stubbornness stop me from pursuing you. He's giving us his blessing."

How'd he know I'd fall in love with his sister? "His letter to me read about the same, in a bit more colorful language and a threat about haunting me if I failed to keep you happy." Through tears and watery smiles, they shared memories, both painful and healing.

Each nurse and aide encountered stopped Kendra in bidding her and Thad farewell as Conner wheeled her to Daeron's room before discharge. Word had spread after Kenson's sketched outline of her bravery and her deceased brother's heroic feat, making her part novelty, part heroine.

Daeron remained belligerent over his confinement, grumbling about hospital smells, food, and money, despite the military picking up the tab.

When she revealed her engagement ring in a subdued excitement, his calculated assessment of Conner ended with, "'Bout time you made an honest woman of her. I wondered if I was going to have to kick your ass when I got out of here."

Outside, late morning sunshine highlighted pink, yellow, and purple blooms to fill the atmosphere with new hope. A peace he'd never known twined in his heart and mind, firming his resolve for a new and better life.

Riding on an energy high never before experienced, he rushed to pull the SUV in the patient loading zone. Never had his future looked so promising, so hopeful.

He'd spent most of his life studying how to read people yet worried now that his excitement had blurred his judgment. Anticipation over Kendra's return home dampened his palms. What if she wasn't ready for the things he'd done?

Excited chatter filled the vehicle while his muscles tensed until blanching knuckles and tingling fingers made him soften his grip on the wheel.

Three years ago, anger over Billy's choices had forced her to run. Though it appeared she'd forgiven herself and her brother, the additions he'd made might open the wounds instead of providing the intended balm. He'd know soon after she walked in the house.

When in the garage at last, he closed his eyes and took a deep breath. Time to dive in. "Stay put, Kendra. You're not going to exert yourself today."

Her smile radiated relief, excitement, and a bit of exhaustion, despite the early hour. Who sleeps well in a hospital bed? When he opened her door and stepped close, her arms circled his neck.

"Carrying me over the threshold isn't supposed to happen until after the wedding."

"This is post-injury care. You can move around in the house, but I'll take the dogs out. We may not be married yet, but consider yourself owned, lock, stock, and barrel." Setting her down in the foyer and placing Thad on the floor, he smiled." He didn't realize he'd held his breath until she stepped farther into the great room and gasped.

"Oh! It's beautiful. When—" She rushed to pull the seat out, grimacing with the use of her left arm.

"It was delivered yesterday. It's a parlor grand, similar to the one you use to play."

"I love it. I've been sneaking in to play the piano at St. Marks for years."

"Yeah, I know. When I'd finally tracked you down and spoke with Father McKinley, he said he left the music room unlocked because of you. He used to sit in the adjoining space and listen for hours."

"These are my books, from home?" Thad rubbed against her calf as she sat and placed her fingers on either side of middle C. The soft, feathery notes were pure, bell-like, lacking the tinny component common to some models. A sonata she'd enjoyed as a young girl filled the house with peace.

"Yes, your parents are back home now. Marc helped relocate them." Conner sat beside her, carefully circling her shoulders and pulling her close.

Her fingers froze as she canted her body toward him.

"My parents?" Teardrops jeweled her eyelashes, expected and unavoidable, painful to witness.

"Yeah, I think its past time we both faced them." Careful of her wound, he snuggled her against his side and smiled as her body lost tension.

"I don't think they want to see me again. Billy and I had such a terrible fight before he left the last time. Mom said I was wrong. Then when he died, she blamed me for distracting him." A sob slipped out, joined by another. Soon, his shirt bore the evidence of her grief. "I'm sorry."

Conner scooped her up and carried her to the couch. "Grieving takes time, sweetheart. Tears won't happen just once. It's a process."

"I understand why he went, it's just, I was so heartless and cruel." Trails of moisture stained her cheek, each drop releasing a fraction of the toxins that had caged her spirit and encapsulated it with armor tougher than ballistic-grade Kevlar.

"I know, Kendra. I do understand."

The long-awaited catharsis, begun but far from completed, would help clear heart and mind and allow the grief process to heal the pain she'd buried so deep in her wounded spirit.

A portion of his own body's venomous moisture dampened her hair in an attempt to purge the virulent cancers of regret and remorse, her unspoken forgiveness accelerating the mending of his soul.

Minutes stretched out while shadows flickered across the hardwood floor. They needed this time, this adjustment of reconciling the past in order to look to the future.

When her well of heartbreak dried for the time being, he reminded her of the times they'd swam, snorkeled, and gone scuba diving. "I haven't been diving since I left the military." Being honest with himself, he hadn't gone because it was something they'd enjoyed long ago, together. He couldn't tolerate the memories. Maybe now things would be different.

"I don't have equipment anymore." She sniffled against his chest. "But I'd love to go again."

"I have gear. We can go when you've healed." Sweeping a lock of hair behind her ear, he traced the tracks of her tears. "Day after tomorrow, we'll go and visit your folks."

Thad's excited yips, playing with a recovering Krystal, brought her attention to the newest modification in the corner.

"Holy shit. How did I not see that? When did you have time?"

Helping her up, Conner shadowed her movements to the three-hundred-gallon, saltwater tank tucked against the back corner of the great room. "Tapped into some friends. This was already set up, just relocated. The seahorses were added this morning."

"Wow, I love these soft corals, they're beautiful." Her shoulders shook with random snivels and each poorly contained whimper. "I remember when you helped Billy and me set one up. This looks so much like it."

Turning her to face him, he wondered why he'd ever thought of resistance. The love shining through her eyes breathed new life and new hope into his world, a world of forgiveness and peace.

"Will you stay with me when I go see them? They love you, too." Barely whispered words betrayed a shared history.

"Absolutely, I have a long way to go in making amends."

Chapter Twenty-Three

Thad cuddled in Kendra's lap as she snuggled in Conner's arms. A warm southern breeze slid through the screened porch where they sat wrapped in a soft blanket. Moonlight filtering through low-lying clouds gilded the pup's hair, silver highlighted with gold, its fur feathering from nature's breath.

She'd never felt such peace. "I was nervous today, coming home."

"I love you, sweetheart. Nothing will ever change that."

"I've always loved you, Conner. You just never saw it, never saw me. Even when I was half-naked."

"You've always existed as part of me, Kendra. I'd thought of you as a sister growing up. Then, when you walked in Ambrosia, well, that just blew me away. I tried to resurrect that sibling feeling, but you obliterated it in two seconds. Afterward, our situation was an obstacle. It took me a while to realize you can't put feelings on hold."

"Are you hungry?" Kendra squirmed with the thoughts warping through her mind.

"Seriously? After all we've eaten?" His expression declared him hungry for something else, something they hadn't enjoyed yet.

"Huh, you'd think I was pregnant." Her cheeks heated. *That definitely shouldn't be in my thoughts.*

"Kinda like putting the cart before the horse, wouldn't you say?" Conner brushed the hair back from her face, denying the ability to hide.

A quick inhale. "You're such a tease."

"I wanted our first time to be without a threat hanging over our heads." Slipping his hand inside the blanket, he opened the top button of her blouse. "How's your shoulder feeling?"

"Um, fine. Hardly notice 'em at all." The heat in his gaze forecasted his intentions before his touch grazed her collarbone.

"It's about nine or so. Tired?"

"Not in the least."

"Good." In one agile and smooth move, he stood, carnal intentions written in his hooded gaze. His warm breath feathered her hair and warmed her face.

The distance to his bedroom seemed to grow with every step. She'd waited so long.

"It's time we spent the night in my bed." His eyes promised both sensual torment and pleasure, intensifying to a point that would end with sore muscles, a hoarse throat, and a very happy camper. Each step carried her closer to her dream of not only complete surrender but also experiencing the fulfillment of Conner's release.

Through the living room and down the short hall, her excitement built one kiss at a time. He brushed his mouth across the crown of her head while rumbling in his chest forewarned of long-standing hunger. Fascination and recent history advised Conner would take his time with teasing and keeping her on edge, attentive to every movement, every plea, both voiced and nonverbal.

Beside his bed, he hesitated a breathless heartbeat. "I love you. I've dreamed of being buried deep inside you."

Her thoughts spun, unable to process the promise in his eyes. Excitement and anticipation shut her mind down after centering on his obvious objective.

Thick and soft, the rug warmed her toes when he set her to stand.

"Tonight, we join as one. You are mine for all time, against any that would stand against us."

"I've always been yours." Perhaps the world only saw the hard exterior he presented, the man who'd accepted responsibility for three younger brothers when barely a teenager. His sensuous smile, the huskiness of his laughter that promised endless pleasure, the gentleness of his caresses and deep abiding passion, all belonged to her.

"I'm possessive, territorial, and not always easy to live with." Slowly, he reached for her. With a well-defined patience, one blouse button after another slipped through its hole in a teasing pretense of restraint.

"Neither am I. But I'll always love you."

Her gaze dropped to the erection tenting his slacks, noting his deep, throaty chuckle that broadcast confidence and resolve.

Soft silk whispered down her arms, sliding to a heap on the floor. Her desire to speed progress and slide greedy fingers beneath his shirt to feel the smattering of hair gave rise to action, only to be stopped with a word.

"Not yet." He knelt before her and removed her shoes, his gaze freezing her in place.

Those words had stilled her actions while his fingers slid beneath her waistband back and forth before unfastening the button. The repetitive grind of the zipper teeth sent tiny frissons of electricity through her abdomen.

Warm hands brushed down her thighs, then each calf, removing her socks and leaving her naked to his ravenous gaze. When he stood, she was helpless to look away as he removed his clothes and left them to pile beside hers.

"I'm no expert," It didn't take a genius to understand. "Slot B will never adjust to the size of peg A." A swath of anxiety grew as she fingered the gem about her neck. She wasn't aware her jaw dropped until his touch gently closed it.

"When properly prepared, as I will ensure, we'll fit together perfectly. Those muscles have an amazing ability to stretch."

She trusted him, completely, irrevocably.

He was taller by at least a head, his breath warm across her face. Very lightly, she grazed his wide, muscled chest with the lightest stroke of her fingers. He'd always been her white knight. Now, he'd sweep her into a world of passion and anticipation, a world of sensual delights built on a love strong enough to last eternity.

Whisking her up into his heated embrace magnified anticipation until the flutter in her belly grew to a full-body shiver.

"Cold? Pain?" His nostrils flared and eyes widened as he noted her inability to remain still.

"Not cold. Pain from wanting." Hell. Just the way his tongue glided along his lower lip made her squirm.

He smiled, then laid her out gently, reverently, then nudged her legs apart.

His expression became serious, demanding. "Kendra, if at any time your shoulder hurts, you say so, understand?" The tenderness of his touch betrayed the boundless craving in his gaze.

"You're going to keep your good arm out to the side. The other will rest on the bed. Understand?"

"Yes." Her entire body trembled. Conner in single-minded pursuit mode was a force to be reckoned with. Her body didn't stand a chance, not that she intended to resist.

On the contrary, she designed her subtle shifting to entice, advance his timetable, and seal their destinies. His feather-light caress under her jawline obliterated her focus, for it was just the beginning of his tactile ploys to reduce her to animalistic responses, controlled by instinct.

"Seems I've waited forever for this." With infinite care, his barely there touch grazed downward to her breast.

"Ah…"

"I'd intended to wait. You've been through so much." He molded each breast as if judging their weight before leaning over to take one pebbled nipple in his mouth.

"Nooo. Please, don't wait." The rough pad of his tongue rasped the bud, but she couldn't arch her back as one of his hands held her good shoulder to the mattress.

This incarnation of lust knew all the ways to keep her on the edge of paradise, teasing and torturing before sending her world spinning out of orbit.

Her breath came in quiet pants before his trail of kisses led up her throat, across her jaw, and settled on her lower lip.

"But I can't. I have to have you, tonight. Hence, we'll do this gently, slowly."

The corners of his mouth tilted up, withholding knowledge he'd use to great advantage, gained by a lifetime's experience using fingers, lips, tongue, and teeth. Little nips stung before his tongue soothed a path across her jaw, the sensitive spot between neck and shoulder, and over her breast. He knew every inch of her body, mapped it again and again. Warm, moist breath on sensitive skin explored her every shiver of heated delight.

She'd waited a lifetime for this, dreaming of Conner's possession. Now, it consumed her from the inside.

"Please! I'm going to explode."

When his tongue finally delved within her mouth, she likened it to storming a castle, a quick, quiet approach followed by a demand to take all. The heat spread through her mind then energized her body, firing every nerve, every muscle, and every cell.

"We'll burn together, sweetheart. I've wanted you since the day you walked into my club." Pain entered his voice, tinged with an eternity of longing.

Lying full out over her while suspending the bulk of his weight, he let his body brush against hers, the heat tightening her breasts painfully while her mind formed images of the bliss to come. Her thighs quivered and adjusted to give him more room.

"Please, Conner." In contrast to the cool sheets beneath her, his overwhelming heat stoked the fire within, tightening her stomach to tilt into what he would offer.

"I've waited so long." Years ago, she'd run from her home, her feelings, and Conner himself, afraid to be the one left behind. Now she realized she'd left him to steep in the pits of remorse, marinated with memories, nightmares, and despair.

Tonight, they'd both throw off their shackles, free to live their lives and revel in each other's love. For in her heart, she felt it surrounding them both.

* * * *

Morning light found him unable to leave the warmth of the bed and her eagerness to explore his body. Her curiosity led to them both sated and wrapped in each other's embrace.

When her stomach growled, he realized they'd spent more time in bed than he'd planned. "Hungry?"

"A little." Her pensive tone begged for explanation.

He'd tolerate no more secrets. "What's warping through your mind?"

"We don't always see eye to eye." She slid her fingers over the hard planes of his chest, smiling at his sharp inhale. "I don't always agree with your methods."

"Granted, sometimes we're flame and gunpowder, but when the dust settles, we're no longer separate entities." In time, she'd understand that relationships entailed a give and take as each learned their partner's intimate traits, rubbing off the rough edges until locked together in seamless perfection.

"Do you think Billy's watching over us?"

"At this minute? God, I hope not." From his letter, Billy had prayed one day he and Kendra sought solace in each other's arms, knowing she'd grow into a woman who knew her own mind. Billy's last words had been a chastisement to not hesitate in seeking what they'd both wanted.

"Sometimes, I feel like he's always watched over me.

"Yeah, I know what you mean. By now, he's rolling in the clouds laughing at us."

Chapter Twenty-Four

"What if they still hate me?" Kendra hesitated beside the SUV as if virtual cement encased every inch of her frame.

Conner's ever-soft touch turned her to face him before smoothing her cheek with the backs of his fingers. "They love you, Kendra. And unless I'm wrong, either Marc or Nate called this morning and let them know we were coming." As much as he'd intervened in his younger brothers' lives, turnabout was bound to happen.

She was adorable. He loved the strength that had bolstered her nerve for street life, her courage to pursue what she wanted, but most of all her heart, that precious, most vulnerable organ she'd consigned into his keeping.

Regardless of how her parents felt about their union, Conner would keep her, protect her, and love her until his last breath. The loving part was uppermost in his mind after the most incredible night of his life.

Her wooden movements thawed slightly with each step up the brick walk leading to the door until her raised hand halted six inches from the formidable oak barrier. "I can't, Conner. I just can't."

The vulnerability in her gaze pleading for understanding as she glanced over her shoulder tore through his own trepidations. Crowding close, he nuzzled her neck with her back snug against his chest and his hands circling her waist, holding her smaller, delicate fingers.

"Of course, you can. We can do anything together. You're not alone here and will never be again." Allowing compassion and strength to seep from his frame in warm degrees of kindness, sincerity, and passion, he felt her body soften.

"Should we just meet them today and not tell them we're getting married?"

"I think they deserve to know the entire truth after all this time. I believe—"

The massive door opened, spilling warmth to brush across their faces and fond memories lending courage to forge ahead. Though she appeared to have aged decades since he'd left for his last tour, love shone from the older woman's gaze, distilled in the crystalline tears adorning her lashes and cheeks.

"Please, come in." Mrs. Bower murmured the plea, uncertainty written in her azure-blue, tear-brimmed eyes. Her chignon held a little extra gray, and she'd lost a few pounds, but her smile was as warm as ever.

Behind her stood Kendra's father, his large hand wrapped around his wife's waist—whether supporting or holding on for strength, Conner couldn't determine. "We've waited so long for this."

The first sob in Kendra's chest broke free when she stepped out of Conner's arms and into her mother's waiting embrace. "I'm sorry, Mom. I'm really sorry."

"Oh, baby. Don't apologize. It was just as much my fault. We were both hurting."

Time seemed to fall away as Mrs. Bower drew her daughter into their home. Her husband stepped forward and clasped Conner's hand, his own eyes misting. "Good to have you home, Conner. Thank you for seeing her safe."

After a fatherly hug, the older man led them to a spacious great room, so similar to the one where they'd gathered many times over the years.

"Please, let's all sit. We want to hear everything about you two. Colonel Kenson told us about your bravery and your injury." Happy tears marked her mom's excited speech. "We called each morning but didn't come to the hospital. We didn't want to force your hand."

"I wasn't sure you'd want to see me after..." Kendra's gaze drifted off with her speech, unable to give voice to the words obviously shredding her heart.

"Nonsense, baby. Your leaving was just as much our fault as yours. We didn't handle things well, either." The elder woman continued to rub her daughter's back.

Conner sat on the other side of Kendra, who was now enveloped in her mom's arms. A glance around the room proved important things hadn't changed, as if keeping the same knickknacks and photos would deny their son's death. How many times had he and Billy sat in a similar room, watching TV, talking, making plans, or laughing over his younger brother's antics?

"The aquarium, the piano… you kept them both?" Kendra's amazement surprised her parents, judging by their frowns.

"How could we let those things go? We prayed you'd come back one day." Her father smiled as he nodded to his wife, then Kendra's hand.

"Oh! Oh my. You're getting married? Heavens." Both women started another round of happy sobbing, enveloped in each other's embrace.

"Well, I see much has changed, Conner." Mr. Bower's smile belied the admonition.

"So, you approve?" Kendra's small voice contained a daughter's hope and a fiancée's love.

The corners of her father's mouth kicked up in a smile. "Approve? Of course, we approve. You couldn't have found a better man."

Conner stood with the older man's approach. A deep sigh released pent-up anxieties and quiet misgivings attached to his shoulders.

"Welcome back to the family, Conner." Mr. Bower offered his hand, a welcome home and a peace offering.

When the women separated, a small celebration entailed food and a bottle of champagne, the afternoon filling with wedding plans, discussion of their future, and gentle, if cursory, explanations of the past. Still, it all danced around the remaining stigma attached to Conner's back.

Guilt over not delivering a personal explanation reached a crescendo. Conner set down his drink, his fingers shaking while something else rose up in his throat, vile and choking. Any parent would want the details of their child's death, yet he'd denied them that simple basic decency.

Billy's dad, with his son's eyes, same set to his mouth, took his glasses off and pinched the bridge of his nose, just as he used to do prior to delivering an important announcement. "I know that look, Conner. I saw it in Colonel Kenson' face the day he came here to tell us our son was gone. It's guilt." The depth of emotion conveyed through pupils and lenses, filled with a sorrow buried deep in the mind of a father's love, brought a misty veil to Conner's own gaze.

"It was on my watch."

"Kenson sent him out on a solo mission. He couldn't say what, but that is what got Billy killed." The older man rubbed a hand over his jaw, the other hand clenching tight on his thigh.

Kendra's mother offered her love through words and the light touch of her hand. "It wasn't your fault, Conner. We don't blame you. We never have. War, whether open or covert, steals lives and souls they've touched. Time and family can help us heal."

"Conner, we took you and your brothers in when your mom died and your father went to prison. We've watched you all grow into men we're proud to call sons," Mr. Bower added. "We've lost Billy, nothing can change that, but we've gained our daughter and our boys back."

With the last of the tension drained, complete and utter peace surrounded them, forgiveness he'd never expected to earn was given without request.

* * * *

Thank you for reading Whispers After Death.

Callie, Dani, and Kendra have joined forces with the Croftons and learn of another prodigy being held captive. Can they free her and root out the source of the organization imprisoning young women before Kenson uncovers their secrets? Follow their journey in Mind Hunters as the Crofton men band together and hunt the predators preying on their women. Book four in the Mind Stalkers Series.

Mind Hunters

Aria curled her chapped lips between chattering teeth and bit down against the pain. The air was thick with the stench of rotting vegetation, and something more sinister that didn't bear considering.

Sharp electric needles from the shock collar surrounding her neck should've lost effectiveness with time and distance from the institution. Stabbing sensations making her neck muscles twitch lessened to a bearable prickle. If she ever found herself in a position to return the favor, she'd turn the level up to ten and walk away.

Continued jostling of the truck bumping down the rutted path magnified her curiosity as to their destination.

And what smells so bad?

In consideration of the potholes and slow speed, it stood to reason they traveled back roads to parts unknown. She'd tucked in behind three long and shallow crates, contents unknown, then settled in the corner to think. The smell proved a strong enough deterrent to closing her eyes.

She needed strength, focus, and a knife, the last she hadn't handled in years. Would muscle memory prove adequate for defense if needed?

If they caught her, death would be a mercy not granted for many days. Her least-favorite captor always took great pleasure in relating details of her intended final destination, buried in an unmarked grave with no one the wiser. Not that she had family who'd care. She hadn't seen her brother since they were kidnapped and separated eight years prior. Did he survive? Escape?

Sneaking past the guards and into the back of the covered truck had drained the last of her reserves. If only she knew where they were going.

Restlessness pushed her to crouch and make her way toward the tailgate. Her heart hammered in time with each sensation zinging along her nervous system. At least pain had decreased to the point she could think.

If she remained stationary too long, the vehicle might stop and the driver catch her before she ducked out of sight. If she jumped out too soon, she'd be lost in the swamps, eaten by one critter or another.

Terrance, her self-appointed tormentor and soon-to-be executioner lived for the day of acting without restraint. He'd described the humiliation to come in vivid detail.

Lifting the canvas flap and peering through the shadows confirmed her suspicions. Little more than multiple rutty tracks with knobbly weeds extended beyond the bend in the snaking dirt trail.

Thick trees straddled the road with dense underbrush reflecting the truck's taillights. The tracks grew weedier until disappearing. Grinding gears preceded the engine's deep rumbling and altered pitch with forward momentum jarring to a snail's pace.

Without internal debate, she hopped over the tailgate and let the momentum carry her further in a tucked roll. Coming to a stop in knee-high grass didn't lend comfort with the thought of other creatures that would call the foliage home.

The sweet pungent scent of ozone warned of an approaching storm, which would enhance the electric shocks delivered by her collar even without contact.

Ahead, the truck turned into an opening her vision couldn't define, its taillights disappearing when it slowly picked up speed.

If homes existed nearby, she witnessed no soft glow filtering through the shadows to define their presence. No mailboxes or signs of civilization dictated the truck's destiny anything but an isolated dumpsite or a clandestine meeting. Neither situation appealed to her.

Lack of geographic knowledge strengthened the logic of following the road forward, yet when she passed the tracks where the truck had turned, curiosity got the best of her.

Again, she saw no sign of civilization, nor had she heard the grumble or purr from another engine.

Low grinding of the brakes and bright red taillights signaled the truck halting. If they were making a transfer of some kind, they'd likely return on the same path.

She waited, listening to the sounds of deep-throated frogs, crickets, and a screeching *kee-aah* as perspiration plastered her collar length mahogany hair against her scalp. Rotting vegetation and something more ominous warned her to stay alert despite exhaustion dogging every step.

Increasing wind whipped her bangs across her face. If rain caught her in the open, it would amplify the current of her collar. Common sense suggested she seek shelter.

Common sense sucked eggs.

In the distance, deep southern accents grumbled about dead weight and shit jobs. A chalkboard-type screech like that made from a crowbar opening a crate overrode the night avian's communication.

Minutes passed as she stood immobile, torn between wanting to know the truck's contents and fleeing to relative safety.

Thumps from dropping each crate on the ground heightened her curiosity. Were they preparing to bury something?

Bodies?

Reily's Books

Romantic Thrillers
McAllister Justice Series
Tender Echoes
Digital Velocity
Bound By Shadows
Inconclusive Evidence
Carbon Replacements
Shattered Reflections
Remnants of Evil

Moonlight and Murder Series
Shifting Targets
A Critical Tangent
Pivotal Decisions
Seeds of Murder
An Unlikely Grave
Deadly Interception
Love You To Death

Bayou Murders Series
Perfect In Death

Psychic Thrillers
Mind Stalkers
Bending Fate
Silent Depths
Shadow Guard
Whispers Beyond Death
Mind Hunters

Paranormal Romance
Immortal Lovers Series
Unholy Alliance
Blood Union

Standalone paranormal romance
Tiago

Reily Garrett is a writer, mother, and companion to three long coat German shepherds. When not working with her dogs, she's sitting at her desk with her fur kids by her side.

Author of chilling suspense and snarky romance, her stories span the distance of romantic thrillers, paranormal romance, and erotic romance. Regardless of genre, each book delves into a dark and twisted imagination yet is tempered with romance and a touch of humor.

Reviews by Kirkus Reviews, San Francisco Bay Review, and BestThrillers.com best describe her work:

"This could be James Patterson, Lee Child, and Tess Gerritsen rolled into one, but the dark, twisted methods used by the serial killer could surprise even those readers..." - San Francisco Bay Review

"...steamy, seductive police procedural..." - BestThrillers.com
"...well-researched thriller that remains romantically genuine throughout." - Kirkus Review

Prior experience in the Military Police, private investigations, and as an ICU nurse gives her fiction a real-world flavor. Find Reily at reilygarrett.com.

Made in United States
Troutdale, OR
10/22/2024

24042676R00130